# MICA HIGHWAYS

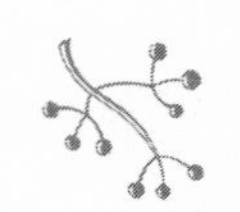

Also by William Elliott Hazelgrove

TOBACCO STICKS

RIPPLES

MICA

# HIGHWAYS

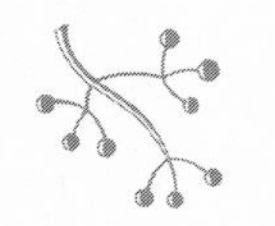

William Elliott Hazelgrove

Bantam Books New York Toronto London Sydney Auckland

This is a work of fiction. Names, characters, places, and incidents are either the product of the author's imagination or are used fictitiously. Any resemblance to actual persons, living or dead, or locales, is entirely coincidental.

A Bantam Book / November 1998

MICA HIGHWAYS



Book design by Laurie Jewell



**Library of Congress Cataloging-in-Publication Data**
Hazelgrove, William Elliott, 1959–
Mica highways / William Elliott Hazelgrove.
p. cm.
ISBN 0-553-10639-2
I. Title.
PS3558.A8894M5 1998
813'.54—dc21 98-26141
CIP

*Published simultaneously in the United States and Canada*

---

Bantam Books are published by Bantam Books, a division of Bantam Doubleday Dell Publishing Group, Inc. Its trademark, consisting of the words "Bantam Books" and the portrayal of a rooster, is Registered in U.S. Patent and Trademark Office and in other countries. Marca Registrada. Bantam Books, 1540 Broadway, New York, New York 10036.

---

PRINTED IN THE UNITED STATES OF AMERICA

BVG 10 9 8 7 6 5 4 3 2 1

*For*
*Kitty and Clay*
*and in memory of*
*Granddaddy*

*Thus with the year*
*Seasons return; but not to me returns*
*Day, or the sweet approach of ev'n or morn . . .*

—Milton

# MICA HIGHWAYS

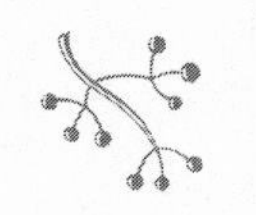

# PROLOGUE

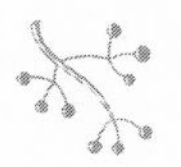

A country road
outside Richmond, Virginia

*April 4, 1968*

The oiled .44 lay next to the man's thigh like the muzzle of a dog. The warm air funneled into his shirtsleeve and ruffled the material in the roar of wind. Spring had come with heat reserved for June and the air was damp. The man rested his elbow and kept his eyes on the narrow two-lane. Twilight rimmed the pines and tinged the cooling highway a simmering pink. The road sparkled a last time before the blanch of headlights snuffed it.

The man glanced at the soft yellow of the radio. . . . *Martin Luther King was struck down by an assassin's bullet in Memphis, Tennessee. Mr. King was staying at the Lorraine Motel . . . sources close to the investigation say they have recovered a rifle . . . Mr. King's death a tragedy . . . April 4, 1968.*

The pines melted into the night and the highway flattened to gray. The man drove hunched forward with farm houses and tobacco barns rushing by in flashes of ramshackle porches and monoliths reflecting the moon over the trees. The man drove farther into the countryside and didn't turn to look at the white-columned house on the hill. The crackly voice rode the wind as the red needle crept past seventy-five, then eighty-five.

*". . . there's no rioting in Richmond now, but we expect some trouble . . . downtown Richmond is empty and all the stores are closed in anticipation of what's already happening all over the country . . . I'm standing on Main Street and there is not a soul to be seen . . ."*

The man pushed down on the accelerator. A festooning tail of red dust followed the Dodge Plymouth as it floated on the speed of one hundred miles an hour. The white dashes zipped into his rear-view mirror, and the whine he heard distantly. He went down into a valley and saw the light.

The garage shadowed the moon sky as the car skidded to a halt on the gravel. The man picked up the .44 and rose from the car, the barrel low by his knee. The weight of the gun swung clumsily as he ran past two sentries with pointed gas pumps and globes of lunar light. The light from the upstairs window shone on the hood.

The man ran through the splintered front door and into darkness. Climbing the steps, stumbling, falling against the wall, he strained toward the light seeping under the door. Gold touched the tips of his shoes as he raised the .44 and cocked back the hammer two clicks. He groped for the handle, heaving his weight against the door, bursting into the yellow-lit room. A far window curtain rippled surprisingly. On the side a small table lamp flickered a short spurt of current in repeating undulations. He stiffened and held the heavy gun waist high as blood sucked on his loafers stickily.

The curtain tufted again.

The black man lay on his stomach with hands clenched beneath his starched white shirt, his back bloodied with buckshot. A bottle of bourbon was between two juice glasses on a low coffee table, the whiskey bisecting each glass perfectly. An open pack of Lucky Strikes lay next to an ashtray where two cigarettes still smoldered. A silver lipstick case gleamed.

His shoe slipped on the floor when he turned to the woman ten feet away. Acid burned in his throat. He knelt. The yellow dress was consumed by the red flow from her chest. One arm arched back across her forehead, blond hair flipping silently in the breeze. One of her high heels had come off, her toe holding quiet possession. . . . Even now she was quite beautiful.

A shadow loomed over him. He glanced up, raising the .44 as a shotgun swung through the darkness, cracking against his skull. He fell to his knees, the world blinking out . . . forever.

# CHAPTER ONE

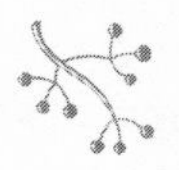

Southampton, Virginia

*August 1998*

Sunshine dappled into Granddaddy's bedroom. He felt the spot of sun as something reassuring, listening to the birds trilling outside the window, open every night of his life. Granddaddy lay in the quiet moment of waking. He sat up slow-slowly with the ember of a dream repeating itself and he rested with one arm back, eighty-some years of flesh smelling like the aged cloth inside his shoe box of fifty years. Years that made linens tear like tissue, leather crack like cardboard, turning the oil-brushed tools in his garage into dark pieces of metal reeking of a distillate between gas and kerosene. The house was full of antiques and he was too, he thought before this moment of sitting up.

But something was different today. *My grandson is coming.* It was the grandson he had seen maybe five times in the last twenty-five years; but then, Granddaddy barely saw anyone except for the visits to make sure he wasn't rotting away in the Virginia heat. At least this wasn't a death visit, he reasoned as he squared the sheet and blanket of the pencil-point canopy bed into which he had been born.

He urinated and began filling his bath. The steamy water clouded the edges of the mirror and sweated the base of the toilet tank. The soaking bath was his own contribution to staying alive. The medical contribution was the grocery bags of skinny white vials in the garage. His water system had broken down—although they called it leukemia. He took the white chemotherapy pills, twenty-five to a vial. *Like candy,* he almost said, stepping his saggy, short body into the warm, giving water.

He couldn't remember the last time he had been sick. It was only because he couldn't pass his water that he drove himself to the hospital. They wheeled him around on a gurney, taking tests until he told a long-faced doctor he would come back when he finished raking his grass.

But it was his belief that the baths kept him in good health. It was just his radiator system malfunctioning. After all, his car was well over eighty years old and the only cars that old were antiques with special permits. Sooner or later a car would develop problems. You could keep a car going a long time, provided you took care of it. He had dealt with engines all his life and he knew cars.

After Granddaddy put on his ironed-stiff white shirt and red bow tie he went to the kitchen and had a bowl of corn flakes under the buzz of the kitchen clock twenty years new. He finished his corn flakes and washed the bowl, putting it in the drying rack, next to his lunch and dinner plates. He recycled the same dinner plate, fork, spoon, knife, and coffee cup and rarely went into the cabinets.

The rotary phone on the wall clattered.

"Halo!"

"Is this *Mr. Austin Turin*?"

Granddaddy nodded, looking at the kitchen clock again.

"I reckon so."

"Mr. Turin, I am pleased to tell you you've just won our grand prize of *five thousand dollars*!"

Granddaddy tilted his head.

"Uh-huh."

The voice chuckled.

"I said, sir, that *you* have been drawn from our national sweepstakes as the lucky winner of *five thousand dollars*!"

Granddaddy bobbed on his knees.

"You say I won five thousand dollars?"

The voice laughed broadly.

"I know it's hard to believe, Mr. Turin, but *yes*, *you* are the *lucky winner* and you can either take five thousand dollars in cash or that amount in prizes . . . which would you prefer, sir?"

Granddaddy scratched his brow.

"Reckon I'll take the cash money, course I don't know what the prizes would be."

"That's a *smart* decision, Mr. Turin, and we'll get that right in the mail to you!"

"Where you callin' from?"

"We are located in South Dakota, sir—"

"Alright, now, you be sure to write my name big on that envelope, see, because we been havin' trouble with our mail and I thank you, bye."

Granddaddy hung up the phone. He wanted to get his oil changed and he looked at his wristwatch. The phone rang behind him.

"Halo!"

"Mr. Turin, I think we were disconnected, you see I need some more information before we can process that check!"

"Now, I don't want you to be using all your money on long distance, see, so you write me and tell me what you need and then I can send it to you, bye now."

Granddaddy turned off the light over the kitchen table and started into the den. The phone called him back.

"Mr. Turin, I just need one item and then we can proceed."

"Uh-huh, now what's that?"

"All I need is a small processing fee, it's a nominal sixty-nine dollars, and if you just give me your Visa or MasterCard number then I can—"

Granddaddy rested his hand on his hip and bobbed once, stretching his black knee-high socks. "Now, you want me to give you sixty-nine dollars so you can send me my prize?"

"Yes, that's right, you see—"

"Tell you what I am going to do for you and that's give you some advice. You should get yourself another line of work, young fella, because nobody's goin' to give you something for nothing . . . even if you promise something. Now, I been sellin' automobiles all my life and I couldn't have sold one automobile if I didn't show them the product *before* I asked for the money, so I wouldn't keep calling here because you are wasting your company's money on a customer who is not going to buy. If I were you—I would look for a product where you are selling something people can see . . . Halo! . . . *Halo!*"

Granddaddy hung up the phone.

"Reckon I didn't win the prize," he murmured, walking through the pine-walled den into the garage with the door hushing out the cooking smell of the house.

The morning-cooled gas-and-oil redolence of the garage started him humming. He walked down the aisle of automobile parts in shoe boxes, hatboxes, NAPA boxes, boxes of no description, containing lights, ignitions, spark plugs, valves, bolts, screws, solenoids, distributors, carburetors, cylinder heads, pistons, a crankshaft, a camshaft.

He passed three red carts with tools wedged and piled and picked up six quarts of oil and a filter. He twinged with irritation when he couldn't remember what time his grandson said he was going to arrive. He glanced at his watch steamed with permanent condensation, unable to distinguish anything without his glasses.

"Coming for a job," he muttered in the garage gloom.

He stacked the oil and filter carefully on the white Deepfreeze stacked with TV dinners, then went back inside. Granddaddy walked into the living room and found the paper with one o'clock scrawled, reminding him of the pen that lost its ink on the last word. He crossed to the antique postal desk. He reached into one of the slots and pulled out a photograph. The picture was of a young couple sitting before a fireplace with flowers in the firebox. The fireplace was not blackened and Granddaddy wondered if the house was new. The woman was short with blond hair. His grandson had on a dark suit, looked to be in his mid-thirties with brown hair jetting back at the temples.

Granddaddy put the envelope and picture in the desk. He reached into another slot and picked up the phone bill stamped and sealed. Granddaddy walked out the front door,

Hush Puppies scuffing burned-stiff grass. TURIN reflected dully on the tube of tin at the end of the drive. Morning light lay on the dew-touched road.

Granddaddy smelled bacon frying somewhere as he pulled the mailbox open, paused, then reached in. A single postcard lay in the center. The postcard reflected shiny red in the sun with the Stars and Bars of the Confederacy in blue relief. Along the bottom in scripted letters was: WELCOME TO RICHMOND VIRGINIA—CAPITAL OF THE CONFEDERACY. He turned it over. His address was printed in stiff block letters as if a child had written it.

Granddaddy stood for a moment by the leaning mailbox post. He glanced at the postmark, then slipped the phone bill into the mailbox and pulled up the red flag. He walked down the tarred drive and dropped the postcard into the aluminum trash can next to the house.

The phone rang as Granddaddy opened the garage door.

"What in the world," he muttered, walking into the kitchen. "Now, I told you not to call again!"

The line hollowed air. He could hear breathing.

*"Halo!"*

"Need money, Jack."

Granddaddy looked at his watch, bobbing slightly, touching the skin just below his right eye.

"Now, I have paid you good money—"

The receiver clicked dead. Granddaddy tapped his belt with his forefinger, holding the phone tightly against his ear. He placed the phone on the wall, then stood looking into the backyard. He put on his horn-rimmed glasses and looked at his watch again—the dial browned with age and the noon hour rubbed away completely—deciding he had enough time to change his oil before his grandson arrived.

*Charlie Tidewater*
*500 Lake Shore Drive*
*Chicago, IL*
*August 21, 1998, midnight*

*Matthew,*

*Just a quick note. I'm taking off for the South. Been a long time . . . over twenty years. No job and no marriage—guess I don't have a thing to lose now. My granddaddy is still down there so I'll be staying with him. I don't know really what I'll do down there except visit my mother's grave. Nineteen sixty-eight was a hell of a long time ago to go asking questions, but I guess it's time. My granddaddy must be well into his eighties by now. Well, take care. Say hey to all the guys.*

*Charlie*

# CHAPTER TWO

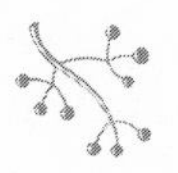

Southampton, Virginia

*August 1998*

The wind howled and shook the panes of the hundred-year-old house. His mother carefully wrapped him in a heavy wool blanket, smelling slightly of the smoky scent of burnt cork. She created a hood and laid him on the couch, then turned off the light and sat down. He saw fire dancing in the glass door of the wood stove and watched ghosts flicker and play on the ceiling. His mother hummed quietly and the wind was far away. He lay wrapped in his warm blanket, his mother's voice flowing around him, the northern lights above. This was his first memory.

Charles Austin Tidewater drove down the highway and watched the sun kiss the blue mountains of Virginia, glancing off barns rotted and unused, bringing to life a rusted tractor that had driven over the rows years before there were highways. A steeple, white and needle-sharp, punched up above a town, waiting for the sun to eclipse the mountains.

Charlie thought about the South he had been away from for many years. It was his mother who had told him about the Scotsman who came with a crest of arms to hack out a plantation along the lowlands of the James River. One son became a commodore who slipped between Union ships in the cover of a Confederate night. The other son was a gruff Confederate artillery sergeant decorated by Jefferson Davis for turning around the second battle of Bull Run.

His mother would take her finger from the genealogy chart of cursive script and Charlie would touch the later names. He always wondered what happened to his family after the war. It seemed his history stopped when the South lost its fight for independence. Charlie was fourteen when his father took him into the industrial mouth of the North—settling in Chicago for a career in the tactile applications of adhesive to boxes, cigarettes, packages, and other commodities that used the gluey bonds his father sold—Charlie repeated the tales of his ancestry at least once a year, embellishing their exploits as cold winters made the dreamy hot land more of a mirage than a memory. He passed the winters this way and on his fourth winter up north his father died.

Charlie watched the spots on the gray-baked two-lane. The road began sparkling when he crossed the Virginia line and he wondered why the roads in Illinois never glittered this way. Charlie wondered how it had come to be that he was on a Virginia highway in August. Less than six months ago he was married, living in a suburb of Chicago, chasing the fluctuations of Wall Street.

It all had just fallen apart when he called his grandfather.

"Hey, Granddaddy."

"Halo!"

"Granddaddy, it's Charlie—your grandson."

"*Hey boy,* now, how you doin'?"

His grandfather sent a Christmas card every year with a crisp twenty-dollar bill folded inside. The Christmas card was always the same SEASON'S GREETINGS with a little drummer boy. The twenty-dollar bill looked like it had just come from the mint.

"I'm doing fine," Charlie said, looking around the office he was packing to leave.

The booming southern voice was a strange tonic to the soft office click of Quotrons. He picked up a glass paperweight; a small, suspended globe.

"The question is, how are you?"

Charlie held the globe and watched Matthew Torev weave through the brokers' desks. There were only five glass-walled offices for twenty brokers. He wondered who would get his.

"Well, I'm still here . . . now, when you comin' down?"

"Actually, I was thinking of coming down there next week to look for a job—"

"Ahhh, now, what day you thinkin' of comin'?"

They talked about dates and times.

"Well, come on down, boy! I'll leave the door unlocked for you, bye."

The phone clicked in his ear. He smiled. To his grandfather, a long-distance call was still like going to the Ritz. Charlie looked up. Matthew Torev was in the doorway. He set the globe on the open slate of his desk.

"Everything all packed up?"

"I think so."

Matthew nodded and looked down quickly. They had become good friends in the two years Charlie had been with the firm.

"Do you know what you're going to do?"

Charlie met his friend's eyes behind the round glasses perched midpoint on the hooked nose of a fighter. The only Jew in a WASP firm, he had given Charlie the inside track on the politics of the high-pressure world of stocks and bonds. The Southerner and the Jew; they quickly became coconspirators.

"That was my grandfather on the phone . . . looks like I'm going to take a trip to Virginia."

Matthew slipped off his glasses and examined the lenses.

Charlie paused and looked up at his friend.

"It's probably time I find out."

Matthew set his glasses back in place and nodded slowly.

"Going to find out what happened to your mother?"

Charlie leaned back in his chair, looking at the Chicago skyline one last time.

"I suppose I am."

Matthew touched the edge of the desk, gliding his finger along the polished glass rim.

"Keep in touch, Charlie. Let me know how you're doing . . ."

Charlie stood and they shook hands.

"Thanks, Matthew—I'll do that."

Charlie glanced at his watch as the tall pines cut the sun on the highway. He had been driving since three A.M. and it was almost nine. Charlie let the old life pass out of his mind. He felt the southern sun on his arm and stared at the highway again.

• • •

Three hours later Charlie turned into a forest, going down into the rich greenery of Virginia with insects whining in his window. He turned down the last street of his remembrance.

*He watched with the safety of a child taken out to see Granddaddy in a 1965 vinyl-smelling car lugging down the heated highway, passing gas-for-a-quarter filling stations where Dad stopped to buy cigarettes. Riding down the roads to Granddaddy, who raced cars when he was young and had motorcycles, go-carts, and minibikes in his garage. Mom was in her sunglasses with the winged corners and Dad a young man in the picture albums.*

The shrubbed homes, guarded by towering oaks and dogwoods, crouched behind lawns of sprinklers and mailboxes of reflective lettering. The tires sucked on the tar with a splattering like rain. Charlie saw the brick ranch-style house squatting behind a scorched lawn, a corroded antenna peaking the flat roof. He turned into the drive, noticing patches of dirt in the grass. The memory of Granddaddy's green lawn caused Charlie to check the address on the mailbox with the red flag up.

He glided down the driveway and pulled up cautiously next to the garage, opening the door into the air of a steamy bathroom. The car door was nothing against the insects. He stretched from nine hours of sitting. Virginia was lush and Charlie breathed in the heat, the quiet of the house reduced by the constant rising and falling of life outside.

Charlie walked to the back door, flowerpots of strawberry begonias and impatiens on either side; Virginia creeper climbed the banister of the deck darkened with age and rain. He opened the screen door to the garage. It was the way he always went into Granddaddy's house. No one used the front door.

It was the smell of age with a faint cooking somewhere;

the redolence of his grandfather's house when he was young. *Old clothes and furniture, faded calendars smudged with grease, shoes worn to curled leather, trunks in a hot attic, an old gas-station bay in the country, a Coca-Cola sign from the beginning of the century.* The kerosene scent of the tools rode over his memory. Charlie stared at the melange of parts, bikes, the junk of random things. He walked into the amazing world of his grandfather's appurtenances.

*He sells cars. Granddaddy used to race cars. Granddaddy always has new cars. "He was quite a man in the automobile world at one time," someone had said long ago. Granddaddy pulling up in a Daytona Charger with airfoils on the back and a "Hemi" engine churning under the hood, identified by a friend years later from the photograph in the spine-torn album.*

He heard a car pull up, rev, then expire with an exhausted rattle like cars in black-and-white comedies. Charlie went out the door. Granddaddy spraddled toward him with groceries cradled in one arm.

"Halo, boy!"

"How are you, Granddaddy," Charlie called with hesitant familiarity, shaking the rough hand light in grip.

"Now, I'm sorry I wasn't here for your arrival, but I had to get the oil changed in my automobile and pick up a few things for us to eat," he said, bow tied, white shirt and light blue shorts pressed. "See, I knew if I didn't get it done today, it would be another week before I could get it changed."

He glanced at Charlie with far-set, pale, almost ice-blue eyes. His skin was the color of rich tobacco, creased and marked from summers of Virginia sun. Charlie thought he looked leaner. The hair rimming his head was whiter, more fine like baby hair. Granddaddy pulled down on his collar, bobbing slightly in his Hush Puppies and black knee-high socks.

"Now, how long did it take you to drive out here?"

"Couple days. I slept in Pennsylvania and got up at about three in the morning."

"You stayed at a motel?" Granddaddy asked, turning quickly.

"Sure."

Granddaddy clicked his tongue against his teeth.

"If I was young like you are I wouldn't stay in a motel."

Charlie looked at him, remembering the scent of battle with his grandfather. It was the way he said "motel." *How old was I? Twelve. I just lifted that spoon to my mouth and paused, and his eyes cracked the whip of strict disgust more than words could: Don't smell your food, boy! Then I burnt my tongue not smelling the soup.*

"I was tired."

Granddaddy held out his wide, cracked palm.

"I was younger than you are when I drove across this country to California, see, and do you know I drove for thirty hours straight and only stopped when I fell asleep at the wheel." Granddaddy nodded. "See, I wouldn't think you'd want to waste your money on a *motel* when you could drive through and maybe take a nap on the side of the road for twenty minutes or so."

"People get killed on the side of the road these days, Granddaddy," he intoned softly.

Granddaddy tilted his head.

"Well, that may be, with all the nuts out there! Bunch of them down here now," he murmured, looking to the house next door. "Now, I was in the business of automobiles and people would always say to me, 'How can you drive so far and not get tired?' When I used to drive old Mr. and Miz Fredericks down to Florida every winter he'd say to me, 'I been knowin' you all these years and I still don't understand how you can drive us all the way to Florida and just take a nap!' " Granddaddy shifted the bag of groceries to his other arm and started to build a castle with his hand, laying the moat, the bridge, the towers, his words becoming the walls. "See, I did that every winter and he couldn't understand how I could drive so far—but it was only because I *liked* to drive! I find pleasure in driving the way other people have pleasure in playing golf or tennis or eatin' a watermelon, see. I *like* drivin' an automobile and the longer the better!" The castle was finished and Granddaddy cradled the whole structure. "Been that way all my life."

Granddaddy let his hand float back to his side.

"So, don't you feel bad about not being able to drive straight through. You just aren't a *professional*." Granddaddy cleared his throat. "Now, I understand you have some interviews in Richmond to get you a job."

"That's right," Charlie answered quickly.

Granddaddy looked back to the yard, sun spotting the top of his smooth-tanned head.

"Uh-huh . . . well," he said, raising a wrinkled hand, groceries cradled to his side, "you are from good people and I think you will find no trouble getting a job." He turned, picking Charlie out of the greenery around them. "Provided, you *want* one, see."

"Oh, I want one," Charlie murmured, looking down Granddaddy's yard, spreading out a good acre. "It's good to be back in the South."

Granddaddy bent his knees, bobbing slightly, his hand out for rain.

"Well now, whole lot of Yankees down here. Some right next door." Granddaddy paused, speaking in a lower tone. "They aren't bad people, once you get to know them." Granddaddy adjusted his tie, pulling one wing lower. "I just got out of the hospital, and they came over to see how I was feeling, see."

Charlie nodded slowly.

"You were in the hospital?"

"My water system was giving me trouble, see, so I spent a week with them . . ." Granddaddy gestured to a magnolia tree. "But I had to leave, because I would have died right there with all the blood those people take from you and the gizmos they have going into your arms," he explained, with his wide palm out again. "Would have died of boredom."

Charlie nodded slowly. "What'd they find out?"

Granddaddy waved away modern medicine with a single motion.

"Didn't find a thing! Gave me some pills, but they make me feel worse than I did before." Granddaddy looked at him. "Now, I have to go up the country day after tomorrow to get some files and things, and, if you don't have any interviews—"

"I'll give you a hand."

"Well, like I was saying, I'm not going 'til noon, see, and if you have an interview or something you have to do in the morning you can." Granddaddy turned. "Now, let's go in and I'll show you your room and your bath."

Charlie hesitated.

"Is it a bath or a shower?"

"What's that?"

"I take showers," Charlie said quickly.

Granddaddy's eyes bored through the softening light.

"Well, now, I take baths, showers are no good for the body, but if you want to take a shower I reckon you can—never heard of anyone *having* to take a shower, though. You have to turn on the exhaust fan before you shower or the steam will rot the wood and destroy the ceiling." He paused. "Do you know that I haven't had to repaint a room in this house for twenty years? That's because I have kept the moisture outside the house by keeping the doors and windows shut and not taking showers! I take baths! See, now, that's why I haven't ruined the walls of the house and I would suggest you do the same from now on." Granddaddy patted the top of his smooth head. "Water comin' down on your head isn't good for the body."

"I'll remember that, Granddaddy," Charlie promised, going to his car, taking out the suitcase, duffel bag, and hanging clothes.

"Now, that's a German car, isn't it?"

Charlie looked at the black Mercedes.

"Right," he nodded, remembering the overdue lease payment.

Granddaddy motioned to the car.

"I have never owned a foreign car before, but they must be good, see, because everybody has them. In my day, people only owned American cars, but it's getting so all you see is *Japanese* or *German* or just about anything but American. That's how time's changed," he finished, walking around the side of the garage.

Charlie followed Granddaddy's bowlegged stride into the cooler garage. His voice echoed along the cement floor.

"Now, wipe your feet, boy, before you go in," he instructed, sliding his Hush Puppies on the rubberized mat.

Charlie thought the mat was the one he had wiped his feet on as a child. He swiped his loafers backward, stepping into Granddaddy's hand.

"Wait a minute, boy! You have some mud on that left shoe," he said, pointing to the shoe touching the tawny floorboard of the den.

Charlie held up his loafer, seeing a dirt smudge on the heel.

"Now, you better take that shoe off. You can clean it later, see, that way you won't track dirt in."

He slipped out of his loafers, feeling the cold cement.

"Make sure they out of the way, now."

Charlie carefully lined the shoes by the freezer, then followed Granddaddy in his stocking feet.

*Charlie Tidewater*
*465 Marilee Road*
*Southampton, VA*
*August 23, one* A.M.

*Matthew,*

*Well, I'm here and it's hot. Of course Granddaddy doesn't believe in air-conditioning so I'm up in the middle of the night in my underwear writing this because it's too hot to sleep. A lot of old ghosts here. Smells like age in the house. Like when I was a boy. I'm thirty-nine and I'm back in the room I used to stay in when my mother would disappear and Dad would bring me over. Like the night she died. Did you know she died the same day Martin Luther King was shot? The night after that, Granddaddy took me to get some ice cream. Then they started burning downtown Richmond and we were the only people out.*

*He's asleep now. I wonder if you dream of the beginning or the end when you get to be his age? Dreams of the end . . . or the beginning?*

*Charlie*

# CHAPTER THREE

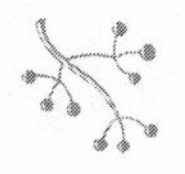

Virginia countryside

*1927*

Austin Turin stared at the animal in the barn, lambency in the headlights, liquescent on the windshield, gleaming off the dark, sinuously curved fenders in such resplendence he felt weak. He breathed in the fusty scent of hay with the gas and oil of the open and gutted Model T. His uncle had let him sit in the seat of the horseless carriage once before, holding the slippery wooden steering wheel, fingering the glass gauge with the needle between numbers and symbols foreign as any European language.

He watched Uncle Edwin and two black men pull out a squat motor and set the greasy mass on the hay-strewn dirt floor.

"Damn, boy, that is heavy," Uncle Edwin declared, smearing greased hands on his streaked coveralls.

"Yes sir, Mr. Edwin. We jes' put that one there in here an' we got ourselves a new car." The tall man nodded.

Uncle Edwin wiped the twilight smudge from his forehead, younger than his thirty-five years. He hooked a thumb on his strap.

"Rufus John, you help Snowball tighten those head bolts down," he said to the wiry boy with the long, shiny scar on his neck.

When Austin came by the garage it was Snowball who explained things and let him work on the engines. Rufus John stared with black, glittering eyes, his shaved head shiny in the garage gloom. Snowball told him Rufus John had found his own father hanging from a sour apple tree behind their farm. Austin could scarcely believe Rufus was younger than he was.

"Hey, boy—didn't your mama tell you to stay away from here?"

Austin shrugged, leaning against the doorframe in the fading afternoon.

"She don't care."

Uncle Edwin kicked hay, scuffing his boots.

"Ain't you 'sposed to be sellin' them shoes, boy?" He spat to the side.

Austin shrugged again with greased hair touching the water-rotted wood of the hay barn.

He wished for the plug of tobacco bulging in his uncle's jaw so he could spat too.

"Reckon I'm done with that job."

Uncle Edwin spat again, wiping his hands on his coveralls, running back his thin hair. He squinted at his nephew.

"You like cars, don't you, boy?"

Austin nodded, trying to contain his excitement. Uncle Edwin ran his tongue over his front teeth, watching Snowball torque down head bolts on an engine. He spat, the decision made.

"How old you, boy?"

"Sixteen."

"You drive a car?"

*"Yes sir!"*

Uncle Edwin paused, squeezing his chin between thumb and forefinger, evaluating the leaping light of enthusiasm in the boy's eyes.

"I get you out of that shoe store and get you a job drivin' a car . . . you come over a couple times a week and help Snowball with these engines?"

Austin jumped off the doorframe, sending a cloud of twilight floating up.

"I'll do it, Uncle!"

His uncle hooked his thumbs back in his straps, feeling the weariness of mechanic, salesman, owner coming in with the dusk; a rifle shot of juice stained the sandy dirt again.

"Alright, boy. You just drive Miz Rita and Miz Myrna where they want to go. . . . You sure you can reach the pedals? Alright, then, car is in the garage and you come every day at two o'clock to take them where they want to go. Sisters are peculiar in their ways, but they'll give you a nickel a day if you do them proper. And then you git on over here and help Snowball in the garage."

Austin jumped in the doorway again, losing the years he was trying for a moment ago.

"I sure will! Thanks, Uncle!"

• • •

"*Boy!* You sure you can drive this automobile?"

"Yes, ma'am," Austin replied, breathing the scent of verbena, glancing in the mirror at the two sisters crammed in the backseat with high-collared nineteenth-century dresses, shawls, and fans.

He adjusted the spark advance, the engine smoothing as they climbed the red-dirt road into the high yawn of sun.

"You look awful young to me to be driving," Miz Rita quipped, dabbing her nose with a handkerchief, waving old perfume.

"Oh, don't go that way, boy! That part of the city is close to the dump and *heaven knows* how many germs."

"Sister, just tell the boy where to go."

"I will, Sister, if he will just slow down . . . the dust of these roads is horrible. *Slow down, boy!*"

"Yes, ma'am."

He let up on the throttle, riding the brake lightly, tasting fine grit.

"I just know it's a bad day for germs . . . we never should have gone out—forget the market today, young man. Let's go home!"

Austin swung the car around, running up on both sides of the dirt road, jumbling the sisters together, staring down the burnt ruts. He squinted into the baseless light, unbounded except for a man and a plow horse on the curve of horizon.

"*Germs.* Sister, I can just feel the germs today."

Austin skirted the breach of Richmond, coming in the side roads to the sisters' home, turning into the sand alley. He stopped the car outside the garage and let the sisters out, helping the splotched and bony hands with the canes.

"Here's your nickel, boy."

Austin took the handkerchief with the coin inside.

"Thank you, ma'am."

"Hurry, Sister! There are germs *everywhere* today."

Austin stood with the dust hot in his nose, holding the nickel and watching the sisters dodder to their back door. He turned around to a red ribbon and sunshiny hair.

"Well, I declare, Austin Turin, you drive the sisters around now, do you?"

He shoved the nickel in his pocket with one eye closed and one on Tamara Drake. She had been walking slowly down the sidewalk. She sashayed over with her robin's-egg blue dress taking color from the black Hudson.

"My, I didn't know you could *drive*."

"Course I can," he retorted, eyeing the girl already called the belle of Richmond, having won the annual state-fair pageant.

Austin had seen her at the fair, where he had ridden his motorcycle to watch the stock-car races. She stood on the platform in the shimmering sun, a princess among dust and cattle. Austin couldn't help but stare. She had blossomed into the most beautiful girl he had ever seen. That had been months before, but now she was here, with eyes the color of a calm Mediterranean sea.

"I suppose you couldn't give me a ride in your auto?"

The pause was a glance toward the sisters' shuttered house.

"Reckon I can."

She ran around to the other side, then they were shooting across the quiet summer streets. He looked over, watching the whip of flaxen hair flailing light like an urgent jockey. Austin pressed hard on the floorboard, improving his hand.

"Tamara, you want to go on out to the Pamunkey River? I got a boat out there with a motor."

She brushed back her hair.

"Oh, that would be grand!" She paused. "But I don't have a swimming suit."

"Don't matter, we'll just ride around," he said, turning the sisters' car out of town.

They broke free of the last home on the outskirts of Richmond, passing people who saw the black Hudson flashing a young man with his elbow on the window and a girl with hair smoothed back into the streaming light.

Tamara pulled her head in the window.

"I declare, I would just give anything for some beer . . . do you have a cigarette?"

Austin squinted down the country road.

"Don't have a cigarette, but I might have some bootleg whiskey in that old boat."

Tamara's eyes lit, hot, leaping green in the car's shadow.

"You do!"

Austin grinned, gunning the sisters' car just ahead of the churning dust cloud.

"Reckon I might at that."

The boat roared like a wounded steel beast. There was no muffler, just a rusted pipe spitting sparks above green algae. Tamara sat while Austin yanked off the spark plug, pouring gas in the cylinder, wrapping the soaked cord-rope around the flywheel. He pulled tirelessly in the breath of bog decay around the shores of the Pamunkey, tearing new blisters, opening old ones, scattering birds from the trees with a single roar.

Tamara waited and sipped from the fruit jar in the bow, feeling the rough plank under her legs and the blot of blue material. Already she felt the small fingers of delight, the tingling rolling up her spine from the charcoal-tasting spirits.

Austin's body jumped with the white cord whipping over his shoulder.

"Is your boat broken?"

"Just about got her," Austin muttered.

Tamara took another gulp of the whiskey.

"Well, I declare, take your time—"

The motor deafened her just then. Austin grinned and jumped onto the seat, steering the boat across the green plain, feeling wind and the white-foamy rush below his right hand. He watched Tamara turn into the wind, thinking she was a goddess with her hair smoothed back. He steered toward the middle of the river, slowing enough to take the fruit jar she handed him, her eyes softly hot from the alcohol.

"You swim?" Austin yelled, tasting the chicory in the whiskey.

"Not really," she mouthed back.

Austin held the jar down, steering across the river in a white swath.

Then they went slower, the motor puttering, spitting. Tamara faced the bow again and sipped from the tea-colored jar. Austin watched her lean out over the nose of the boat, skimming her hand along the slipping green.

Shade was a line across the river and the mason jar was half empty.

"I appreciate you bringin' me out here," Tamara drawled softly, leaning back, chin toward the sky, her firm, round legs stretched out.

"My pleasure," he murmured, sipping the warm alcohol.

He guided the boat and felt the push of the whiskey. Suddenly the world was in front of him and he was on a wave looking down. The summer day and the beautiful girl lying casually in his boat giddied him up until he thought he could open the day and take out all its luscious treasures.

"I'll have my own car soon and we won't have to take the sisters'."

Tamara looked up, her eyes richer than the green Pamunkey River.

"Are you buying a car?"

"Sure I am." Austin nodded. "My uncle's goin' to sell me one, hell, he'll probably give it to me." He took one of the treasures. "He says I'm his best mechanic and he's goin' to put me to sellin' soon."

"Really?"

Austin upended the mason jar and nodded the way his uncle did when a customer asked if a car had a good engine.

"I'll have me a car soon and then . . ." He paused, letting himself go further with his dream, taking all the golden day had to offer. "One day, I'll get my own garage and sell cars from my own place and it'll be bigger than my uncle's place!"

Tamara shook her head, tipping the jar to her small mouth.

"You have it all figured out, Austin Turin."

He looked at her, then shrugged.

"I'm just runnin' off at the mouth—guess that old whiskey got me that way."

Tamara looked at him intently, coming across the boat suddenly, taking his hand in her soft palm.

"I think it's wonderful that you have dreams," she whispered, the whiskey warm on her breath. "I have my own dream too."

Austin felt his hand in hers, warmth coming up from his shirt.

"What's your dream, Tamara?"

She stared at him, the leaping light in her eyes more beautiful than the day.

"Well, if you promise not to laugh."

Austin crossed his chest solemnly.

"Promise."

"Well, I'd like to be—I'd like to be a *movie star*."

Austin stared at her and then he saw her again.

"You could do it," he said solemnly.

Tamara held his hand tighter in both her palms.

"You think so? Mother says I can. She says I'm just as pretty as any of those girls in the pictures and she has a friend in Hollywood who says she can set me up with a screen test."

The boat came to a halt under the shade of a tree. The sun dappled and danced in the green flecks of her eyes.

"I'd put you in a movie," he said, huskily.

Tamara squeezed his hand, whispering.

"We'll both get what we want—I just know it."

She leaned back and Austin turned quickly to the motor.

"All set?"

Tamara nodded, getting back into the front of the boat.

"Let's go as fast as we can!"

Austin pulled the rip cord and opened the throttle. He crisscrossed the river several times, jerking the boat around with Tamara laughing as they hydroplaned crazily from one side to the other. She stood suddenly with her arms wide. Austin cut back on a turn, but it was too late. Tamara flipped out like an acrobat. He turned the boat again, grabbing her hair as she went under.

"*Whew!*" she called, flowing with the boat. "I declare! That whiskey has just about knocked me down!"

"You be careful there, Tamara," he said, helping her into the boat with the dress a skintight blue.

The water left her face smooth and aquiline in the afternoon light.

"I just love going fast!"

Austin turned to the motor sputtering a rainbow of gas in the leaky boat.

"Let's see if I can get this old crank goin' again," he murmured, turning the throttle to the gunshot of a blue backfire flame.

The cylinder head and gas water flamed invisibly.

"C'mon, Tamara, reckon we better get out of the boat."

"But I just got back in."

Austin watched the flames lick across the bottom, whipping for the gas tank in back. He grabbed Tamara around the middle, jumping over the side as flames engulfed the boat.

"Damn! Thought that leaky carburetor might get us in trouble," he said, spitting out river water.

Tamara kept her arms around his neck while he floated on his back, stroking toward shore through sun-warmed water. He could see pearls of water dabbed on her smooth skin, a fine cluster on the bridge of her nose.

"Oh, and what a shame!" She laughed out loud. "We were having such a lovely time."

There was a blast. A flaming gas can arced into the water, hissing as it disappeared.

"Reckon that's about it for that boat."

"What'll you do?"

Austin kept swimming, turning to look for the shore.

"Build another."

"You know how to build a boat?"

"Build the motor."

Her eyes held the iridescence of the water as they flowed in their backwater movement.

"You must be mighty smart."

He grinned.

"Some."

Tamara looked at the boat disappearing into the flat green.

"I am so sorry we lost the whiskey."

"More where that came from."

"Oh, good," She hugged his neck. "I do love whiskey."

They reached the shore, walking up to the muddy bank. Tamara squeezed water from her hair as they climbed into the sisters' car and drove for Richmond through the forest gloom.

Austin followed the dusty white line cutting right, then left, in the glare. The alcohol slowed him down on the dark curves, though he expertly handled the big Hudson's tail swings on the loose dirt. Tamara cheered for him to go faster. He glanced in the rearview mirror, staring into the glimmering darkness.

"Somethin' back there."

Tamara turned around.

"I don't see anything."

"Keep watchin' . . ." Austin kept his eye on the mirror. "There."

"Why, I believe you're right. . . . Is that a car?"

Austin could see the black shape flitting through moon shadows.

"Reckon so . . ." Austin muttered, gunning the Hudson.

"Why doesn't he have his lights on?"

He shrugged.

"Bootlegger, probably. . . ."

"He's coming closer."

Austin glanced up and saw the grillwork not twenty feet away.

"Damn that boy's got an engine in that thing."

He opened it up, barely making the turns. Austin looked behind. The car was barreling toward his back bumper.

"Means to bump us," he nodded, skidding on a turn.

"He's still coming!"

The car was dead behind them and Austin could see a man's arm outside the window. He started zigzagging and the black car followed perfectly.

"Going to hit us—hold on, Tamara!"

The road whipped suddenly to the right. Austin jerked the wheel, knowing he had turned too hard and too fast. The big Hudson lifted onto two wheels, headlights picking out branches and leaves of a frozen moment and they became a carnival car, perfectly balanced, and then the world began its sickening rotation. Austin held tightly to the wheel as the car rolled over in a slow-motion groan of metal and shrieking glass. Something hit Austin in the back of the neck. He heard Tamara and then she went away and the world rotated again. Then it all just stopped.

Austin lay against his door with Tamara in his arms. Her head was on his shoulder as if they were a couple watching a movie. There was silence after shattering glass and crushing metal. The car was on its side with the radiator hissing.

"You alright?"

Tamara's head moved slowly.

"I . . . I think so . . ."

"Looks like you're cut . . . don't look deep," he lied, able to see only a dark slick on her arm.

"I'm alright," she repeated, trying to sit up. "I didn't think the car would ever stop turning over!"

"Me neither. Reckon we'll have to climb out your window."

He helped Tamara to the window, pushing her up in her damp dress. She sat on the edge of the car, then jumped. Austin smelled raw gas as he climbed down. Pale light filtered through the lather of tree branches and gleamed on the bumper. They walked through the forest to the road.

"Just a scrape."

"I knew it wasn't bad," she lied, then started crying.

"What? What is it? Are you hurt?"

"I . . ." She sobbed, wiping her eyes with the back of her hand. "I lost my purse."

"Oh."

Austin turned back to the tree line.

"Alright, tell you what—you stay right here and I'll go get it."

She brightened, wiping her nose again, more beautiful with the glisten on her cheeks.

"Oh, would you?"

"Just stay here."

He went into the woods and came upon the hissing car with the gas vapor stronger. White puffed out the sides of the hood. He stepped on the driveshaft and weaseled his way in the window. Austin felt around the broken glass until he found the purse wedged between the seat and door.

He made his way back to the road.

"Oh! You got it!"

"Yep." He nodded, handing it to her. "Looks like it didn't even open up."

She took out a brush and started stroking her hair.

"Guess we better get walking," Austin said, staring down the road.

"I wonder what time it is?" She looked at him. "My folks will be worried sick."

Austin jammed his hands in his pockets.

"Mine too."

"Why do you think that car was trying to hit us?"

Austin spat in the dust.

"Reckon only he knows that."

They had walked for twenty minutes when a truck came

from Richmond. Austin waved it down, walking to the side of the motor purr, seeing six men in the bed of the truck. A spark flared under a wide-brimmed hat.

"Where y'all headed?"

Austin turned.

"Ran our car off the road and tryin' to get back to Richmond."

The country man looked down the road.

"Just passed a car goin' hell-fo'-leather fo' Richmond."

Austin nodded.

"Reckon he run us off the road."

The man regarded him solemnly.

"Bootlegger," he nodded to Austin's expression. "Y'all get in and we'll see if we can get your car on the road."

Two of the men in the cab got in back with the others. Austin and Tamara rode up front until they reached the curve in the road. Austin walked with the men to the tree line.

"She's on her side, is she." The driver nodded his brimmed hat to the black mass shining beneath a low moon.

"Reckon we all push, she ought to fall over," Austin said.

They tramped into the woods, taking positions against the car, illuminated by the truck lights peeping through the trees. They pushed and pushed, rocking the car on crackling glass. Another truck pulled over and two more men helped. This was after Austin and the men darkened their shirts in the night air.

With the two extra men the Hudson groaned, then fell to its wheels. The driver of the truck nodded to the car, now without one smooth piece of metal.

"Think she'll start?"

"Reckon so."

Austin wrenched open the door. He cranked the motor

over once. The man with the brimmed hat spat into the brush.

"Y'all be careful, now," he said, straightening up. "Dance down the road if y'all want to come along."

Austin stepped out and let Tamara in the driver's side.

"Mighty nice of you, but we better get on back."

The truck swung away and Austin started driving for town. The car could only turn right and he had to back up for left turns. The next night he told his uncle about the police in front of Tamara's house at two o'clock in the morning. He didn't tell his uncle about Tamara turning to him when they saw the police, turning to him in the dark, delicious privacy of the car, kissing him on the lips.

"Thank you, Austin Turin. I had a *wonderful* time."

Uncle Edwin listened to his story in silence on the way back from bailing him out of the police station. He didn't say a word until they reached the garage and he turned off the motor.

"I did you a favor here now, boy, and one day I'll ask you for one."

He didn't speak of the incident again until two years later.

*"Boy!"*

Austin looked up from the workbench in the barn. Uncle Edwin stood in the doorway against the evening tide in the shirt and tie he wore to sell cars.

"You graduating tomorrow, aren't you, boy?"

"Yes sir." Austin nodded, putting down the file he was using to smooth valves, but not before he ran his finger over the rough side.

"You plannin' to go off to college?"

Austin shrugged.

"Thought about the academy."

Uncle Edwin leaned against the doorway, the slide rule in his top pocket, jingling coins Austin couldn't see.

"Boy, you 'member when I got you out of that county jail?"

Austin nodded, a slow grin escaping.

"Yes, sir."

"An' you 'member I told you one day I was goin' to ask you a favor, boy."

"Reckon I do."

Uncle Edwin spat in the dusk-colored dust.

"Callin' my marker due."

He took a step into the garage, looking at his nephew.

"Anybody knows automobiles the way you do, boy, has no business wasting time in *college*. They ain't goin' to teach you anything you need to know. If it was anybody else, reckon I wouldn't be sayin' this, but you have a mind for automobiles that I never seen and reckon it's important to say my piece." He paused as Snowball walked across the barn door. Uncle Edwin tilted his fedora back, hands resting on hips. "Yo' daddy want you to go?"

"Daddy's been up in the country, five years now."

Uncle Edwin nodded.

"In that log cabin, is he?"

"Yes sir, reckon he don't like town life."

Uncle Edwin was quiet, looking around the shop of used and new automobiles. Snowball was in the twilight gloom, his hammer pinging out the moment.

"Automobile business growin', boy. Ain't no one I seen work out figures on a slide rule way you can, knows how many parts I got in the shop, knows what's wrong with an engine just by listenin' to it. You got a bright future, boy. Stay with me and I put you to sellin'."

Austin lifted the gray file off the bench, fingering the rough surface again, smiling inside for what he wanted to hear.

"Reckon I stay, then."

His uncle spat off to the side.

"Won't regret it, boy," he called back, walking out into the velvet evening.

Austin turned back to the bench, hearing something. He squinted into the barn; Rufus John lay against the wall, smiling in the glaring darkness.

# CHAPTER FOUR

Southampton, Virginia

*August 1998*

Charlie woke and lay in the balmy warmth of the night breeze. Darkness cast shadow on the tangled sheet by his knees, turning his shirt on the chair to dirty linen. He turned toward the gauzy curtains swinging out with the wind and rose up on one elbow. Charlie heard the noise again. The curtains waved like water in a long curl, then fell flat. A dog barked. Twice. He lay down slowly, watching the still cloth. He blinked, then shut his eyes. Hard shoes clicked toward him.

Charlie sat up straight and the shoes stopped. He felt the breeze under his arms. A dried stick snapped him out of bed. The lacy curtains tufted gently, then fell. Charlie stood in the middle of the room. The curtain puffed again, toying with the open page of his journal. He saw the sharp point of his pen. The dog down the street barked once more against the low breath of crickets and Charlie felt his breathing slow. He would prove to himself it was nothing. He took a step toward the window.

*"Hey . . . Jack . . ."*

A shadow was in the cottony light.

*"Hey, Jack . . . I know who you are . . ."*

The voice was hoarse, like a whisper of sand in an empty hall.

*"Hey, Jack . . . tell yo' granddaddy I stopped by . . . I know who you are, Jack. . . ."*

The face vanished and Charlie heard the muffled scruff of grass, the far-off click of hard shoes on cement, then quiet. He went to the window and peeked through the curtains. Charlie looked around the short hedges bordering the house, watching the smooth landscape of Granddaddy's lawn. Nothing.

Charlie woke in sun and threw on his clothes from the night before, walking around to the front of the house, pushing through the prickly shrub, staring at the ground beneath his window.

"It was just a dream," he muttered, kneeling down.

Charlie brushed away leaves and dried sticks with his fingertips. He sucked his breath in sharply, staring at the mossy, damp earth, then touched the footprint in the clay.

*Richmond is a yawning summer-baked ghost of some past glory* went through Charlie's mind as he walked the curving, ascending streets in the breath of morning. He was amazed. There were no people. The teeming throngs of Michigan Avenue had been replaced by a lone man in a khaki suit who nodded to him briefly. There were only the dark dwellings of the previous century with their intense quiet adorning the bricked sidewalks.

There were people, but they were an afterthought, visitors passing through the museum. There was only the bright, fierce heat and the past lurking in the drooping willows and wide, shady porticos. The past dwarfed the people. Maybe that was it, he thought. The present wasn't big enough. People are either of the moment or are forever dwarfed by those who came before.

Charlie reached his car with the groceries and wound his way down the sun-burnished streets. The gate of the cemetery came into view. Hollywood Cemetery was home to a few presidents, Patrick Henry, numerous Confederate generals of note, and thousands of Confederate soldiers lost during the siege of Richmond. It was also where his mother was buried.

Charlie descended into the old cemetery, following the winding road to the high bluffs overlooking the James. The James River Bridge crossed the valley of mossy water in tan ovals. Egg boulders flared in the river, splashes firing around the base. In the distance were the clustered buildings of Richmond. Charlie parked his car. His mother's grave wasn't far and he began walking. It had been a while since he thought of the day when the man burst in on his cartoons and announced Martin Luther King was dead. He was only nine years old, but he knew this was something important. His father took him to his granddaddy's that night.

Charlie turned and recognized a group of headstones. Far away he saw a woman in black bending down. He passed the ornate stones of the nineteenth century, smoothed gray from rain and age. Charlie reached his mother's grave. A faint discoloration had begun at the edges of the marble, a spidery black vein down the middle.

TAMARA DRAKE TIDEWATER
Born July 10, 1933. Died April 4, 1968
Loving Mother and Wife

*The beautiful are broken,*
*And the swift are slowed*

Charlie looked at the second stone, his grandmother's, older, gray, faded. He wondered again at the decision to bury her with her mother, thinking his father should have reserved that space for himself. But he was in a cemetery in Chicago among tract homes, near the suburb of his second wife. She had laid claim to his soul years before.

Charlie touched the smooth marble surface. His mother was screaming again. It seemed every night her voice came through the door and across the quiet light of his boyhood. He would start humming with fingers in his ears, words stabbing his heart as he hugged the pillow. Charlie could hear the low utterances of his father's voice against the background of his mother's virulent soprano. Then there were the memories that made no sense to him. There were the icy dinners, which choked his father's jokes and destroyed his own appetite. All his life he would associate hunger with anxiety. Then his mother became sick and he wondered why his father didn't stay home. His father was a traveling salesman; he would appear on weekends and there would be a thick steak, the yard was cut, a door hinge fixed, lightbulbs replaced. Then he would go away again on Monday. The house was quiet during the week and Charlie wondered if his mother was lonely.

Even when his father was home he was always working. He was a businessman and was about his business every minute of the day. He was the type of man who would talk to a person on the phone while watching television or writing a letter. People simply weren't enough to occupy him. Charlie thought his father was very American that way. They never touched. He could not think of one instance where they hugged or shook hands. He always thought it odd when he saw other boys hug their fathers.

But his mother gave him the gift of his life. They were home together during that part of the day when cars didn't come down the streets and life was somewhere else. She was pointing out a bumblebee pollinating a large purple peony, telling him how bees were good for flowers.

"I want to be a *gardener*," he suddenly proclaimed.

His mother held his hand.

"Charlie, you can be anything and do anything you want as long as you believe you can."

It was a simple moment of growing up, but it was her parting gift.

Now, looking down at her headstone, Charlie leaned over and touched the cool white marble, tracing the lettering. When he looked up, a man with oily hair and wire-rimmed sunglasses stood ten feet away. The man chewed on something.

"She didn't feel much," he said, spatting beyond bruised cowboy boots.

Charlie stood up.

"Pardon me—"

"Wasn't like people don't know your mama . . . good family . . . First Family of Virginia." He nodded in the shimmer of heat, skin the color of raw salmon.

"You ain't shit you ain't FFV."

He hunched down, replacing the pouch of tobacco in his top pocket, the small line pinched in the corner of his mouth. The man ran a hand through his hair, revealing forearms blue with bleeding tattoos.

"I'm sorry, I don't think we've met—"

"Yo' granddaddy, he knows." The man's jaw moved in a slow circular rhythm. "Things he ain't talkin' 'bout . . . but it's been a long time since yo' mama died." The dark glasses tilted up. "Ain't it, *Jack*?"

Charlie shaded his eyes and felt his heart pound beneath his shirt. The man stood in the drone of cicadas, heat rising from the scorched grass.

"Who are you?"

The man hooked a swollen hand on his oversized buckle and shot a stream of brown tobacco juice at Charlie's feet.

"Take care, *Jack*."

He turned, walking slowly away.

"Hey!" Charlie took a step. *"Hey!"*

The man crested the ridge, then disappeared. Charlie stared after him. A faint breeze cooled the perspiration on the back of his neck, the cicadas rilling down to the approaching solstice. The woman in black passed distantly among the tombs.

Charlie walked into the light of August discontent. Granddaddy's rake created a small dust cloud, and he shaded his eyes.

"Now, did you finish your errands?"

Charlie nodded.

"Yes . . . listen, Granddaddy." He paused. "I was at Mom's grave . . ."

Granddaddy stopped his line of dried leaves and twigs. His hands were on top of the smooth rake handle, the sun harsh on his cheek and eye. He brushed a mosquito from his leg, his hand returning to the rake.

"There was this man—he came up behind me and seemed to know things about Mom."

Granddaddy scratched his cheek slowly.

"And last night—I heard something outside the window and thought I saw a man in the curtains." Charlie paused, squinting at his grandfather. "Are you in some kind of trouble?"

Granddaddy slapped his arm, wiping the insect clean.

"You probably just heard some animal," he said, starting to rake again.

Charlie watched him scuffing the ground.

"But the man at Mom's grave—"

"Now, what did he look like?"

"Big, sunglasses, large belt buckle, tattoos on both arms."

Granddaddy reached down and picked up the line of grass, carrying it to a round wire pen. He dropped the dead life on top of a soft mound of decay.

"Could be somebody who worked for me. I was in the automobile business and hired lots of mechanics, see, so he might have worked for me at some time."

"What about the things he knew about Mom?"

Granddaddy paused with the rake, shutting one eye against the sun.

"Richmond's a small town, boy, could be *any kind* of crazy person, see." He held his wide palm up to the sun. "So, I wouldn't worry about it."

Charlie watched him pick up some more leaves and drop them into the burning pen. He looked around at the dying yard.

"Your grass looks like it needs water."

Granddaddy looked at the lawn.

"I have to get the sprinkler out from under the house one of these days."

Charlie nodded. "I'll change and give you a hand."

"Now, don't worry about me, boy, we goin' to be leavin' for the country soon anyway."

Granddaddy started to rake the small line of twigs and leaves again.

"Well, if you're sure you're not in any trouble."

"No, no trouble, boy . . ."

Charlie hesitated, then walked toward the house.

"Just crazy people," Granddaddy murmured, the muffled scruff following Charlie in the dead grass.

The metronome tick of the blinker had been going for twenty miles but Charlie didn't say a word. When he was a boy, Charlie never told Granddaddy his blinker was on, because he thought the clicking green light had something to do with the operation of the car, but now he realized it was the operation of the man.

Charlie assumed Granddaddy knew where they were going. He had swung the car onto the four-lane highway with only a brassy hum escaping his pursed lips, but then he began squinting through his reading glasses at the overhead signs, clicking his tongue, murmuring, "Darn signs, can't make head or tail of them." Charlie pulled out the map from the glove box.

"Granddaddy—I think we just passed I-Ninety-Five," he murmured, studying the map.

"Where?"

"Back there."

Granddaddy clucked his tongue, ducking under the pulled visor as if the road were above the car.

"Now, they changed the durn roads." Granddaddy lifted one hand off the wheel. "I don't even know how you get off this road!"

"It's an expressway. We have to wait for an exit."

Granddaddy pulled at his bow tie and hit the dashboard, leaving a three-finger imprint in the curve of sunburnished dust.

"See, now, that's the problem nowadays. Before, you just had one road going to a particular place. But now, you have *big roads* that don't go anywhere. They just go on by places, see."

Charlie leaned back in the seat.

"I think that's an exit up there."

Granddaddy squinted. "Don't see anything."

"Right there, Granddaddy." Charlie pointed. "It's right there—Exit Twenty-five."

"Now, that's not where we want to go."

"But to get where we want to go we have to get off here."

Granddaddy shook his head.

"No, that doesn't make sense. We're looking for Interstate Ninety-Five—"

"I told you, we passed it back there!"

"Then we have to turn around, not get off at a different street," he murmured.

"Granddaddy, that *is* how we turn around—you have to get off at an exit," he explained, watching the exit zoom by. Charlie took a deep breath. "There's another exit coming up. On the other side will be a ramp to reenter the expressway."

Granddaddy looked at the cars going the other way.

"Now, whoever designed this road didn't have the driver in mind, see," he grumbled. "It's a lucky thing that I am always prepared, because on this durn road no tow truck could get to you! See, I always carry a gallon of water and some tape. People don't do that anymore, but with a gallon of water and some tape you can get yourself to a filling station to be serviced." He glanced at Charlie, his wide hand hovering above the wheel. "See, now, here's the reason. If you blow a hose and lose all your water, and keep driving, your engine will be ruined." His forefinger became a flag bisecting the space between them. "But! With a gallon of water and some tape, you can tape up that old hose and fill your radiator and get to a filling station, see."

Charlie jumped forward.

"Get in the right lane."

Granddaddy looked in the rearview mirror irritably, switching the left blinker to the right.

"I'll do it, but I don't see where we goin' to turn around," he murmured, weaving the car into the horn blare of a small compact. "What kind of nut—"

They watched the white car become a small oval, then an egg as it crested the swell in the highway and disappeared.

"I didn't see him either," Charlie admitted tiredly, wondering if events weren't conspiring against them.

"See, drivers don't *respect* each other today. I been driving for all my life and never had a serious accident or received a speeding ticket, and received a *citation* from the Division of Motor Vehicles saying so."

Charlie looked into his side mirror and saw another white car float out from behind a truck. He looked up as a green sign appeared above a cluster of trees like a flat dirigible.

"There's another exit."

"I don't see no—"

"Right there, Granddaddy!"

"Now, maybe we should keep going and look—"

*"No!"* Charlie pointed. "Get off here!"

Granddaddy shook his head, veering off onto the ramp. They descended into a running line of sun-faded buildings in shades of gray. The trash, the people in doorways, the slow burn of despair breathing up from the streets congealed into an understanding that they had found the bad part of Richmond.

The buildings reminded Charlie of faded drawings where the lines are in danger of disappearing into pale light. The streets were lined with low-slung cars, and a few blackened carcasses had become sitting pieces. Men leaned on bumpers and sat in car seats among the weeds.

"Go left," Charlie directed, rolling up his window in the warm car.

"Lots of them here," Granddaddy murmured.

"Go *left*, Granddaddy."

They passed into the looming shadow of the expressway, moving under the skeleton of girders holding the road aloft from the ghetto. Charlie could hear cars whooshing overhead with the whine stretched out like a passing train. The sun had lost its dimension, becoming a hazy, bleaching light.

"Now, I don't see no road back onto the highway."

"It's here," Charlie muttered, turning around, looking for the road, fully realizing his mistake.

This was one of those exits that for some reason had no return ramp. He began to feel a slight panic.

"Told you that you couldn't just turn around on these roads, but you wouldn't listen to me. Now, you see what you've gotten us into," Granddaddy continued, driving slowly past a man lying on the sidewalk in the heat.

"We'll just find another exit back onto the expressway," Charlie snapped, feeling a pearl of sweat descend his brow.

"Now, I don't know about these neighborhoods, see."

"We'll be fine, the war's over."

"That may be, but—"

"There's a sign for the expressway."

His grandfather glanced at him.

"Why would we go back on that durn highway when that was where all the trouble started in the first place?"

"Because that's how we're going to get out of here!"

"No sir." Granddaddy shook his head resolutely. "Now, I listened to you once, see, and look what happened to us." He held the outside world on the flat of his hand. "We're in the *colored* section of town, liable to get robbed, or hit on the head!" He shook his head again. "No, I'm not going to listen to you anymore or we might end up in the town dump next, see."

He turned down a street of leaning white skeletons bleaching in the merciless heat; monuments to the burnings after King was assassinated. Charlie grabbed his eyes, feeling the pound of blood in his temples. He reached for the air conditioner.

"We don't need the air conditioner, boy," Granddaddy grumbled, snapping it off.

"It's a hundred degrees out!"

"You can't run the air conditioner going this slow, boy, or the car will overheat. Then where will we be? You have to have the proper RPM's to drive the compressor, or you'll end up making your engine work too hard. Now, it's not that warm out anyway, and once we get out of this mess *you* got us in, you can roll down your window."

Charlie felt the smooth tickle slipping down his back and sides.

"I'm rolling down the window," he muttered.

"I told you we are in the *colored section* of town—"

"They probably say the same thing about the white part of town."

Granddaddy shook his head. Charlie turned back to

the window, laying his head in the futile breeze of rotting garbage.

"Roll that window up, boy!"

"No—"

Granddaddy slammed on the brakes and Charlie fell into the dash. They were snugged to the bumper of a tan Cadillac convertible stopped in the road. Two men without shirts stood up in the featureless light. Charlie felt a trickle of fear in his bowels as the black, lanky bodies moved toward them.

"Now, these boys shouldn't be changing a tire in the road," Granddaddy muttered.

"Let's get out of here, Granddaddy," Charlie murmured, watching the men approach the car.

Granddaddy started rolling down his window.

"What are you doing?"

"Rolling down my window—"

The man covered the door with shadow, leaning easily on the top of the car. Charlie saw a mouth surrounded by a wiry goatee.

The other man blotted the light on his side; Charlie saw the evening news with the tragic story of the grandfather and grandson lost in the bad section of town. Granddaddy squinted up at the man.

"Now, y'all should pull your car off the road to change that tire."

Charlie felt his heart hammer his chest. The sweating man on Granddaddy's side nodded, long fingers cradling a distended belly button.

"Got no lug wrench."

"Put the car in reverse," Charlie said mechanically as the man on his side tapped on the window.

Granddaddy pulled at his bow tie.

"Well, I'll tell you what I'm going to do," he announced, with his hands still on the steering wheel. "Since y'all are blocking traffic anyway and our way through, I'm going to let you use my lug wrench, and that will help you get the tire on your automobile changed faster, see. My lug wrench is in the trunk and—"

Charlie felt his throat constrict, a high, unnatural squeak escaping. He grabbed Granddaddy by the arm, keeping a thin smile on his face, speaking like a mannequin through clenched teeth.

"Granddaddy! What the fuck are you doing?"

His grandfather saw for the first time the sweating, tremulous person of his grandson.

"Now, what kind of language is that to use around people you don't know, or around me, for that matter."

Charlie heard another tap on the glass. It sounded like a gun barrel against the window. He turned slowly, rolling down the window a hairline crack to see a scraggly beard and few teeth.

"Hey, man, we ain't goin' to do nothin' to you. Just goin' to fix our ride and then be on our way."

Charlie smiled. Granddaddy opened the car door.

"Now, I'm just going to help these boys with their tire."

Charlie watched him, then opened his own door into the stifling heat. Cars roared on the distant expressway. Several people were sitting on a brown car seat in the shade of the trestle, bottles glinting in their hands. Charlie walked back to the trunk.

"Granddaddy."

"Hold on, boy," he murmured, going through the organized trunk with his white sleeves still cuffed and pressed.

"Give them the lug wrench and let's get the hell out of

here," Charlie hissed by his ear, keeping an eye on the two men in front of Granddaddy's car.

"Now, I'm going to let these boys use my lug wrench and then we'll go on," he continued, picking up the iron tool. He stood up from the trunk. "Now, do y'all need any water? I always carry a gallon just in case my radiator hose breaks."

"Don't need none fo' my radiator but sure use a drink for myself," the man by Granddaddy's window nodded.

Granddaddy eyed the water.

"Reckon it's alright for drinking."

He walked to the rusting Cadillac beached on three wheels and hiked up his shorts, examining the car on one knee.

"Hmmm . . . y'all jack this car down, see, and we can get that tire off a whole lot quicker! You don't have anything to torque against with that wheel in the air."

The man with the goatee let the car down. Granddaddy stayed on one knee in his shorts and knee-high socks, methodically loosening the bolts with the lug wrench.

"Alright, now, put it up."

He pumped his arm, hot metal groaning against the clicketyclick of the jack. Granddaddy stood up, brushing his knee with a quick slap as Charlie walked up. He turned abruptly.

"How are y'all today?"

The men on the car set under the viaduct murmured a raspy reply. Granddaddy turned back to the car.

"Now, tighten those bolts crossway, see, so your tire will seat properly."

The young man moved fast with the lug wrench.

"Bring it down," Granddaddy nodded, watching the car float down to the street.

"Y'all better get this on to a filling station, see, and get that tire properly inflated so you don't have another flat."

"That's exactly where we goin'." The skinny man nodded, handing him the lug wrench.

"Now, I'm glad to have been able to help y'all and I was wondering if you would help me now," Granddaddy said, bobbing slightly with the lug wrench to his side. "See, the reason we came upon you is that we are lost, my grandson got us this way," he explained in a low voice. "So, we need to know which way is best to go to get back to I-Ninety-Five."

The man with the goatee pointed a skinny arm down the road.

"Go on and you see another sign for 'spressway."

Granddaddy nodded slowly.

"Alright . . . I think we can do that," he murmured. "Well, I want to thank you for the directions, and I'd get that car to a filling station where you can get your spare patched," he said, shaking hands with the men.

"Thanks for letting us use yo' lug wrench," the tall, skinny man nodded. He turned to Charlie suddenly. "See, I told you, man, you alright now."

Charlie felt heat in his face and smiled uneasily.

"Y'all have a good day," Granddaddy called, walking back to the open trunk.

"Now! They were nice people, see," he said, shutting the door as the Cadillac pulled away.

Granddaddy began to drive, floating one hand up.

"See, you help people and they help you. Now, this is the highway that boy was talking about." He turned toward the expressway arrow. "It just goes to show you, you never can tell about people." He flattened his hand on his chest. "See, now I would have *thought* we have some trouble, but now they give us directions, and we help them with their automobile, see."

He paused again, beating the air in his finale.

"So! In other words, you never can tell about people, can you?"

Granddaddy looked at Charlie slumped against the door, thinking he looked pale, placing his hand back on the wheel. He nodded to himself.

"No sir, you never can."

# CHAPTER FIVE

Virginia countryside

*1998*

Charlie watched the ramshackle houses with people waving on porches become fallow tobacco fields. An abandoned gas station flashed by. He rested his elbow on the open window of the car, the Virginia warmth filling the open windows, ruffling his shirt and picking at Granddaddy's shirtsleeves.

"Now, that's where I grew up."

Charlie looked outside the car to a white-columned house topping a gentle rise. The house looked curiously unreal.

"You were born there?"

Granddaddy nodded, the steering wheel secured with one hand high and the other resting lightly on the horn.

"That's right, I grew up there for a time."

Charlie turned around to the glimmer of antebellum life, a toy citadel on a hill.

"Do you ever go there and see if it's the same?"

"Lord, no."

Charlie looked at his grandfather.

"Aren't you curious about the place?"

"Reckon I'm not," he murmured. "Been abandoned for some time."

Granddaddy slowed, then pulled off the highway to a squat white-brick building. The structure was without company and floated against the mazy backdrop of country sky. Granddaddy parked the car next to an island of cement, the ripped pipes of dead gas pumps glinting copper. A man stood by the door; Charlie could see a bright red feather in the band of his hat.

"There's Jigger Hix." Granddaddy pointed. "Good old country boy, keeps an eye on the place for me when I can't get up here."

The car motor was louder in its absence. Gravel and glass crackled beneath their feet.

"Halo, Jigger," Granddaddy called, shaking his hand.

"Don't think I met this one."

"Now, Jigger Hix, this is my grandson, Charlie Tidewater, who has come down from Chicago to get himself a job."

"Welllll," Jigger nodded, shaking his hand, a grip like a piece of dense wood. "Mighty fine to meet you. Your granddaddy been talkin' about you for years and I see you a lot better lookin' than your granddaddy!"

He laughed in a rumbling, hoarse voice.

"Reckon he is," Granddaddy murmured, walking to the door.

Charlie stared at the two men; Jigger Hix's short-sleeved checked shirt, baggy pants pulled high, and his granddaddy

in a stiff white shirt an
them in the hot, remors
have been surprised to se

"Now, isn't that son
Granddaddy. "I know I loc

Granddaddy walked in.

"Reckon you forgot."

Charlie looked beyond
wrecked cars; headlights a
among brown weeds and wi
pines rimmed the back of the

"You comin' in, boy?"

Charlie walked into the bui … dust and the kerosene scent of aged motor oil. Light streamed through dust-coated glass, spiderwebs mazing sun-split front windows. Charlie walked into a car bay with hydraulic-lift holes still in the floor. Two fifty-gallon drums, OIL stenciled on the side, were against a wall with an S-curved pump frozen halfway. Jigger Hix leaned against a grimy counter, smoke zipping up through the light, ashes falling to the floor.

"Yes sir, your granddaddy is quite a character," he nodded. "I tell you a story about your granddaddy—I bought many a car from him, yes sir, an I 'member a fellow from up the country came in, a colored fella, and he said to your granddaddy, 'I want to buy that old Nash you have there on the back lot.' " Jigger shifted his weight. "Your granddaddy said, 'You can have it, but it has a bad battery in it, and that's going to give you some trouble.' " Jigger Hix smoked blue again, his long ash falling before him. "So this fella—he says, 'That don't matter, I want to buy the car anyway.' So your granddaddy gave him a right fair price, as I recall, and this fella drives away. Jest about an hour later we see that old Nash come back down the highway and pull in to the front.

and walks up to your granddaddy and
e a car with a bad battery!' " Jigger Hix
, your granddaddy says, 'I told you that.' And
. An' this boy says he didn't, an' that he's goin' to
attery with him! So, he takes a battery off the counter
starts like all get-out for his car. Well, next thing I know, your granddaddy is running out there with a pistol—big heavy son of a gun, course I didn't even know he had one." Jigger Hix rumbled and shook his head. "Well, this boy saw him comin' and jumps into that car and goes screeching down the highway like all get-out! So, I run out there and your granddaddy is staring after him with that pistol, and I say, 'Austin! You weren't really goin' to shoot that boy, were you?' " Jigger Hix paused, his watery blue eyes flooding over behind his glasses. "An' he looks at me, and says, 'I would have if I hadn't forgot the bullets!' "

Jigger's cigarette collapsed and he slapped his knee.

" 'Would have if I didn't forget the bullets!' Can you believe that? They don't make them like your granddaddy anymore." He laughed again, shaking his head. "No sirree, your granddaddy is quite an individual, yes sir, that he is . . ."

Charlie heard Granddaddy and looked into a room just larger than a closet off the near bay. Papers splayed across the top of the desk; a faded calendar with a couple smoking cigarettes in 1968 hung on a wall. A tin washed-out DRINK COCA-COLA thermometer caught the door light above a black safe.

"Now! I want to put these drawers in the trunk," Granddaddy said, flipping through yellowed files.

Charlie unhinged the drawer, the weight making him hurry to the car. He set the drawer on the bumper. Charlie looked at the moldy yellow files. He opened a dirty manila folder to crackling invoices, ink-faded checks, smudged receipts, Studebaker advertisements from 1934. A datebook filled with the faded lines of a fountain pen flashed through the pale sun.

*Call John Henry back on new cars due on Tuesday . . . Flowers ordered for opening . . . Don't forget to pick up present for Tamara . . . Doctor's appointment on Friday for Tamara . . . Call councilmen on zoning . . . Uncle Edwin called . . . Get Snowball to hire new mechanic . . .*

Charlie put the appointment calendar into the file, seeing the edge of a black-and-white photograph. A tall black man and a teenager with slicked-back hair leaned against a pale car. The older man smirked and wore the brimmed cap Charlie had seen in movies.

"Boy! What are you doing out there?"

He put the file back, leaving the picture. After the last drawer was in the car Charlie wandered around the building through copper light slanting in from the picture windows. He opened a door; a narrow stairwell climbed darkly to a second floor.

"Hey, Granddaddy—this is that apartment you used to live in, right?"

Granddaddy appeared next to him.

"Nothin' up there, boy," he grumbled, closing the door.

"Didn't you live up there for a time?"

"Uh-huh," he said, walking outside.

Charlie walked to the window and saw Granddaddy and Jigger Hix talking by the car. He turned and climbed the stairs with the open door behind, the heated air of an attic rushing toward him. He opened the second door and stepped into the snuffed lambency of undisturbed years. The room was a sepia-toned photograph of parlors and living rooms in nineteenth-century homes. Two end tables with rose-glass lamps bordered a sofa with a rusty spring piercing the back cushion.

Charlie stepped on creaking floorboards. His dust-coated reflection hung in a mirror over a tarnished brass bed. A stove and a refrigerator sprouting a cooling coil secured the far wall. The sun went behind a cloud and left a stain in the wood floor like something below the surface of water. The hard roof light streamed back in. Charlie turned to the windows in their lightless dimension, seeing something he couldn't place, but felt in the void he was seeing.

They filled the car with parts until the body sagged on the back wheels. Jigger Hix locked the door and drove off in a loud Falcon that fit with his hat and Camel nonfilters. Charlie and Granddaddy rested against the car, staring at the garage with the faded STP emblem tacked on the corner.

"Reckon that does it."

Charlie squinted, brushing off dust and paint chips.

"You sold the place?"

"Uh-huh."

Charlie picked up the picture from the corner of the trunk.

"Who's that, Granddaddy?"

He took the picture, one side of his mouth growing.

"That's me and a good old boy named Snowball—best mechanic you ever saw and a loyal friend."

"You ever see him anymore?"

"No—reckon he's probably dead—lived upcountry last I heard." He looked at the sun glare on the crinkly gloss. "Now—that's the Ford coupe we hopped up and raced bootleggers with."

Granddaddy blinked, holding the picture at arm's length.

"I was a good-looking cuss," he murmured.

"You look like a hood."

Granddaddy kept his eyes on the picture and grinned.

"Reckon I do."

A shot of hot wind stirred up a small cyclone of dust. Charlie looked up to the eaved windows.

"You lived here for a while?"

"Long time ago," he said.

Charlie looked at him.

"With Mom?"

"For a little while," Granddaddy answered, slamming the trunk.

The country wind blew down the road again.

"How come you and Mom didn't get along, Granddaddy?"

He rubbed dust off the trunk latch.

"Now, what makes you think we didn't?"

Charlie shrugged.

"Just something I picked up."

"We got along," Granddaddy murmured, turning to the crumbling building dried out from heat and time. "Once upon a time . . . we got along."

*Charlie Tidewater*
*465 Marilee Road*
*Southampton, VA*
*August 23, evening*

*Matthew,*

*Maybe I shouldn't have come down here. The South will rise again. I met a guy today who should have that on his T-shirt. I was at my mother's grave and this strange man comes up and starts talking about her like he knew her, and what's more, he seemed to know something about the way she died! Then he just walked away.*

*Then Granddaddy took me out to this old garage in the country where he lived with my mother when she was a little girl. Something went on out there. Upstairs there was an apartment and on the windows were crude iron bars. The whole place, Matthew, felt bad. Really bad. When I was a boy, Granddaddy used to take me through the field of wrecks behind the garage pointing out the black widow spiders nesting in abandoned cars. He used to say to me, "You stay away from those spiders, boy. They can kill a grown man." Then he would point to the red diamond on their undersides. "The females are the poisonous ones . . . you want to stay away from them."*

*Charlie*

# CHAPTER SIX

Southampton, Virginia

*August 1998*

The shadow gloom of evening was under the backyard trees, with cicadas, crickets, and june bugs shhhhhhsing across the yard like sand in a tambourine. The canopy of leaves held the light up from the ground and Charlie leaned back and could feel the South in the long evening of dissipating heat.

The door sprung behind.

"Now, here you are! Thought maybe you left," Granddaddy joked, sitting down in the lawn chair of crisscrossing sheaths.

"No such luck."

Granddaddy rested his hands on the plastic arms.

"Nice evening tonight."

Charlie nodded slowly, watching the light melt.

"We don't get evenings like this up in Chicago."

"Reckon not."

The insects unified, then backed down to a steady pulse. Charlie heard Granddaddy shuffle his feet, tapping the lawn-chair arm.

"Now, you say you and your wife split up?"

"Yes."

Granddaddy cleared his throat.

"How long since you separated?"

Charlie looked into the specters dancing in the treetops, remembering the morning when it rained so intensely.

"About six months ago."

Granddaddy turned to him.

"Now, what kind of trouble did you have?"

Charlie paused. *The snow-covered window. The blue flicker next door. A tumbler of scotch just below his mouth in the darkness. Sybil had walked upstairs. Charlie could hear the bathroom door closing and he was drinking from the bottle again. All he did was bring the bottle up again.*

"We grew apart," he replied, meeting Granddaddy's eyes.

A locomotive rumbled the evening with a deep chord. Charlie could hear the clack of the cars. He imagined the freight train slipping through the old warm night and felt restless.

"Now, what happened to your job?"

Charlie paused again, another memory reel cuing. *Sunlight slanted across his open desk. He had never noticed the glare before. Ron Jennings closed the door.*

*"So, what are we going to do here?"*

*"I don't know, Ron . . . what are we going to do?"*

*Just touching forty, Ron was a health-club man. Health and money. They went together.*

*"I think we both know the answer to that, Charles."*

*"Why don't you tell me the answer."*

*"Okay. I see the way you want it, then." Ron stood. "Have your desk cleaned out by the end of the day."*

*Even though he knew it was coming, the force still buckled his knees.*

*"Fuck you, Ron," he muttered.*

*Ron reeled the smile out.*

*"You did it to yourself."*

Charlie looked at his grandfather.

"I wanted to consider other opportunities."

"Uh-huh, you quit, then." Granddaddy nodded.

"I quit."

Granddaddy pointed his finger to the sky, stabbing the scattering darkness.

"Now, I would have kept my job and looked for another one, see, that way you could get paid while you doing it."

Charlie looked into the trees.

"Didn't happen that way," he murmured.

"Now, have you found yourself another girl?"

"No."

Granddaddy turned.

"Well, *that's* your problem! You need to find yourself another one, boy."

"I don't want another relationship, right now."

"Seems to me you afraid to get back in the saddle?"

Charlie heard the slap before he saw Granddaddy wipe the mosquito off his forearm.

"Why don't you?"

Granddaddy ducked his head.

"Boy, I am too old to even be *thinking* about that!"

Charlie smiled slowly.

"You're what . . . thirty-five, forty?"

"Little older than that," he murmured. "But now, you're a

young man. No use in waiting around, see, go on back out there and get yourself a girl, you don't want to wait *too* long or no one will want you then."

Charlie watched the faded white doghouse take on the night glow against the foliage of tree limbs. He could smell the honeysuckle and crape myrtle bordering the back of the house.

"I just want to get my life back on track."

Granddaddy spread out his hand.

"Lives don't wait for people."

Charlie splotched a mosquito on his ankle.

"This one is going to have to."

"You remind me of my daddy," Granddaddy grumbled, turning away from him. "He wasn't interested in money or things other people were, see, but he had a whole lot up here," he said, touching his temple.

"He's the one who lived in a log cabin?"

Granddaddy turned back, eyes and teeth flashing in the summer dark.

"Yes sir. That was after he came back from looking for gold out west, see." Granddaddy paused, shaking his head. "Wasn't much of a father. But he could teach. I used to run into people who say to me, 'Do you know your daddy taught me history in a log cabin up the country when I was a boy?' " Granddaddy held his hand up to the whispering tide. "See, now, you don't know how you affect people's lives until later, but he affected a lot of people, I'd say."

The dark was around them completely. Granddaddy tapped the chair rhythmically with his left thumb. Charlie heard another train.

"I was thinking of going into Richmond and looking around; would you be interested in coming along?"

Granddaddy turned like he had been stung.

“*Lord no, boy!* I wouldn’t go into Richmond at night!”

“I’ll be careful,” Charlie assured him, leaning forward.

“I wouldn’t go in there,” he murmured, looking off. “I don’t even go there during the day, much less the night when you don’t know *who* you liable to run into.”

Charlie nodded again, standing from the lawn chair.

“I’ll be careful.”

“Now, boy,” he called, raising his hand. “I’m going to bed, so I’ll leave the key under the mat here for you.”

“Okay.” Charlie hesitated. “I’ll see you later, Granddaddy.”

“I wouldn’t be so sure of that,” he murmured.

Charlie walked to the side of the house, seeing only Granddaddy’s shirt in the lawn chair; a ghost without head or body.

# CHAPTER SEVEN

Virginia countryside

*1928*

"You gone and pulled the guts out of that automobile, boy!"

Austin took the wrench from Snowball under the light of the hanging bulb with moths flying softly around the circle of yellow in the barn door. Uncle Edwin walked up out of the darkness, shaking his head. He stood next to Rufus John cleaning a spark plug with a wire brush.

"Now, I said you could have the car, boy, but you gone and took the carburetor all apart, and you ain't never going to get it together the way you found it."

Austin took another wrench from the oil-sheeny hands, breathing raw gas from the carburetor he had just replaced.

"Just fixin' to make it faster, Uncle."

Uncle Edwin spat on the dirt floor. "You goin' to make it

faster alright, boy—make it move faster right to the junk heap."

Snowball looked over the hood, his grin shiny against the darkness.

"Mistah Edwin, he know what he doin'. I ain't seen no one who can 'member where a part come from like he can or tell what's wrong with a car jest by listenin' to it."

Uncle Edwin stood with his hands in his back pockets, his vest open, tie loosened against the sales day. Rufus John handed Austin the spark plug.

"You fixin' on beatin' those bootleggers, ain't you, boy?"

Snowball grinned again under the shadow of the hood while Austin bent closer to the engine. Uncle Edwin stood off to the side, his belt buckle glinting. From the field there was just the yellow light and three men in the mouth of the car.

"He goin' to beat 'em, Mistah Edwin. They ain't beat him by much and now with this new engine them bootleggers goin' to be givin' us all that money!"

Austin stood up, wiping sweat and grease from his forehead, the wrench shiny by his face.

"Just intend to make them work a little harder for their money, is all."

Uncle Edwin spat again in the dust.

"When you goin' to help me sellin' cars, boy?"

"Give it a start, Snowball."

Snowball swung around into the seat, kicking the engine to life in the high-raftered barn.

"She purrin'," Snowball nodded, revving the engine in the echo of the barn.

Austin stood looking at the 1927 Model A Ford coupe. He flipped the wrench in his hand and let the motor die into the low crickets. He looked at his uncle.

"Reckon I'm ready to sell some of them Studebakers."

Uncle Edwin paused, spatting softly as he walked into the young night.

"Don't beat them bootleggers too bad, boy."

Austin turned off the flush of sandy dirt. Black cars were parked along the sides of the road. Matches flared and occasional stars spiraled to the ground. He could see the bootleggers turn as he rolled up without lights. The figures lounged against the cars, marring the smooth lines of chrome bumpers. Austin could hear the guffaws.

"You come back for another whippin', boy . . ."

"You bringin' back the same bucket of bolts, boy . . ."

"Better git another nigger mechanic, boy . . . you need help!"

The bootleggers laughed. Austin could see bottles on the bumpers of the cars. He stopped behind the last car with the sweet tobacco crop blowing through the open window. A cigarette floated toward them, becoming a man with a hat.

"You and yo' niggers back for 'nother whuppin', boy?"

Astringent whiskey and stale tobacco breathed hotly in his window. Austin tapped his wheel, slightly pursing his mouth.

"Reckon I am."

"Sure hate takin' your money, boy."

"Hate givin' it."

The hat came down, glittery eyes reflecting like a cat along a tree line.

"Same rules, boy," he nodded, taking the money Austin had clutched during the ride out, a month's wages from the garage. "Floyd goin' to be holdin' the money in Richmond. You get there first and it's yours . . . sure y'all want to do this, now?"

Austin looked at Snowball with the chewed floppy hat pulled down and Rufus John in the backseat.

"Reckon so."

"Alright, then," the voice drawled. "You pull on up on the outside over there, boy." The man paused, staring into the backseat. "Ain't you Rufus John?"

Austin nodded. "He's with me."

The man showed missing teeth.

"Knew yo' daddy, boy." The man swore, leering into the car. "Preachin' all that shit up the country—you a preacher too, boy?"

Austin looked at the man.

"Told you he's with me."

The man looked at Austin, something flickering across his eyes under the hat. He spat below the car. "Course, nigger don't preach no more." He looked into the backseat. "Does he, boy?"

Austin felt his throat tighten, then the man grinned and walked away. He watched the lanky figure melt back to the cars coughing small clouds over the cooling fields.

"He goin' to race, Buck?"

"He just can't give us enough, boys."

Austin glanced at Rufus John, seeing the strained whites of his eyes.

"Don't pay that old redneck any mind, Rufus, we'll take care of him," he muttered, pulling the car onto the bank, holding on to keep from sliding toward Snowball.

"They tryin' to put us behind by leaving us off the road," Snowball grumbled, his eyes gleaming straight ahead.

Austin could feel the men looking through the car windows lined to the tobacco fields—hats pulled low, bottles flashing in timed rhythm like a row of dominoes.

"C'mon, boy . . . don't get too far behind . . ."

"Better git that nigger walkin' now to get you a tow, boy!"

Austin glanced over, squeezing the ball of the shift, feeling the tightening spasm of his foot on the clutch.

"Hold on, Snowball."

Rufus John slumped down, muttering just as the man threw down his hat. Austin heard it as a curse as he popped the heavy-duty clutch, smashing down on the accelerator. The engine sucked air and gas, exploding in the sudden combustion of open valves, surging electricity, flooding gas, blasting forth violently like the roar of an animal from a long sleep.

Austin jerked the wheel toward the road, back tires losing ground, fishtailing, finding traction while second gear passed to third, blasting through to fourth, lunging past the cars in the middle of the luminous swath with the roar in both windows.

The dirt road swung away to a curve. Austin jumped down into third, winding out the engine, jerking Snowball back against the seat like a puppet. The moon road disappeared into a flick of tree shadow, cars so many phantoms running under a black cloak with lights not powerful enough for the speed. Austin heard the leader downshift. He jammed down on the accelerator, cutting low and picking up speed, hugging the inside of the dirt turn, knowing the bootlegger had cut too wide with too much speed. He navigated the last turns through the trees, coming out into the fields, on the clear road to Richmond.

"We got 'em! We got 'em! We surely do, Austin!"

He glanced into the mirror, bearing down more on the engine, going cleanly up to fourth gear. Austin turned to Snowball.

"Reckon—"

His neck snapped back and the coupe went into a tailspin. Austin fought the wheel, fighting the wildly fishtailing car, getting control just as a tree scraped the front right bumper.

"He done rammed us!"

Austin looked behind and saw low headlights not three feet away.

"Hold on, Snowball!"

The car flew at them again; Austin braced himself as their speed increased and the back wheels started to lose traction. The bump was harder this time.

"Son bitch!"

Austin saw the ditch alongside the road and felt a sickening loss of control as roadside gravel disallowed gravity and the car careened sideways. He jammed down a gear and touched the brakes lightly, shooting crazily across the road as the car came back to earth. When he looked up, Buck was in front of him.

"He goin' to win," Snowball muttered.

Austin jammed down into third gear and stomped on the accelerator, winding the engine before going to fourth. He saw the car was ten feet away and he could come no closer. Buck had his elbow resting on the driver's-side door. The flask flashed up. The road swung right and zigzagged back, the horseshoe curve clear in the night, the moon a stripe of blue on the far road.

"Ain't rained in a while, has it?"

Snowball's eyes flared white.

"You ain't thinkin'—"

"Reckon so," Austin murmured, hopping from the road onto a sun-packed row, riding the curved mud like a railcar with dry cornhusks popping down in fast relief.

"I seen *everything* now!"

Austin didn't look at Snowball. He couldn't see three feet in front of him for the tawny husks slapping back against the windshield in the glare of headlights, shearing away on the fenders and slapping against the side windows. He was counting to himself, having taken the turn many times, knowing that if he didn't slow and turn at the right moment he would shoot across the road into the next cornfield. That is, if he didn't smash right into Buck's car.

"How you goin'—"

*"Ten,"* Austin finished, jerking the wheel to the left, touching the brake slightly, his spirit falling as the wheels hit hardened mud ridges. He jerked back against the momentum, falling out of the husks into a glare of light, knowing he had turned too soon, and that Buck was about to hit him. He braced against the wheel, seeing the coupe careen into the far field. Austin turned back, skidding onto the smooth road to Richmond.

"Hot damn! We got him, Austin! We got him!" Snowball sang, looking behind at Buck's car resting in the cornfield.

"Reckon we did," he murmured, keeping his eye on the sparkling road.

"It's all yours, boy," the man said, handing Austin the grease-stained envelope on the dark corner with the bootleggers still pulling up. "You do something to your engine, boy?"

Austin spat in the dirt.

"Made few 'justments."

He and Snowball started walking to where Rufus John slouched with his long arms in his coverall pockets.

"Hey, boy, you and your niggers come on out and we'll race you again!"

They kept walking, teeth flashing between them.

"What you going to do with the money, boy? You got a girl?"

Austin grinned, the way he did when she counted the money wad.

"Where did you get all this *money*, Austin Turin?"

He shrugged on the flowery porch with the yellow cast

from the parlor window playing across their feet. The money glowed faintly on the swing.

"Reckon I found it, Miz Tamara."

They sat in the light from a red line over the trees. The porch swing barely moved; radio music floated on the close night air.

"You didn't find it. Did you rob somebody?"

Austin laughed.

"Not so loud! Mother will hear us and if she saw all this money she'd think you were *bootlegging*!"

"I ain't running no whiskey," he said, smelling the faint mist of tangled scuppernong climbing the latticework on the porch.

"That's not what I hear."

Austin looked over the railing, remembering not to spit the tobacco tucked under his lip.

"Reckon I just take their money," he murmured, seeing the yellow coupe glowing under the willow tree.

"Well, if you think I'm going to marry you because you have money—"

He stretched his legs from the porch swing, crossing his arms.

"I do."

Tamara stood up, her gold hair catching the dusk. She was the best-looking girl in Richmond, Austin nodded, thinking it was only logical a man should find the best-looking girl, then try and get her. The hot, flowery dusk was thick in his throat again like dust from the fields. The scent of the willow tree, the honeysuckle, roses, flowers he didn't know, had become aisle markers of their swiftly passionate courtship.

"I told you! I'm going to Hollywood to become a movie star."

Austin gave up and spat into the honeysuckle.

"Oh, that's so disgusting!"

"Sorry," he muttered, scooping up the oily money.

"Mother is taking me for a screen test next week in California!" She looked at him with feigned tragedy. "I . . . I don't know if we're going to come back."

Austin eyed her coolly.

"Going off to be a movie star, huh?" He stood up off the swing. "What about the plans we talked about?"

"Oh," she said with a slight twist of her shoulders. "I was a child—we were children. Why, I've known you all my life, Austin Turin—we couldn't *possibly* marry!"

He closed one eye, seeing the faint yellow of his car, smelling the night again.

"That ain't what you said that night out on Hull Street Road, on that bootlegger whiskey—"

"Shhhh . . . if Mother hears—"

"Uh-huh, or the night in the barn where—"

"Alright, I've said a few things—"

"Done a few too."

She drew herself up.

"But that doesn't change the fact I'm going to Hollywood to become a *star*!"

Austin rose, standing in the tie and shirt Uncle Edwin had given him for selling. He held the money loosely, touching the railing of their courtship, the swing, breathing the balmy air of his summer romance.

"What happens you don't become a star?"

"Mother says I'm the most beautiful girl in Richmond and—"

He shut one eye.

"This your mother's idea, is it?"

"No!"

"Wager it is."

She stood against the raging sky with her figure saying more than she could to Austin.

"Maybe you should just go!"

"Maybe I will, *Miz Hollywood*."

Austin stomped down the steps toward the coupe and glanced back to the porch. Tamara was gone and he saw the stout figure of her mother in the doorway. She shut the door slowly, the lock clicking across the summer night of memory.

# CHAPTER EIGHT

Richmond, Virginia

*August 1998*

Charlie walked on the intensely quiet street under low-hanging trees, a lingering scent of flower petals in the warm breath of dusk. He passed ghostly magnolia and willow trees, balustrades of wisteria and honeysuckle, azaleas and Virginia creeper—all verdant scents of a society resting in the quietest, hottest part of the night.

The swaying hoop skirts and the jingle of horse and buggy on the sloping city streets passed Charlie on his own imaginative journey. He felt the long hot summers those people of another time had passed, the four years of lingering death. He heard the hammering of a blacksmith mixing with the *hyah!* of the groom floating in the window of a Southern belle waiting in some cool anteroom laid with rugs and glass.

Charlie walked with the shadows of his own ghosts. *"Do you know that your people have been here three hundred years and they had plantations up and down the James River? Do you know your great-great-grandfather was a blockade runner and that he wrote about it in a small book no one ever read?" His mother's voice followed him: "Oh, yes. We used to see the old veterans in the parks when I was a little girl. They would wear Confederate caps or they would put up their flag—of course, they all died by the time your father and I appreciated them."*

Charlie heard music. The dulcet sound played out along the velvet air passing between columns of pale alabaster from a portico in deep night shadow. He could see a porch swing breaking across a yellow window dreaming out the music. The splash of white swung between the columns like a railroad signal.

But it was the colored cat with one eye gleaming that stopped Charlie on the sidewalk next to the black iron fence. The cat lay on his side, his fur speckled black. He switched his tail once, whipping it back to the sidewalk where only the tip betrayed any agitation.

Charlie was about to step around the cat when it rolled to its back, meowing loudly. The swing stopped. There was a moment of complete quiet. Charlie faced the glare of feline suspicion, incisors flashing another plaintive cry.

"Is Old Boy blocking your way?" a liquid voice of long vowels called out.

Charlie turned from the cat, searching for the voice, calling over the iron fence garrisoned with a solid barrier of vines.

"No, I can go around."

She came on slippers, in reality some flat shoe, but the swaying dress made Charlie think of the movies where the

Southern belle has tiny feet in slippers. The gate squealed as she came toward him. Old Boy stretched his neck to watch her until he found it necessary to roll.

"He is a lazy thing."

"I suppose he's just enjoying the night."

"Well, he should not be so rude as to block the sidewalk."

Old Boy was unceremoniously scooped up, his head just below the long sheen of hair.

"That's alright."

Old Boy turned and stared at Charlie with a Lilith gleam; the voice could easily have belonged to the cat as well.

"You aren't from Richmond."

Charlie shook his head, noticing the soft eyes blinking in the slow way he gave to being from the South.

"I was born here, but I've been gone for a long time." He looked beyond her to the house shimmering under the blue cast. "I heard your music and stopped."

She turned, diamond eyes of Old Boy facing Charlie.

"Oh, that's Daddy's. He *loves* his Vivaldi."

Charlie stood in the soft darkness without wondering when to walk on. He closed his hand around a hitching ring on the iron fence.

"I think Old Boy was just guarding the house for me," she said, kissing him between twitching ears.

"I'm sure of it."

The low purr of night was between them. She turned back to the gate.

"I was wondering . . ."

She turned again.

"Is there somewhere to get a drink—or a bite to eat—around here?"

She regarded him as if he had just spoken a foreign language.

"There are several good restaurants down at the slip," she offered.

Charlie nodded.

"The slip?"

"Down by the river . . ." She waved airily then let her hand drop; Charlie kept the image of her slender arm pointing down the street for an extra moment.

"I'm sorry, I'm not being very polite . . . but what do they eat in the North?"

Charlie smiled.

"How do you know I'm from the North?"

The nose wrinkled, two delicate eyebrows descending.

"You talk like you have a boxcar in your mouth, besides, you look like a Yankee."

"What—"

"You look cold, thick, that's what it is, you look thick."

Charlie looked down at his waist.

"I don't mean that." She laughed, rocking Old Boy gently from side to side. "You have an aura about you, like someone who could be buried in problems and then get up the next day and just begin again."

"Thanks, I must seem a little phlegmatic, I've felt that way for a long time."

She took a delicate step back.

"My! I'm going to have to go to a dictionary after talking with you. 'Phlegmatic,' that's a word I've heard but I never really knew what it meant."

Charlie paused and considered in panic that he really had no idea what the word meant.

"Well, it means—slow, yes . . . slow. I'm pretty sure, maybe, I suppose I shouldn't use it if I'm not completely sure of its meaning . . ."

Charlie felt the rough sensibilities of the North against

the mellifluous churn of the slower climate. Glittering eyes regarded him.

"So, let me guess, Michigan?"

Charlie smiled. "Close, Chicago."

Her eyes lit with a lazy intensity.

"The Art Institute, basketball, football . . . Saul Bellow."

"Saul left . . . but that sums it up."

She rubbed Old Boy's neck.

"I've always wanted to go to Chicago . . . it seems like a man's city, though."

Charlie nodded slowly. "I never thought of it that way."

"What's it like?"

"Well, it's cold, and then it gets colder." Charlie paused. "Then it snows."

"Sounds divine . . ." she murmured. "I get so *tired* of the heat."

Charlie looked around in the warm, flowery night, resonant crickets hiding in the bushes and grass.

"That's what people say about the winters in Chicago."

"You must go to the Art Institute all the time."

Charlie nodded.

"Every day."

She looked at him from the corners of her eyes.

"Well, I would go every day if I lived there."

He held his hands wide.

"You should visit."

She turned quickly to the cat.

"You wanted somewhere to eat?"

"Right." He nodded. "Whatever is fine," he added, wondering why he felt thoroughly unhinged with this woman.

"Straight on down the street, the Union Stop."

He nodded, seeing no glint on her left hand.

"What kind of a place is it?"

"It's a cafe. You could get a hamburger or whatever."

"I'll check it out," he called, watching the full curves of her figure as Old Boy peered haughtily over her shoulder.

"Tell them Minnie sent you."

Some sense of triumph came to him.

"Minnie?"

"Yes, Minnie," she called. "Have a nice evening."

Charlie felt the lack of a hat to sweep down, but bowed slightly, seeing a faint shadow on the sidewalk.

"Thank you, ma'am."

She was ascending the stairs, one hand raised. The dress passed between the portico columns toward the swing. Charlie walked slowly, touching the low heat of iron fences under trees older than the century.

# CHAPTER NINE

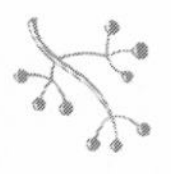

Southampton, Virginia

*August 1998*

Charlie drove down the driveway with his lights off. The outside air was damp with early morning as he steadied himself at the door and pulled the key from under the mat. The five scotch and sodas he had drunk earlier caused the lock to jump right, then left; he nailed it in the center. His feet were louder in the garage. He stopped at the door and touched a wood splinter along the frame.

Charlie turned back to the garage door. It had opened easily. He crept into the shadowy light snowing from the den windows. Two wing chairs and a cream sofa were specters in the darkness. He saw the long hallway to his bedroom and sensed movement. A floorboard creaked. Barely breathing, Charlie picked up a heavy silver lighter.

"Granddaddy," he called in a hoarse voice, stepping around the chairs in the kitchen. Something glinted on the far side of the dining-room table. To the right was the foyer and the beginning of the hallway. To his left was black. Charlie froze, his skin reaching into the darkness. He turned rigidly, a mannequin facing destruction. A figure slipped past him.

Then the dark exploded, a white flash sending him onto the kitchen table and across the falling chairs. A shadow rushed by, hard shoes clicking in the garage, then quiet.

Charlie lay motionless. A pale figure crossed to the doorway; then light blinded him.

*"Am I shot?"*

"Don't reckon so," Granddaddy grumbled, walking into the den, a long, lead-colored pistol in his right hand. "Don't think I shot him, either," he murmured, returning in his boxer shorts and sleeveless T-shirt, laying the oily gun with the long barrel on the kitchen table. "Now, are you alright?"

"Yes, I think so . . ." Charlie sat up, feeling like he had just been tackled. "You shot at him?"

Granddaddy looked in the dining room.

"Must have been a burglar—they wanted that silver, see."

Charlie saw a candelabra lying on the floor.

"Now, it's a good thing you came home when you did, you surprised him, see." Granddaddy walked to the far end of the dining table. "Uh-huh, there it is," he murmured, tapping the wall below the window.

*"What?"*

"The bullet, see, I was aiming too high, I was too late with my aim." Granddaddy bent down. "Now, how in the world did this get here . . . must have been goin' to take this old lighter too."

Charlie shook his head.

"No, I had that."

Granddaddy stared at him.

"I used it as a weapon."

"Not much of a weapon," he murmured, taking it back into the den.

"Aren't you going to call the police?"

Charlie heard Granddaddy go into the garage.

"What's that?" he called back.

"*The police!* Aren't you going to call the police?"

Granddaddy walked into the kitchen and picked up the heavy pistol.

"Now, what in the world for?"

Charlie stared at him.

"You just had somebody in your house and you shot at him!"

Granddaddy pressed his lips together.

"No, don't reckon so, doesn't look like he got anything."

"But you have to file a report."

Granddaddy shook his head.

"No, don't think I'm going to do that," he finished, turning off the overhead kitchen light.

Charlie stared at him, then followed down the hallway.

"I think you know who he was, Granddaddy."

"Don't know what makes you say that," he said, walking with the pistol barrel even with his knee.

He turned in the door of his bedroom. "Now, you better get some sleep," he nodded, tipping the gun toward his door.

"Granddaddy—" Charlie paused. "What kind of trouble are you in?"

Granddaddy's pale blue eyes hardened.

"Now, I reckon, that's my business."

Charlie stared at the old man holding the pistol by his bed.

He nodded to his hand. "Where did you get the gun?"

Granddaddy raised the pistol; forged metal harsh against wallpaper and carpet.

"My daddy gave this old Army Colt to me . . ." He looked at Charlie. "Had it all my life."

The door shut behind him. Charlie went to his bed and lay down. He reached behind his head, then switched on the bedside light that flicked several times from a loose contact. A dirty envelope was propped against the lamp base. The cold, oily scent of a garage was in the paper. He thumbed open the flap.

**Negro Man Disappears**

*Times Dispatch*, Sherwood Anders,
(Local Correspondent), Goochland County

A local Negro man, Rufus John Jr., has been missing for three days and authorities and his family have no idea where he might have gone. The local sheriff, Junior Pairs, does not think foul play is involved but said he wasn't ruling anything out. "The problem is nobody's seen much of him for a while. He is one of those college Negroes who's been traveling around for the civil rights and all and he opened that church and been giving lots of speeches to people that aren't from around here. You ought to ask those people if they seen him." Rufus John Jr. is the son of Rufus and Tilly John.

Charlie stared at the date, the night rhythm of the crickets outside his window casting fire to his memory of a dusky April evening in 1968.

# CHAPTER TEN

Virginia countryside

*1929*

"So, you goin' to get her, boy?"

Uncle Edwin stood in the barn door with the light ash of evening settling behind. He rubbed his day-old stubble, a confirmed bachelor of almost forty years, not understanding what his nephew was going through, but seeing the light step missing since Tamara Drake had left.

Austin stayed under the hood of his car, arm torquing the last spark plug home. His uncle pulled the chewed, whittled pencil from behind his ear. He examined the stub he used to calculate the cost of options, extras, and financing on the back of a receipt, an envelope, a business card. He tapped the pencil lightly against his palm.

"Well, good, boy! I don't want you moonin' all over the lot no more—ain't goin' to sell no cars poutin' around!"

Austin fitted the oil-filler cap to the manifold, hearing the dirt spat of tobacco before it jumped in the corner of his eye. He wasn't sure when he had decided, but he woke that morning knowing he would bring Tamara back if he could.

"Yes sir—seen some lovesick dogs in my time, but I *never* thought you gave much a hang about anythin' didn't have a crankshaft under the hood . . ." Uncle Edwin paused, a strut against the frame of the doorway, still patting the stubby pencil against a callus. "Course, she is about the prettiest damn thing I've seen in Richmond . . . didn't she win the pageant a couple years back?"

Austin nodded, standing up from the hood and dropping it into place. He jumped onto the seat, roaring the motor to life, blue plumes rolling across the streaming lambency.

Uncle Edwin slipped the pencil back, smoothing thin hair by his ear, scratching his cheek. He watched his nephew throttle the engine.

"Yes sir. Go get her, boy, so I can get you back to work! We got lots of cars to get fixed and you ain't goin' to make your livin' off just racing them bootleggers."

Austin jammed the car into gear and paused. Staring into the Western sky in the barn doorway. His Uncle didn't take his hands from his pocket or pull his vest together. Austin waited with the car vibrating through him, perfect timing of his own soul engine.

Uncle Edwin faced the yellow work light on the chair. He spat into the barn.

"I know you goin' to California, boy. Your job be waitin' for you when you come back. But you better start sellin' them cars. Wives want to be supported and sooner or later them bootleggers are goin' to get tired of racin' or prohibition goin' to end. So don't tell me what you're goin' to do in California, because I know you comin' back."

Austin stared out to the sky raging over a line of country trees. He had never been out of Richmond, had never left the South.

"Ain't like your pa. I don't worry you'll go off and not come back, now."

Austin could hear the slow crickets in the shop barn. Uncle Edwin nodded, still looking at the yellow light.

"But hurry on and bring her back, boy. Snowball pout the whole time and I won't be able to get a lick of work out of him until you come back. Been shorthanded since Rufus John got sent back to county."

Austin kept his hand on the live shift.

"Now, you go on, boy. I'm goin' to go turn off that light and when I turn around you'll be that much closer to comin' back."

Austin looked out to the dying sky, revved the engine once, then let out the clutch and left his uncle in the velvet evening. Uncle Edwin listened to the whine of the throttled engine, then went into the barn and snapped off the light. He walked out, staring into the west where Austin disappeared, striking light against shadow, smoke shafting down from his nose and mouth.

Austin passed into the western light curving over the horizon. He gunned the engine to its limit, city lights falling away. He smoked a cigarette and wondered where he would get gas in the middle of the night. He passed few cars on the highway running to the state line where another state highway began. He drove with the slipping center lines disappearing, leaving him with sand along the shoulders.

*"Mother says I'm going to be a movie star. I can sing on the radio and Mother says if I can sing on the radio here, no reason why I can't sing in Hollywood. Besides—they always want a pretty girl!"*

Austin burned his cigarettes into dawn with the car shadow just ahead. He thought of the owner of the gas station in the mountains he woke when he noticed the curtains above the gas pump. He knocked lightly on the unlocked door. The old man descended, suspenders collapsed to the side, amazingly fresh for the three-o'clock hour. He pumped the globe full of gold fuel and listened.

"So, yer goin' to get her, are you?"

He said this, looking down at his work, bugs swirling around the bulb over the door.

"Reckon I've got to try."

The old man fit the nozzle back to the pump, waving away the money Austin pressed on him.

"Consider that a wedding present, son," he called, turning out the light.

The door closed. Austin drove into morning, the wrinkled, torn, pieced-back-together Western Union telegram on the seat.

*"What do you mean you goin' to Hollywood?"*

*"Mother says it's just for a screen test."*

*They moved gently in the cover of porch shade.*

*"You'll be comin' back, won't you?"*

*"Of course. It's only for a test. Then I'll be back."*

*"Don't trust your mother."*

*"Don't worry."*

*"Still, don't trust her."*

*The closer snuggle on the porch with the pit in his stomach; the safe cloak of romance torn off just as he asked her to marry him. He was desperately on his knees, not understanding her tears and refusal, saying she had to find out first.*

*"Find out what?"*

*She put her head down, wiping tears from her cheeks.*

*"Find out what?"*

*But she couldn't talk, leaving him on his knees by the swing with her steps going up the stairs. She was gone. The maid shook her head, saying she had instructions to close up the house indefinitely.*

Austin buried himself at his uncle's garage, ignoring the hollowed-out feeling that killed appetite and ruined sleep. He felt his uncle's eyes watching him when customers walked off the lot. Even racing the bootleggers had lost its glow with no one to share his triumph. He had simply lost meaning and was astounded to find he couldn't live without her.

The telegram became bright, then turned to a glowing sheath as day turned to night and back again; West Virginia passing to Oklahoma, to Arizona on the third day. The road of occasional cars became bumpy, losing itself to sand and sagebrush with the needle of his gauge bouncing across the white *E*.

The man at the single-pump gas station asked him how much water he was carrying across the desert. He came up with a gasoline can and filled it from the slop sink inside the bay.

"I seen more of you greenhorns cross the desert without so much as a *canteen* and some of 'em ain't been seen since," he grumbled, placing the gas-smelling can at Austin's feet, knocking back the bent and scuffed cowboy hat. "Don't drink all of this at once, parcel it out. You break down, and they all do, or the road gives out on you, you'll need every dang drop."

When Austin asked him about gas, he pushed the straw hat farther back on his head, scratching matted snow-white hair.

"Reckon you can get some gas at Joe's. He's an Indian feller and has a station of sorts with a tank . . . he's just on the other side, go slow, don't burn up all yer fuel hot-roddin' across 'cause you'll never make it to Joe's." He spat, walking to the shade of his chair by the door.

Austin drank half the gas-tasting water when the road became the dirt of the raw West. He hadn't slept for three days and many times he thought he saw buildings on the horizon. Thought became speech and dream became reality. He spoke aloud several times, having a lively conversation before the bumping slowness of the sand woke him.

When night fell over the flat expanse, turning it into a pale blue slate tabletop, thought became dream as he urged the lone yellow coupe down the deserted highway. Austin came to a stop in the sandy brush, and slept hugging the wheel, a glittering play of stars dying into the atmosphere over the dew-covered car. Star dust sprinkled down on him as he slept; not waking until the fireball tipped the desert sky of cool glitter.

Austin stumbled out of the car and urinated, looking up into early morning. He listened to his water splattering the sagebrush, realizing he would remember wetting the sagebrush of the West long after the moment passed.

He was back in the car quickly, not stopping until he was outside the address in Hollywood on the Western Union telegram.

*HAD SCREEN TEST. MOTHER SAYS I WILL BE A STAR. MOTHER SAYS WE ARE STAYING. VERY SORRY.*

*ADDRESS IS THREE TWELVE SYCAMORE HOLLYWOOD. ALL MY LOVE. TAMARA.*

Then he was there, not waiting for the morning to come, knocking on the door of the bungalow with *312* hidden behind a palm tree. He knocked with the six-hour sleep of four going on five days, forgetting what he had planned for ninety-six hours to say. The car heat popped behind him, a bit of sage wedged in the bumper. He ran a hand over his chin stubble, pushed back his hair, and hoped he didn't smell of cigarettes and sweat. The morning broke somewhere behind with rose light touching the door. He jammed his hands in his pockets, feeling the balm of a land where it was never cold. He saw the curlers of Tamara's mother.

"What are *you* doing here?"

All veiled innuendo was cast aside.

"I've come to take Tamara back, Miz Drake."

The curlers dipped in the crack of the doorway.

"You've wasted your time. She's not going back."

The door shut, but Austin had his boot inside.

*"Mama. Let him in!"*

The pressure on his boot increased.

"*No.* Tamara, go back to sleep. I won't allow you to do this to yourself. You are going to be a star—"

"Mama—open the door."

"Don't! You will regret this—*he sells cars, for God's sake!*"

Austin pushed his boot in more, wedging a shoulder to the door.

*"Tamara!"*

"You will regret this for the rest of your life if you go with him now."

"I don't care, Mama! Let me through—"

There was scuffling, then the door flew back. Austin melted to her. The warm, golden hair with the indescribable smell of her was on his shoulder. They were together. The breath of sunlight lay over a highway that crossed a continent, slipping over the desert, sparkling on bridges, touching cornfields, breaking over Uncle Edwin's shrouded garage.

Austin looked over Tamara's shoulder as her mother cursed him from the shadow.

# CHAPTER ELEVEN

Richmond, Virginia

*August 1998*

A timorous rain stained the sidewalk the color of grocery wrap and sogged the magnolias that brushed against Charlie's shoulder. He ascended a march of steps, protected by a guard of antebellum columns, the state library smelled like a can of shoe polish.

"May I help you?"

Charlie pulled down his sunglasses, then took them off.

"I'm looking for a newspaper—from a long time ago."

She had the straight blond hair and an ankle bracelet of a University of Richmond coed.

"What paper?"

"Richmond *Times Dispatch*."

She pushed her books to the side with tattered pink nails

and pulled out a thick binder. She paged through, trailing a pink finger.

"Microfiche," she announced, clapping the book shut. "To your right. The drawers are numbered by year."

Charlie thanked her and passed through a square of sunlight into rows of card-catalog drawers. His footfall snapped back at him from the marble above and below. He walked to the cabinet and stopped at the years 1967–68. He pulled the wide drawer open and found a box marked APRIL 1–15. Charlie turned to the oversized screens with roller handles, carefully threading the tape onto the wheel. He snapped on the light. The screen effloresced, a small fan humming into the marble quiet. Charlie turned the crank slowly.

The headlines blurred by as the rain beat time on the high ceiling.

An hour later he had found nothing. Charlie took the article from the night before and laid it on the table. He turned the crank past the headlines of April 4 and went through the back pages. He rotated his hand slowly and stopped. The name of the correspondent jumped out at him as if someone had shouted into the echoing quiet.

**Cross Burned in Front of Negro Church**

*Times Dispatch*, Sherwood Anders,
(Local Correspondent), Goochland County

A series of racial incidents has been attributed to a Klan thought to be active in this county. Reliable sources cite mysterious church burnings, and a recent spate of kidnappings where Negroes are beaten, tied up, then left along roadsides or in fields far from their homes as evidence of Klan activity. The latest incident involved a cross set on fire in front of the Second Baptist Negro Church, recently opened by Rufus John Jr. "Of course these racists are trying to intimidate me," he said in a recent interview. "I have participated in sit-ins and have done work personally for the Reverend King and will continue to push for the civil rights we deserve. I returned to my home state from college even though I know the oppression that exists here. They lynched my grandfather, who was a man of God, but they will not quiet me the same way." Sheriff Junior Pairs of Goochland County thinks it is the work of outsiders. "We don't have any trouble with our Negroes out here and I don't understand what all the fuss is about. If it's anything, it's probably some of these freedom people trying to stir people up when there's no trouble to begin with." The sheriff went on to say that there was no Klan operating in Goochland County as far as he knew. "You might have some of the local boys getting liquored up, but we are just a small, peaceful country town . . . we just don't have the problems you people seem to think we do."

Charlie wrote on the back of an old business card. He turned the crank until he reached April 5, 1968. He scanned the headlines.

**King Is Shot, Killed at Memphis Motel**

**Automatic Rifle Found in Area; Curfew Imposed**

**Violence Erupts in Many Cities**

**Law and Order to Be Kept in State, Governor Says**

Charlie slowly turned the pages and stopped. There, in the right-hand corner of the last page of the first section, was a picture of his mother. It was her wedding photo.

Tamara Drake Tidewater, 35, died peacefully at her home after a long illness. Mrs. Tidewater descended from the Turins of Richmond and was a longtime resident of Richmond. She attended Washington College for Women and taught briefly at the local high school. She married Charles Henry Tidewater of Goochland County, who worked for Dow Chemical. She is survived by her father, Austin Turin; her husband; and her son, Charles Tidewater.

Charlie studied her picture. Her hair was short and curled inward. A strand of pearls curved above a V neck. Her smile was radiant. Charlie looked at the headline of Martin Luther King's death. His mother was gone again. He was back watching the cartoons in the den of his childhood. He remembered the shadowy dusk outside, the crickets pulsing just below the open window over the garden, the tree shadows. The man was coming on the television announcing to the world Martin Luther King was dead. He ran to tell his father the news.

*Tamara Drake Tidewater, 35, died peacefully at her home.*

*Charlie Tidewater*
*Richmond Library*
*10 Capitol Square*
*Richmond, VA*
*August 24, noon*

*Matthew,*

*I hope you are sitting down when you read this because you won't believe it. Someone broke into the house early this morning and Granddaddy pulled out a gun and fired a shot at the guy! Then I went into my bedroom and there was a dirty envelope with an article in it from 1968 about a black man named Rufus John who disappeared out in the country. Obviously someone risked getting shot to get this information to me. Things are getting stranger by the minute down here. I went to the library and found another article about cross burnings in the country around that old garage Granddaddy lived in. Then I found my mother's obituary. It said she died at home. I was at home, Matthew. She wasn't.*

*I'll write you when I find out more.*

*Charlie*

# CHAPTER TWELVE

Richmond, Virginia

*August 1998*

The rain broke to a finicky dribble, the heat of three o'clock on the streets by noon. The sun steamed the air. Charlie walked through the gossamers of time beneath the magnolias, hanging dogwoods, and willow trees, stepping on sedge in the cracks of the green-stained sidewalks. The James River was pale in the distance.

The cat was on the sidewalk. Charlie stopped. He could feel his shirt sticking to his back. Old Boy yawned a shark's mouth, then rolled to his back.

"Is he obstructing your way again?"

The porch swing didn't move, but Charlie could see a splash of color behind the portico columns.

"No . . . well, actually yes." Charlie shaded his eyes. "But I could go around . . ."

"You look mighty hot," she called from the wisteria and honeysuckle bordering the house. "Would you care to rest in the shade?"

Charlie nodded to the cat panting slightly in the heat.

"Yes, I would," he called, stepping over Old Boy, one paw jerking as if in final repose.

Charlie passed through the squeaking iron gate. His shoes were loud on the painted planks, walking toward Minnie, who wore an organdy blouse and a surprising jean skirt. He sat carefully on the banister of the porch. Minnie piled her hair on her shoulder, pulling back the brassy richness of wheat.

"Did you find your restaurant last night?"

"Yes—thanks . . . I'm Charlie Tidewater, by the way."

"Minnie Barrek. Judge Barrek is my father."

Charlie smiled. "I should know this."

Minnie shrugged, smiling.

"In this town people do. I don't think outside of Richmond people much would care." Minnie breathed in deeply and brushed the dot of orange resting on her neckline. Charlie watched the ladybug take flight. "Tidewater . . . that's a Virginia name."

"My mother's maiden name was Turin."

Minnie mouthed the name, arching her eyebrows into the small shelter of her hair. A door sprung wide and Charlie felt the vibration of the steps.

"Daddy, I'd like you to meet Charlie Tidewater—he's from Chicago."

Charlie stood and met the long hand breaking from a jet-black suit. Flossed silver crowned a strong bridge and hawk eyes; the mustache and eyebrows defied sixty-odd years of washed pigment.

"Judge Barrek."

The judge settled into a wicker chair, crossing his legs, dabbing his mouth with a white handkerchief. His black eyes snapped over Charlie.

"And how is the great city of the North?"

"Hot, now."

"How was your lunch, Daddy?"

"Fine, fine."

He pulled a cigar from his top pocket; the blue smoke hung in the still air of the porch like an uninvited ghost. Charlie watched his eyes do a slow inventory of the yard.

"Visitin'?"

"I'm down here interviewing for a job. I'm staying with my grandfather."

The brows touched once.

"What's your grandfather's name?"

"Austin Turin."

Judge Barrek glanced at the perfect plug of blue ash.

"Oh, yes." He nodded slowly.

He leaned forward, ashing over the banister. The movement was swift, like a younger man's.

"I think I bought a car from your grandfather . . . once." He turned to Minnie. "Mr. Turin was a car dealer at the corner of Broadway and Twentieth Street, I believe." The judge swung back to Charlie.

"He had a daughter . . ."

"My mother." He nodded quickly, feeling a surge of blood from the way Judge Barrek said "car dealer."

The judge leaned farther back, depthless eyes looking just beyond Charlie's head.

"Yes, that's right, she died some time ago," he continued slowly, as if reading from a book. "An illness of some sort, wasn't it?"

"Yes."

Judge Barrek unclasped the cigar.

"She was a teacher," he explained to Minnie, then turned to Charlie. "Short of that I don't know—I must say I know nothing of the Tidewaters. Are they from up north?"

"No, Charlottesville."

The judge took the cigar back to a resting spot just above the wicker arm.

"Ah, country folk. Sometimes I think the only families I know are the founding families."

"I think the Turins are in that elite group."

The judge tilted his head.

"Are they, now?"

Charlie felt he was being drawn out of a hedge.

"So I am told."

"Well . . . I didn't know that." He turned to Minnie. "It just goes to show, Daughter, that you can't know everything."

Minnie laughed, touching her father's crisp sleeve.

"Oh, Daddy, you always say that, but you know most *everything* about everybody."

Judge Barrek looked at Charlie and smiled.

"I suppose that is true."

He unfolded his legs and stood in a two-time motion. Charlie rose.

"I have to get to the courthouse, Daughter," he announced, lowering his face slightly for Minnie to kiss his cheek, then turning to Charlie and shaking his hand.

"It was nice meeting you, Mr. Tidewater, please give our best to our brethren up north."

"Will do, sir," Charlie returned, feeling the quickness of the hand. "But I will be down here awhile."

"Well," the judge said, without looking, "then so much the better."

Charlie listened to his footsteps go back into the house. Minnie smoothed her skirt and settled into the porch swing. Old Boy came down the hot sidewalk, meowing against the heat, and collapsed below the steps.

"May I get you some lemonade?"

"No, I'm fine."

She moved the swing, rubbing her finger, glancing up swiftly.

"Daddy can be very intimidating."

Charlie looked at her. "Really . . . I didn't notice."

Minnie paused. "I think he believes he should know everybody who even walks past the house . . . ever since I moved back he acts like I was just coming out again."

She stared at him, her eyes a fragile chartreuse against the slats of the swing.

"He handled the entire divorce and acts like it never happened—of course, Cole's family was just fit to be tied when Daddy made him sign away all visitation." Minnie squinted out into the sun-drenched yard. "He says it's like we were never married and that I shouldn't think of myself as a divorced woman." She looked up almost shyly. "And I guess I don't."

Charlie nodded slowly.

"I don't think Sybil will go for that."

Minnie's face brightened.

"Your wife?"

"Ex."

Minnie tilted her head slowly, eyes changing like a marble in sunlight. "Maybe men and women should stay apart."

Charlie shifted his coat to his other arm.

"That would solve a lot of problems."

"But then, we would all just wither away," she said slowly.

"I think we are damned to it."

"Did you like being married?"

"I liked being with her."

The dimples came back to her smooth cheeks.

"I like that." Minnie glanced at her watch. "Well . . . I'm sorry." She stood up. "I have to go pick up my daughter."

Charlie walked to the front of the porch with her. He paused, then turned.

"Would you consider going to dinner tomorrow night?"

She stared at him.

"With *you*?"

"Unless you have a better escort, then I will gladly just pay for the dinner."

She smiled slowly.

"You aren't some sort of serial killer?"

"Nope, I'm looking for a job."

"Hmmmm . . . Okay."

Charlie nodded. "Great . . . about seven?"

"That sounds fine," she said at the door.

"Nice talking to you, Minnie."

Then he was in the sun-shot day, walking down the sidewalk. He reached the heated gate and swung it open, latching it quietly on the other side. He looked back at the white-columned southern home. A sprinkler whipped silently around. Old Boy slept on in the sun.

# CHAPTER THIRTEEN

Virginia countryside

*August 1998*

The white Impala crackled across the loose gravel, warily crossing in front of the garage window, mirroring a white car and the highway, a russet field rising beyond. The man saw no car approaching from either direction of the vanishing white lines and rolled to a stop. He strode across the drive, stepping between two dead gas pumps.

A sheaf of greasy hair creased his forehead as he jimmied the door. Inside the garage it was close to dark. His boots sanded the cement, still slick from oily residue. He went into the small office and struck a match, squatting in front of the scratched safe. The match turned to a pin and he struck again, holding the flame while he jerked the aluminum-colored handle. He spun the tumbler, pulling on the handle again.

*"Shit."*

He said the word fast, like a pop can opening. He hesitated, then went past the barrels with OIL stenciled white. He took the steps two at a time and barged into the room, going to the window. He smoked slowly and pulled the whiskey from his back pocket. He held the bottle below his mouth, cigarette smoke curling in front of the pint.

"Goddamn."

He said this without effect. He felt calm from the dusty domesticity of the sofa and lamps. The warm light made him sleepy until the memory of the safe twisted him around to the window. The single pane shattered with the blood slick and bright inside his arm. He thought about prison. Three meals a day didn't sound bad.

The cigarette died under his heel and he turned to the field of wrecks glinting to a stand of tall pines. He kept his eyes on the trees and nodded.

"Treatin' me like a nigger," he muttered in the gloom.

His eyes went back to the trees, then he was down the steps into the cool air of early-evening dew. The man looked down the highway trailing into the distance, then crossed to the side of the garage, following a path between the twisted metal hunks. He didn't feel weeds catching him or briars clinging to his jeans. If a man watched from a distance he would see a rolling progress like wind crossing the field.

The insects were louder as he approached the cedars and firs. He looked back to the garage, then cut left, wondering about the passage of time.

"Thirty years, Jack," he muttered, the swishing of his steps louder in the forest quiet.

He saw the circle of trees beyond the woods. The man paused, then squeezed between two pine branches. He struck another cigarette. The weeds looked the same with no break he could discern. He hunched down on one leg, smoking pensively.

He sparked his finger.

"Jest like a nigger."

The man's voice was small outside. He held his cigarette below his chin; night was on the land. From the road there was the white Impala by the abandoned garage. Stars in the east. A person walking by could stare into the peaceful field of wrecks, unaware of the man casting his decision; a voice lost in the agrarian night.

Eight-year-old Charlie stood with his feet pale in the river. The forest was black and cold at his back, peopled with beasts that hooted and tittered from the trees. Granddaddy stood along the curve of saffron leaving the riverfront. The twine jerked in his hand. He pulled the fish head through the shallows while the crab held on with a pincer, skittering in the sand until Granddaddy swooped him from the water.

"That's a good one," he nodded, holding up the angling spider, then walking back to the crate by the river.

Charlie tossed out his fishing line, the fish head plopping into the colored water. Granddaddy swished into the shallows with his pants rolled below his knees, the cuffs perfect, his feet white and hairless in the water. He threw out his line, holding it by his waist like a kite.

Charlie could smell fish, reminding him of the rickety dock where Granddaddy kept his boat. The bay smelled like the ocean, but it was quiet, with stinging nettles and crabs Granddaddy pushed out of the way.

"We goin' to have some good eatin' tonight, boy!"

Charlie nodded, feeling the tug on his line. He brought the line in slowly, the crab slipping dark above the smooth evening water. Granddaddy swooped him again.

"You one good crabber, boy," he said, going back to the crate. "Looks like you goin' to need another fish head."

Granddaddy walked to the bucket, parting phosphorous surf wash. He tied on the fish head and Charlie watched.

"Granddaddy?"

"What's that, boy?"

Charlie looked out to the still water.

"Where'd Mom go again?"

Granddaddy paused, holding the fish head, then continued to wrap the line.

"She gone to the hospital, boy, and when she comes back she'll be well again," he answered, walking over with the fish head.

"Now, watch out and don't get blood on your clothes."

Charlie watched his grandfather's thick hands tie the line, pulling to make sure it was tight. They were brown and aged, unlike his father's hands, which were white and soft.

"Throw it on out there, boy!"

Charlie swung the line out, watching the ripples of washed light radiate from the center. Granddaddy held his line to his waist, tugging every few minutes. A gull broke across the sky. Charlie looked at his grandfather.

"Why does she always get sick?"

Granddaddy tugged his line, puckering his lips.

"Now, boy, your mother has a disease, like a virus . . . same as when you get sick, see. . . ." He tugged the line again and nodded to the water. "The place she goes to is real good . . . they'll make her better soon."

Charlie nodded slowly, tugging his own line, shooting

ripples into the mirrored water. Black birds soared across the sky and the lowlands of the Chesapeake Bay pulsed with life.

"You got another one, boy!"

Charlie started pulling in the string, line falling wet against his ankles. Granddaddy waded out and picked the crab up by a pincer.

"Biggest one, yet!"

"Sure is!"

Charlie marveled that his grandfather could pick up a crab without fear. He carried the crab to the crate and put the top on.

"Well, I think we have enough. We better get on back now, boy."

They put their gear in the trunk and the crabs in the backseat. Granddaddy started the car, driving through the forest gloom. Charlie sat in the seat, feeling the sunburn from the long day. He lay back against the upholstered seat, hearing the funny ticking noise of the crabs.

"They aren't going anywhere, boy."

"I know, I just wanted to look."

Granddaddy ran his hand across the back of the seat.

"Crab almost got you there!"

Charlie shouted and laughed, leaning back against the strong arm of his grandfather. He watched the road sparkling in the slanting light.

"Granddaddy . . ."

"What's that?"

"Why does the road sparkle that way?"

Granddaddy squinted at tiny prisms flaring in front of the car.

"Well, now, that's the mica, see, they use mica in the gravel." He paused, lifting a broad hand off the wheel. "See, now, when I was younger, I used to think all the roads sparkled that way. But when I traveled the country, see, I realized only our own sparkle that way," he said, looking over.

"Oh." Charlie nodded, watching the glitter play on the two-lane highway.

Granddaddy put both hands on the wheel and nodded to himself.

"Only our own," he murmured.

When Charlie woke they were in the driveway.

"Now, these goin' to make good eatin'," Granddaddy called, walking ahead of him, wiping his feet on the rubber mat. "Make sure you wipe your feet now, boy."

Then the crabs were red and orange, caked with the Old Bay seasoning that smelled sharp. The newspapers were spread out on the picnic bench and Granddaddy had a glass of beer trickling a large stain. He sipped the beer, set it down, and took a crab off the top of the mound.

"You ate crabs before, boy?"

Charlie shook his head.

"Thought your daddy take you crabbin'," he murmured. "Well, you take the crab here, boy."

Charlie watched his thumb go under the white belly.

"See, that lever there . . . you take it out, then you pop the shell, see." Granddaddy shucked the crab out of its shell. "Then you break it in two, see, and you don't eat all that there, boy." Granddaddy wiped the inside of the crab clean.

"Now, break it again, and look at all that meat, boy."

Granddaddy scooped out a hunk of white meat.

"Go ahead and try some of that now."

Charlie touched the crabmeat to his lips experimentally, then popped it in his mouth. The Old Bay seasoning burned, but the crab melted on his tongue. Granddaddy nodded.

"Right good, isn't it? Now, you take one and try it yourself."

Charlie reached into the pile and pulled out a large crab, making sure the pincers were away from him. He turned the crab over and found the lever.

"That's right, now pull that lever out, see, and you pop that shell off."

Charlie wedged his thumb under the crab and pulled at the shell.

"Now, you got to pull hard, boy," Granddaddy added, neatly cleaning his crab.

Charlie pulled harder on the shell, but it remained firmly glued to the body. Granddaddy took another sip of his beer.

"Now, go on, boy, don't be afraid of it, just *pull* on that shell with all your strength, see," Granddaddy instructed, demonstrating the technique on another crab.

Charlie nodded solemnly, took a deep breath, and pulled on the shell as hard as he could. The shell cracked open, flying from his hand with a spray of crab intestine following. Charlie's hand was empty. He looked up slowly at Granddaddy; a fine mustard of crab guts was sprayed across his white shirt. Charlie stared at him, horrified with what he had just done. Granddaddy picked up the crumpled shell that had landed in front of him.

"Well, now, boy," he began slowly. "Reckon that's one way to do it," he murmured, handing him the body of the crab. "Next time I'll know to duck, see," he said, his pale eyes lightening.

Charlie began to giggle. Then Granddaddy was chuckling. Charlie howled, laughing so hard he woke himself up.

He stared into the afternoon light, dropping his foot from the sofa he had fallen asleep on. Charlie sat up groggily, glancing at his watch as he heard the freezer open in the kitchen. Granddaddy landed two frosted packs on the counter.

"Why don't you let me get us dinner tonight?"

Granddaddy glanced at him as he walked in.

"Now, I make the dinners, boy."

He pulled the stove door open; preheated waves rolled under the overhead light.

"Granddaddy, do you like pizza?"

He turned the knob on the stove, injecting the silver food into the mouth.

"Now, don't worry, boy," he said, carrying the dinner boxes to the trash. "I'll do the cooking here."

Charlie looked at the phone. The TV dinners were bad enough fully prepared, but Granddaddy didn't get the heating right and the center of the food was stone cold. He waited until Granddaddy walked out to the garage, then snatched up the rotary phone.

They were on the back porch when the doorbell rang. Charlie pulled out his wallet, but Granddaddy was already moving through the house. He reached the foyer as Granddaddy opened the door.

"Now, what can I do for you, boy?"

Charlie looked over his shoulder and saw the broad flat box of the pizza.

"Who you callin' *boy*, old man?"

"Granddaddy, I ordered a pizza—"

"I'm sorry, boy, but you have the wrong house."

Granddaddy shut the door on the opening mouth. He turned to Charlie with disgust in his blue-steel eyes.

"I told you that I was—"

The doorbell rang again. Granddaddy turned from one crisis to another, opening the door to glimpse an indignant, sweating African American holding a steaming pizza just below his chin.

"I told you, boy—"

*"Who you callin' boy, motherfucker?"*

Granddaddy shut the door again. The doorbell chimed through the house as Granddaddy stood guard. The doorbell rang and rang, then Charlie heard the footsteps leave the porch. He ran for the back door, circling the house, reaching the skinny man in the red-and-white shirt.

"That motherfuckin' old asshole! I kick his motherfuckin' ass all over the place! Who he think he is callin' me boy, stupid white old motherfucker!"

"He's my grandfather. Here's a twenty—keep it," Charlie said, taking the flat box from him.

"I ought to kick his motherfuckin' Confederate ass," he grumbled, pocketing the seven-dollar tip.

Charlie walked back around the house.

"*Now!* Who told that boy to bring a pizza here?"

Charlie sat down at the table.

"I did."

He plopped down the bright pizza box on the picnic table. The redolence of sausage, pepperoni, mushrooms, and onions wafted out.

"I wanted some pizza—you want a piece?" He flipped the lid back; a small white ghost floated in front of Granddaddy's eyes. "Take a piece if you want one."

Charlie burned his tongue on the steaming cheese, dropping it on top of the cold dinner. He looked at Granddaddy.

"What—"

Granddaddy shook his head.

"You are one hardheaded person!"

"Look who's talking." Charlie nodded to the box. "Why don't you just have a piece and forget about it?"

Granddaddy looked at the open box for the first time.

"I don't eat that kind of food."

"What kind?"

*"Junk food."*

Charlie pointed down at the tray of compartmentalized food.

"What do you call those things?"

"Whole lot more nutritious than that," he murmured, jabbing two fingers down at the offending pizza.

Charlie reached for another slice.

"Now, what is in that mess?"

"Pepperoni, sausage, onions, mushrooms, and extra sauce."

"Well, now, you get a lot of different foods on that pie, at least."

Charlie wiped his mouth with his napkin.

"Why don't you have a piece of this pie—it won't hurt you."

Granddaddy pointed down at the pizza.

"Now, will you have enough left then, boy? I don't want to take your food, see."

"I have plenty," he nodded, dropping a piece on Granddaddy's cleaned aluminum tray.

Granddaddy looked down, then picked up the pizza experimentally.

"Now, I don't believe in eating junk food."

"Go on, it won't stunt your growth."

"Might stunt something else," he murmured, taking a bite.

Charlie watched him chew the pizza, setting down the piece on his tray.

"Well . . . what do you think?"

Granddaddy ducked his head, touching his napkin to his mouth.

"Right good."

Granddaddy pointed to him and wiped his mouth again.

"I know what I wanted to ask you, boy. I have to go back up the country again tomorrow and pick up some things I forgot and I was wondering if you wanted to accompany me?"

Charlie looked at him.

"I thought we got everything."

Granddaddy shook his head slowly. "No, I forgot a few things. Now, you don't have to go if you have other things to do, see."

"I'll go."

"If you have an interview—I don't want to take you away from that."

"I don't have an interview."

Granddaddy picked up his piece of pizza. "Then, we'll get an early start and get up there in the morning, see, before it gets too hot."

Charlie nodded, watching him take another bite. He wiped his mouth again, setting the pizza down.

"Right good," Granddaddy murmured. "Pizza is right good food."

# CHAPTER FOURTEEN

Virginia countryside

*1931*

"Uncle Edwin?"

Austin's uncle looked up from the newspaper in an office yellowed with invoices tacked on walls around pictures of girls next to new cars, leaning against barrels of Standard Oil, partly obscuring the 1931 calendar floating in the middle of the wall fracas. The January wind banged outside, irritating his uncle.

"What is it, boy?"

Austin ventured into the cubbyhole office of the shop barn they went to many times to confer with clients on the sale of a car, *Jim, I don't know how I can do this and make money, but I'm going to do it,* breathing from the walls after years of selling cars with his uncle. He had been promoted to vice president of sales, which didn't mean a thing except Austin got business cards with VICE PRESIDENT OF SALES.

"Wonder if I could talk to you about somethin'."

His uncle squeaked back, slipping toward the wall in the peeling-green swivel chair that allowed him to catch a wink with hands clasped, chin down in prayer, boots on the desk blotter that hadn't seen light under the mountain of invoices, work orders, bills.

"Sho' boy, you sell that last Studebaker?"

Austin nodded, pulling the tie loose on his neck.

"Yes sir, that's what I wanted to talk to you about."

His uncle swung his boots up on the desk and flared a match in the corner darkness, rolling blue clouds into the detective-style desk lamp. The wind banged the shop door as the pressure in Austin's chest rose. What he had rehearsed, what he had heard himself say twenty times, had vanished in the evanescent second of a cooling match. The harsh wind pounded the door again.

"Go on, boy."

Austin took the deep breath of his aspirations, readying himself for the foray, seeing the pinwheel stars of the desert in the cool morning and having the same sentience of powerlessness against the tide of life. When he had decided to talk to his uncle he didn't know. The same way he didn't know where his audacity originated, or his pluck in knowing he would be successful. He could only follow the wind slamming against the door in syncopation with his own marching drummer.

"Uncle, you know I've sold every Studebaker on the lot."

The peel of fire moved up and down.

"An' I reckon I could sell as many as you can get."

"That a fact," came coolly from the corner darkness, two thin shafts of smoke streaming across his mud-crusted boots.

Austin sat up in the sagging chair. His arms felt heavy and awkward as he leaned forward.

"Saw that application you got from Studebaker . . . invitin' you to come out to the factory to talk about a dealership."

Boots thudded against the desk.

"Them boys always sendin' me their applications."

Austin nodded, feeling the hunch of his shoulders, the uselessness of his arms and hands. The effort of his charge had already put him out of sync. The only thing to do was plow through to the other side. He began to speak rapidly.

"I know you got the shop here and the car lot and that you ain't goin' to take them up on their offer . . . I know you been real good to me and I appreciate it, I really do, ain't no one done for me what you have . . ." Austin took a breath, hearing the wind bang the door again. "But I was just wonderin' . . . well, just wonderin', if you wouldn't mind, that is, I was just wonderin' if you'd mind if I went out and had a talk with those boys and see what they had to say. Just talk and see what they're always flappin' about with their brochures and things, just talk about some things and I wonder if you'd mind if I did that . . . Uncle?"

The cigarette died under the desk, and there was his uncle's creased and worn face squinting in the desk light. It was the face of long nights counting out greasy bills and hours on the lot with the sun on the back of his neck and brow. It was the face that turned a hay barn and a few old cars into a successful business and now saw trouble on the horizon. Uncle Edwin knew this was the ending to a day portending things to come.

"You movin' fast now, ain't you, boy?"

Austin gripped the arms of the chair, braced for battle.

"You drive off to California and come back with your girl from Hollywood. Then y'all go on down to Jacksonville and get married—I give you a new car for y'all's honeymoon, then you come on back and get yourself an apartment on the Boulevard. Start sellin' cars with me and makin' money hand over fist. More money than them bootleggers could give you and learnin' the automobile business while you're at it, I might add. You been movin' fast, boy, *fast*!"

"Yes sir." Austin nodded slowly, keeping his eyes on the squinting face of destiny.

"I let you and Snowball use the shop for hoppin' up your car to go race them bootleggers—and I know you been beatin' 'em for a while now, boy! Don't *tell* me you ain't been gittin' good money from them too," he continued, changing tactics in midstream, laying out a careful string of mines.

Austin nodded slowly, knowing his uncle was pointing out what he would stand to lose.

"You been right good to me, Uncle, and I ain't sayin' I'm goin' to do anything, I just wondered if you mind if I talked to these old boys if you ain't goin' to."

His uncle paused—the metal sign squeaking above the shop door. He leaned back slowly into the descending darkness, cracked a match with his thumb, and lit another cigarette, exhaling tiredly. Austin rested in his corner, limbering up for the next charge, but seeing his uncle suddenly as a man resigned, wondering if this had happened while he was sitting there.

"And now you want to get yourself a Studebaker dealership . . . is that it, boy?"

Austin heard the words he himself had never spoken. They came from darkness.

"Just want to talk to them, Uncle."

His uncle breathed in tiredly and lit a cigarette. Two long blue shafts rolled out from the shadows.

"Uh-huh . . . how old you, boy?"

"Twenty-two."

His uncle picked up the tie hanging outside his open vest on the bridge of his stomach. He examined a grease spot, the wind gusting under the shop door, scurrying fine sand around Austin's chair.

"I been like a daddy to you, Austin . . ." He looked up. "Your pa still in the country in that log cabin doin' Lord knows what out there?"

"He teaches," Austin bristled.

"Teaches who? Niggers and poor trash."

"He teaches history."

The glittering eye was on Austin.

"He lives in history, boy, and your sick mother lives in the city with your support—not his—I know you been givin' her money."

Austin slumped from the one-two punch, but knew his uncle's hits were ineffectual. His uncle shook his head slowly.

"What makes you think those people goin' to give someone just twenty-two years old a dealership, boy?" He motioned down to the desk. "You been readin' the papers? We are in a depression, son! Ain't *no one* takin' risks now."

Austin faced him evenly.

"'Cause I reckon you'll help me."

The boots crashed to the floor, clearing the desk momentarily, invoices and work orders landing softly underneath as the first petals of his dying business.

"Damn!"

Uncle Edwin was standing up, leaning across his desk with his hands below the desk lamp. He bore down on Austin, light cutting under his nose.

"Why would I help myself to lose the best damn car salesman and mechanic I ever had?"

The winter quiet had come into the office. The cold cars of the still-young century gleamed outside. A single light burned over EDWIN'S GARAGE, and a few flakes had started to fall, lying delicately on the curve of a car fender without melting. Inside, in the corner of the hay barn, the older man and the young man faced each other, both knowing they were following their own scripts. Neither could stop the wind outside the shop doors now.

Austin faced the soft windows of human instinct, helpless under the march of time and finality.

"'Cause I know you will, Uncle," he said quietly.

Uncle Edwin stood behind his desk with the calendar of his life behind. He stared at Austin and shook his head slowly.

"Damn, boy."

He faced Austin with his hands in his back pockets; the fight now over, the wind smashing away at the small shop barn for the victor. He shook his head again.

"Damn!"

Austin felt the crease of his suit tickle the back of his knee. He watched the man speak into the silver teardrop, enjoying his opportunity to playact in the drama of his life, complete with new cars, new suits, new hats, new dresses, new houses, new furniture, new success, and soon, any day, any hour, any minute, a new baby.

The man signaled Austin to get ready. He stepped closer to the boom, clearing his throat silently, glancing at his watch, thinking about his next meeting. He didn't really take advertising seriously because the real selling was done by the man on the lot. His business manager thought radio advertising was a way to bring in more business. Austin wanted to hurry. Men from the bank were coming and he had a meeting with the new salesmen.

The man nodded again, notching up his voice.

"And *you* are the *youngest* man to have a Studebaker dealership? How do you account for your *amazing success* at selling these *outstanding automobiles*?"

Austin leaned toward the microphone, holding the script, speaking crisply, the way the man told him to.

"These 1933 Studebaker *coupes* are what's amazing! These cars with automatic speed control, spark advance, and front and rear heaters are selling themselves! I just show people the fine lines of these new cars and I can barely keep them on the lot!"

The man nodded.

"Well then! I guess the only thing to do is let the people know where they can buy these *amazing* cars!"

Austin leaned closer, his lips grazing the perforated steel.

"Well, that's easy, Two hundred Broad Street. That's where you can find Turin Studebaker . . . and, you can find *me*!"

"Cut! Alright. That was fine, Mr. Turin. That one will be ready for broadcast tomorrow."

Austin adjusted his crisp bow tie, already walking for the door, twenty-dollar shoes clicking on the tile floor.

"I have to get back to the lot, just let me know the times it will run."

"Will do, Mr. Turin."

Austin jumped into the back of his black Studebaker.

"How'd it go, Mr. Turin?"

"Fine, Sam . . . fine," he nodded, picking up the morning paper to make sure the prices of his cars were correct.

"You like doing those radio spots, Mr. Turin?"

"I like making money, Sam," he murmured.

"Well, you're good at that, Mr. Turin!"

Austin didn't hear this last statement, checking his watch again.

"Could you step on it, Sam? I have a meeting with some new salesmen."

"You got it, boss."

They reached the long structure with wet paint still on the showroom windows and the TURIN STUDEBAKER sign flickering the letter *N*. Austin reminded himself to tell his secretary to call the electrician.

"Mr. Turin, I need a quote on—"

"Mr. Turin, are we going to get the new line of cars tomorrow?"

"Boss, you got to get me another mechanic, we are just too backed up . . ."

"Mr. Turin, can we give them the incentive price early?"

Austin sprayed out a few fires on the way to his office, referring the rest to his business manager, shaking hands with three couples who recently purchased three cars, stopping by his secretary's desk to pick up five messages, carrying the newly hired salesmen into his office with a sweep of his hand.

Austin motioned the salesmen to chairs, firing off two calls, taking two more, signing five documents that couldn't wait, moving last month's sales figures to the other side of his desk, writing down three more appointments, telling his secretary to call the electrician again. All the while he was talking to the salesmen, dropping the crumbs of sales success for them to devour.

"You never let somebody off the lot without putting them into the car. If you can get them to sit in the car you'll sell them! I have had more sales by just getting the person to take a test drive. You see, they want to buy. They want you to make them feel good about buying the car. That's your job—"

"Mr. Turin, I have Bobby Hicks on the line."

Austin leaned forward and picked up the line.

"Bobby! Of course I know your boss liked the car! Right . . .

we have that color . . . no problem. . . . Let's talk about it, I could give you a corporate discount on three cars . . . I'll see you at the supper club . . . right, thanks."

Austin hung up.

"So, like I was saying, get them into the car, get them to drive it, make them feel good—"

The secretary's voice crackled through the speaker box.

"Mr. Turin, it's Georgia Bain."

"Just a minute, boys—"

Austin snatched the phone.

"Georgia! Tell me what I want to hear."

Austin motioned to the grinning men.

"Well, that's just great, Georgia! When can we move in?"

Austin winked at the men.

"I know the house needs to be cleaned—can't they do that while we're there?"

He laughed, spinning around a black appointment book.

"I can make it about eighty-thirty, no wait a minute, I have Bobby Hicks at seven and that might take a while. . . . Tell you what, Georgia, can you get hold of their people and try and set something up for nine-thirty? . . . Alright, then give me a call back. . . . Alright, fine."

He let the phone fall to the cradle, making a note, signing three more documents he had missed, pocketing a cuff link he had thought lost but was under the three documents.

"Sorry about that, boys, just bought a house—now, like I said—get them to drive the car. Get the wife involved too. Let me tell you, boys, you have to get the wife to want to buy that car. I have seen more deals fall through because the salesman concentrated on the husband and forgot the wife. She's usually the one controlling the pocketbook, and let me tell you—"

"Mr. Turin, it's the Bigg's people—"

Austin snatched the phone.

"Yes . . . right, the dining-room and living-room set . . . I know, I'm going to have a place for y'all to deliver . . . right, thanks."

He looked at the two men.

"And finally, remember, you are selling one of the *finest* automobiles on the road. Studebaker is far superior to the big automakers and I'm not just saying that, boys. See, you have to educate the customer and let them—"

"Mr. Turin, it's Celia!"

Austin looked up.

"Can you take a message?"

"She says it's urgent."

Austin grabbed up the phone. "Yes, Celia."

The small voice was loud enough for the salesmen to hear.

"*Mr. Turin!* Your wife says she thinks she's going to have it today, feelin' the labor pains!"

Austin glanced at his watch.

"Alright, I'll be there just as soon as I can."

"You bettah hurry, Mr. Turin—"

"Mr. Turin, the gentlemen from the bank are here to see you."

Austin held his hand up to his secretary in the doorway.

"Alright, tell them just a minute."

He turned back to the phone.

"Celia, call Henry, tell him to get the car and take Tamara to the hospital and I'll be there as soon as I can."

"You bettah hurry, Mr. Turin, 'cause I think this baby comin' fast!"

"Alright, Celia," he finished, dropping the phone, smoothing his double-breasted suit, walking to the door with the two salesmen.

"Just remember what I said, boys, and you'll do fine!"

"Thank you, Mr. Turin," they sang in unison, pumping his hand even as he was late for his own baby, but the bank couldn't be put off. He needed the money to expand.

Every time he tried to get away something came up. He was selling cars so fast the factory couldn't keep up with him. *Selling cars in a depression year!* But none of that mattered now, he told himself, watching his wife stir.

"Hey, sweetie," he whispered softly, her eyes opening out of the ether, shining with the dew light of exhaustion.

She put her arms around his neck weakly. He could smell the stiff, light cotton of his own suit with the faint leathery scent the cleaners left in contrast to the talcum-delicate scent of his wife.

"Where were you?" she murmured.

He stared at the wall.

"Right here. I got held up for a few minutes by the men from the bank, but then I got here and they had just put you under."

"Oh." She drowsed, her grasp weakening, lying back on the downy pillow.

Her eyes opened more, a soft cast of light on the surface like a kite on a green field.

"You sleep, honey . . . you need your rest."

"Okay," she murmured, turning, the clutched hand touching her cheek.

Austin walked to the door with the relief of a man forgiven for his crime. *It's for her own good,* he told himself in the hallway. *She doesn't understand what it takes to run a business. And it's true that I'm not home most nights and have to work on weekends, but she doesn't mind having a new home, and new furniture, or the new clothes. She just has to accept that we can't always be together,* he thought, turning a corner in the hospital. *Building a business up takes a lot of time and with this new expansion it's going to take even more time. Let's see, what's left for the night. Have to go back and make sure Snowball got the new mechanic hired and see how the boys did today. Those new cars should be in. When is that radio spot going to run? Uncle Edwin was supposed to deliver some cars too.*

Austin approached the large window of the maternity ward. The swaddled baby in the crib had his eyes, though they were more Tamara's color, he thought. He stared at her, feeling the nervous energy of too much coffee, not enough sleep, too many things on his mind.

*She will go on and be a princess among princesses. She will not know hardship and worry and this world where circumstance and doubt can swallow one up. Her world will be protected. Everything I do will be for her. Every car I sell, every dollar I make, will insure her life. All my transgressions and all my shortcomings will be paid for by this little soul I have brought in because she will be the best of me. Her opportunities will surpass any I have known and we will renew ourselves. She will be the leaping light of my enthusiasm, of my love, passion, hope, and dreams. She will dream for all of us as she goes to the finest schools and lives in the finest house. She will marry someone wealthy and who is of her own standing because by then I will have dealerships all over the country. Yes, everything I do will be for her and she doesn't even know how lucky she is.*

Austin touched the glass, then walked out of the hospital, leaving a single moist print over the young life.

*Charlie Tidewater*
*465 Marilee Road*
*Southampton, VA*
*August 25, seven* A.M.

*Matthew,*

*No shots have been fired and no articles left on my pillow since I wrote you last. But I did call up the reporter who wrote that article and I'm meeting him tonight. And then I have a date. She's a one-hundred-percent southern belle. Anyway, it's for dinner. Did I tell you Granddaddy still has a black-and-white television? Same kind I was watching when they announced King was shot. I remember—I went looking for my dad to tell him and walked down the hall. I heard these voices of men in the darkness just short of the living room. The voices stopped and my dad came out and screamed at me and told me to go to my room. He never told me who they were and why he was so mad. But I remember those voices scared me. I'm headed back out to the garage this morning with Granddaddy. Seems he forgot something.*

*Maybe I'll find it.*

*Charlie*

# CHAPTER FIFTEEN

Richmond, Virginia

*August 1998*

Charlie waited beneath Robert E. Lee's horse in the shimmering darkness. The evening had collected behind the trees and statues farther down Monument Avenue. He sat on the marble bench and watched the curving, spiked iron railing forge to night, remembering an earlier conversation.

"Sherwood Anders."

". . . I have some questions about an article you wrote a long time ago—quite a long time ago . . . April 5, 1968."

There had been a long pause.

"Mr. Tidewater, I've written hundreds of articles and that was long ago—"

"My mother died on the same day a man named Rufus John Jr. disappeared."

Sherwood Anders's voice closed down into the phone.

"Rufus junior?"

Charlie uncrossed his legs and looked at his watch again. He looked at the mossy overhanging branches of the willows on the side of General Lee, trumpet blooms scattered on the concrete. The dusk collected in a pool of water reflecting sky and trees. He was tired suddenly. They had risen early to go to the country.

*"Now, I'll just be a minute," Granddaddy called, walking into the garage that afternoon.*

*Sun draped the drive in dull midday languor, a hot gritty dust swirling on the empty highway. Charlie heard Granddaddy in the small room, then he was up the steps three at a time. Through the door he saw burned matches and pinched cigarette butts littering the floor. He stared at the window, a jagged edge of blood hovering in sun.*

"Mr. Tidewater?"

Charlie jumped. A man in a checked shirt and khakis stood before him.

"Sherwood Anders," he nodded, shaking his hand. "I don't know if I can help you." He adjusted his glasses and paused, fingering gray slices in his mustache.

"You brought up someone I haven't thought of for years. . . ."

Charlie nodded. "Whatever you can remember would help."

Sherwood Anders breathed heavily and crossed his legs. "In 1968 I was a reporter trying to make my way up covering the country—it was sort of a training field for reporters," he explained, glancing at Charlie with quick gray eyes, slipping a hand through his longish hair. "I had been covering Goochland for a year and the whole world was on fire, but in my neck of the woods if somebody stole someone's lawn mower then I had to file the story."

He paused.

"Then the civil rights movement came, and Rufus junior. He had been away at college . . . his father, Rufus John, was a local mechanic." He paused again. "Rufus junior was different. Intensely good-looking, charismatic. He had been doing work with King up north and he brought back very new ideas." Sherwood shook his head. "They didn't know what to make of him."

A man walked by. Anders watched him until he was a safe distance away.

"The first thing he did was open up the Second Baptist Church—" He glanced at Charlie. "It had been his grandfather's church at one time before he was lynched in the twenties—"

"Lynched?"

He nodded slowly. "Rufus junior wasn't really a preacher, he was more of a civil rights crusader, but the people came. A few at first, then it began to fill up. That's when folks began to get nervous; they burned a cross in front of the church."

"I read that article."

Sherwood nodded, fingering his mustache again. "But it had the opposite effect on Rufus junior. He preached more radical ideas. I think he saw himself more like his grandfather than his father." Sherwood stopped. "Then he disappeared." He looked at Charlie. "I got a call from his mother and she said he had been missing for a few days."

A car slipped down Monument Avenue and they watched until the sound died into the slight tittering of night sparrows. Charlie turned.

"Then what?"

"I was transferred to Richmond . . ." He shrugged. "I got what I could in the paper, but was never able to follow up."

He stood suddenly.

"I wish I could help you, but that's all I know, Mr. Tidewater." He shook Charlie's hand quickly. "Good luck with your research."

He began to limp away, one shoe scraping the sidewalk.

"Mr. Anders?"

He kept walking.

Charlie stood up. "Mr. Anders!"

He stopped without turning around.

"Do you know why they lynched Rufus junior's grandfather?"

Sherwood turned around in shadow, his glasses reflecting distant light. A gust of wind scattered leaves on the sidewalk. He opened his mouth, shutting it quickly.

"They found him in the home of a white woman."

Charlie listened to his uneven footfalls echo on the street. He was still there after Sherwood Anders disappeared under the trees.

# CHAPTER SIXTEEN

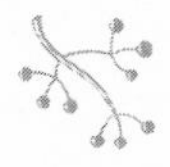

Richmond, Virginia

*August 1998*

Pearl stared into the yard with her arms crossed, a cigarette trailing from fingers dried from years of scrubbing floors. She sat on the back steps the way she did every night when the dishes were washed and the judge was in his chair with a cigar. Sometimes she would dream of her childhood, seeing the world through scudding clouds. Years of toil would fall away and she could smell the honeysuckle by the white lattice.

That was before the judge.

She stubbed the dead butt into the glass ashtray she kept below the sink. Bringing out the glass ashtray was always a pleasure. She kept her ashtray with the silver-backed lighter spit-clean. Pearl clapped the lighter down into a pocket under her apron, the sweet breath of burley tobacco filling her lungs again.

" 'Cause once the judge got you, he got you," she hummed in a low voice, tapping the small white line, remembering the door her mother had pushed her through.

"She do good work," her mother nodded, disappearing forever.

"He sure young then," Pearl murmured, thinking of the man with black eyes and clipped mustache who briskly showed her the room on the third floor.

"This will be your quarters." He paused. "Your mother has done the best she could for herself in the circumstances. It wasn't her fault your daddy was a bad nigger," he continued in the same tone he explained how the silver was to be cleaned. "Do right by me, then I will do by you." He stopped and turned. "But I will not tolerate any uppity nigger," he warned, slashes of light crossing the dark space of his eyes. "The rest of the world can go to hell; here we hold our own."

Pearl stared into the yard. She regarded the small white rabbit the way she did the crickets and scattering light in the trees. Pearl heard the front door and wondered if it would be the man with the flat accent of her cousins in Detroit. He had called once already for Minnie. Pearl shook her head slowly. The judge had just as well given her a room on the third floor.

" 'Cause once the judge got you, he got you," she repeated softly.

Pearl nodded into the darkness.

"Go on, old rabbit," she murmured. "Go on."

The night before, Minnie sat with her father in the butternut glow of a single lamp. The light gleamed on the instep of his shoe; a newspaper shadowed his eyes. Minnie could hear Pearl's brassy voice in the kitchen.

When Pearl sang, Minnie always thought of New York. Even as a little girl she thought of nightclubs where husky-voiced women would sing and fashionable people drifted down avenues between tall buildings. Minnie had collected magazine pictures of New York, Chicago, San Francisco and pinned them around her room as an adolescent. She would walk down such streets and be like the modern women she knew existed outside the dreary confines of the South. She planned to make her getaway at college.

Minnie looked at her father. Cole used to read the paper the same way. The seeds of Cole started when she was born to the judge. Men deferred to her father and blacks melted in his sight. Even when she was less than ten she was Miz Minnie, women called her dear and the world parted in quick declension as she tore down the years of her adolescence to the coming-out party of her sixteenth birthday. Her father brought her down the steps slowly that day upon his arm, the room filled with only the oldest, finest families of Virginia.

Minnie looked at her father. He had made the sound *tsk tsk*. Something displeased him. The world had made another turn outside his domain. Minnie watched him carefully.

"Sad to see families go to pieces this way."

Minnie rested her hands in her lap.

"What do you mean, Daddy?"

"Oh, this Kelly girl has gone and gotten herself in another one of these disgusting movies. I imagine Joe Kelly can barely hold up his head with what this woman is doing."

Minnie considered this her bridge, but the snap of the paper showed the judge was still displeased by the world's intrusion into his bourbon and cigar resting on the tall ashtray of tobacco-colored glass. She decided to wait. Minnie looked into the parlor and remembered returning from college. She had not been able to clear the state with the small liberal-arts college her father picked for her, but she had managed to drive to New York and sample the life that would be hers. Eating outside a bistro on the East Side of New York, she felt life was a warm, flowing stream that swept convention to the wayside like so much dust. Among the winking lights of a New York twilight she took great gulps of her dreams.

Minnie planned her move with three girls in her sorority. They were all to get jobs in New York and would take an apartment together. All she had to do was break the news to her father.

*"You don't want to leave Richmond!"*

Minnie sat quietly.

"Why would you go to that cesspool? I should think not, young lady."

"Daddy! I'm a grown woman."

The judge stood behind his large desk.

"Then you should have a family."

Minnie began pacing, feeling a strange panic.

"There is nothing here for me!"

"Only your family and your heritage."

Minnie shook her head, realizing her dreams were slipping out into the gathering twilight.

"No . . . I'm leaving here."

The judge cast his sentence.

"I will cut you off without a cent."

Minnie backed away, considering walking out the door right then. The judge must have seen this, because he came around the desk.

"At least you can wait until the end of the summer to make your decision, Daughter."

Minnie had turned her back and looked at the open porch door. She knew instinctively that now was the moment. She willed herself to take the step. Five more feet and she would be free.

"I ask only that you delay your decision."

Still she did not move. Her confidence wavered. The judge's voice imprisoned her.

"I only want you to consider . . . just until the end of the summer . . ."

She looked out into the night and began to cry; she knew then she would never leave.

Minnie now faced the barrier of pale yellow newsprint. She saw the ring on her father's right hand. Cole used to wear his college ring on that finger. It was a large red rhinestone with the University of Virginia insignia in gold. Minnie saw Cole's ring for the first time in this parlor.

"Cole Penrod, this is my daughter, Minnie. Darling, Cole is just back from the university and I suggested he have dinner with us tonight."

Cole was all mouth even then. His crew cut stood as a line on the crown of his skull; his mouth flashed large white teeth. He had the largest blue eyes she had ever seen.

"They finally decided Cole Penrod will never leave here unless we kick him out, and so after I let the alligator loose in the commons it was decided that I should pursue other opportunities." Cole laughed over dinner, winking at Minnie and chuckling with the judge.

"Now, Cole's family owns Continental Brick," the judge explained to her, lighting their cigars while she sipped coffee. "And you will be going into the business, I assume."

Cole put his folded napkin to the side, the chunky ring glinting candlelight.

"Yes sir, Daddy and I already talked. I'm going to handle sales . . . he's getting rid of Jim Reedy—never did a good job anyway."

The judge watched him through the smoke.

"Well, that's real good, Cole—honey, you know Cole's family was one of the first families to settle in this area?" He looked back at Cole. "You had an ancestor in Jeff Davis's cabinet, is that right?"

"Yes sir, a great great uncle, that's right." He nodded, tipping his cigar in the silver discus to the right of his brandy.

The judge stood up suddenly.

"I have some briefs I have to go over . . . I'll leave you two young people to get acquainted."

He withdrew and pulled the pocket doors separating the dining room from the parlor. The doors thudded together and the room was very quiet. Cole stubbed out his cigar.

"Never really liked those things."

Minnie nodded. "So your family was in the Civil War?"

Cole smiled and slumped down in his chair.

"Hell, if that's what your daddy wants to hear, then I'll tell him that."

Minnie's eyes came together.

"Now, why would you tell him a lie?"

Cole looked at her.

"I'd tell him my granddaddy was Robert E. Lee if it meant I could meet his beautiful daughter."

*I was charmed by him,* Minnie thought, listening to the tick of the grandfather clock in the hallway. He took her for a ride in his convertible that night and she came home at three in the morning. The judge approved of Cole and through that she got more freedom. He took her to nice restaurants and they drove to Virginia Beach twice. Cole even said he wouldn't mind living in a city like New York. By the end of August she was engaged.

Minnie stared at the blackened brick of the fireplace in the yellowing light. The andirons were brassed along with the poker and chimney sweep she used as a little girl. That belonged to memories of her family life before Mother died. That belonged to life before Cole and the baby.

Their first years of marriage were a blur. They lived in a house on Monument Avenue. She remembered the drone of the television; Cole was always watching sports of some kind. Then she had a baby.

Cole stayed out and she was home with Madelyn. The walks with the stroller across the hot, dead days made her feel she was a ghost on the far side of life. Then she started to smell cheap perfume on his collar. On a late night she came to know the ring. Cole hadn't bothered to wipe off the lipstick smudged in clown relief to the side of his mouth.

*"I won't put up with this anymore, Cole!"*

The whiskey was sharp on his breath and the ring came out of the semidarkness like a gold-and-red comet. That was the first time the university made its intentions known to her. After that the ring was familiar. Sometimes it whizzed her into darkness and she would wake on the floor.

"You tell anybody I hit you and I tell everybody you a liar and how you whored around before!"

She had told him her secret in a weak moment. The abortion was a college girl's mistake and she lived with it every day, but now Cole could do anything he wanted. Minnie came to live with his women and avoided the ring best she could. Then a neighbor saw the ring in action and she woke in a hospital room with her father by her side. She and the baby came home under the judge's roof.

The paper fortress crumbled and dropped to the side of the chair. The judge rubbed his eyes.

"I'm mighty tired."

This was her last chance.

"Daddy?"

"Yes," he murmured, glancing at his pocket watch like a conductor.

"Daddy, I have a date tomorrow night."

The judge snapped time shut. He looked at her, light bringing out creases under his eyes.

"With whom, may I ask?"

"With the gentleman you met today . . . Charlie Tidewater."

"Ah." He smiled, bringing out his handkerchief. "The man from the First Family."

"Yes, I believe he is."

The judge wiped his mouth.

"The Yankee?"

"He is from here originally."

"And been there eternally."

The handkerchief was back in his top pocket. "I don't think it is such a good idea for you to be experimenting."

"It's been six months!"

"A trifle."

Minnie looked down at her hands. "I want to go. I want to get on with my life."

The legs uncrossed and the judge leaned forward.

"What do you call this? This is your life."

Minnie kept her eyes on her chewed-short fingernails.

"No, Daddy, it's *your* life," she answered slowly.

"It is *our* life now, *yours, Madelyn's*—you don't know this man from Adam."

"He's nice."

The judge nodded slowly.

"Cole was nice too, Daughter."

"And you brought him here."

He breathed in wearily.

"A mistake, I now admit."

He picked up the cigar, fingering the smooth, rounded end.

"I just don't—"

"It's for *dinner,* Daddy, not marriage!"

The smoke shot into the lamp.

"I should hope not," he murmured.

The silence was between them and Minnie looked up slowly. The black eyebrows and mustache were lost in the shadows. The judge crossed his legs again, light gleaming on his forward shoe.

"I do not think I can ask Pearl to stay late again."

"I can get a sitter, Daddy."

He put the cigar in the ashtray. "On such short notice? I should think not."

The dark eyes settled on her. They sat opposite each other in the wing chairs like two chess players.

"Madelyn and I will be fine."

Minnie paused.

"Thank you, Daddy."

He picked up the newspaper.

"I expect you home by midnight . . . for Madelyn's sake."

Minnie looked up from the floor. The judge's fingers were around the paper, smoke wicking slowly around the ring.

# CHAPTER SEVENTEEN

Richmond, Virginia

*August 1998*

Charlie strolled under the snow of magnolias along the dimming street. He couldn't reconcile the whispered past life with any sense of present life. The past was so rich and vibrant, while his own age seemed pathetic. When he was married he would stay up and watch the late news, many times thinking the world had gone insane.

A harvest moon sparkled the sidewalk to the porch.

"Hey, Old Boy," he whispered to the figure that stretched, meowed, then reclined again, tail in twitching repose.

"The gentleman caller has arrived."

Charlie stared into the darkling portico, picking out her blouse between structure and void. She flowed down the five short steps.

"Sorry I'm late."

She took his arm at the bottom of the steps.

"Come say hello to Daddy before we go," she whispered.

The house smelled like clothes after a weekend at a cottage. Charlie walked into the sepia room with the blackened fireplace, Queen Anne furniture, round silver-edged ashtrays. A bronze dog sat patiently on the edge of the hearth. In the Midwest the living room would be reminiscent of long winters in lonely farmhouses, but here it reminded Charlie of simmering afternoons.

Judge Barrek rose from his chair.

"The man from Chicago."

"Hello, sir."

Charlie shook the hand motioning him to the rounded white couch. Minnie sat beside him in flowing crepe. The judge leaned back.

"Late for dinner, I'd say," he remarked, flipping the pocket watch from his vest.

"Charlie's taking me to the Tobacco Company, Daddy—they serve late."

"I don't know that establishment—"

"It's down at the slip."

"Ah, the tourist trap," he said to Charlie.

Charlie managed a smile.

"When in Rome . . ."

The judge's dark eyes registered nothing. He studied his cigar, then looked at Charlie.

"I looked up your people and could find no trace of them in the founding families—do you know the exact names of your ancestors?"

The shiny shoe was in front of him. He wondered if all southern aristocrats possessed such pointed black shoes.

"I wouldn't know their exact names . . . sir," he replied, feeling he wanted to snap the smoldering cigar in two.

"We really have to go, Daddy, or I'm liable to starve to death," Minnie announced, rising quickly.

"Nice seeing you again, sir."

"The pleasure's mine," the judge replied.

The Tobacco Company was on a cobblestone street slanting down a hill to the James River. Charlie listened to the mellifluous tones of Minnie's voice as she pointed out shops and bistros. The restaurant was shades of brown; the table by a window swung wide for the balmy night.

"Your father," Charlie began.

"The judge," Minnie answered in a way he couldn't decide.

"He's protective."

Minnie looked out the window.

"I suppose men don't have protective fathers."

"I never really knew my father well. He was always traveling when I was young . . . he died while I was a teenager."

"How sad."

Charlie sipped his Bloody Mary and tasted the horseradish at the bottom. Their shrimp arrived.

"You are an only child?"

"Yes." She touched the cocktail sauce and popped the shrimp.

Charlie hesitated.

"What did your mother—"

"Cancer."

Charlie rested his arms, feeling the buttons in the double-breasted coat he had tried on several times.

*"So you have a date, well, that's good," Granddaddy said, broom in hand in the driveway. "Now, what's the girl's name?"*

*"Minnie Barrek."*

*Granddaddy made a sound through his teeth.*

*"Now, that's high cotton, boy. Judge Barrek's daughter. Now, I heard she had divorced the Penrod boy. He didn't hold a candle to Mr. Penrod, see, who built that brick business from the ground up. But, that's high cotton you have there, see."*

Charlie looked up at Minnie.

"I really don't know how my mother died . . . you see, that's the reason I'm down here."

Minnie's strand of pearls shone dully around her neck. She leaned forward.

"Not to look for gainful employment?"

Charlie paused, then shook his head. "No."

"Out with it."

He considered the gleam in her eye.

"What?"

"Tell me about your mother," she said, leaning back in her chair.

Charlie took another sip of his drink.

"A lot of the things I remember about my mother don't make sense to me." He paused. "Once I was at home, playing in the front of the house and I heard my mother screaming. So I went to the back of the house. I could hear her, but I didn't see her anywhere." He looked at Minnie, then touched the spoon by his hand. "I went in, and the screaming was coming from the bathroom." Charlie looked up from the table. "So, I opened the door and there she was. Just standing in the bathtub."

"What did she do when she saw you?"

Charlie paused.

"She pulled the shower curtain and stood there until she heard me leave."

Minnie looked down quickly from his gaze, then picked up her drink.

"Anyway . . . there are a lot of things about my childhood that I don't understand." Charlie looked at her. "I guess I'm down here to find some answers."

He pulled the newspaper article from his pocket and handed it across the table.

"I found this in my bedroom the other night."

Minnie leaned back and Charlie watched her slender arm parallel the paper-covered table as she read. She looked up suddenly.

"This Rufus John Jr.?"

"Disappeared the same day my mother died," Charlie nodded.

Minnie looked down at the article again.

"Turin Motors belonged to my grandfather—that's where he used to live with his family. I called that reporter and—"

"Wait a minute!" Minnie held up her hand. "*How* did you get this article?"

Charlie paused.

"Someone left it in my bedroom at my grandfather's—there was a prowler—" He hesitated, seeing her expression. "My grandfather scared him off—there's another thing," he said, looking into her wide eyes. "I went to my mother's grave and this man came up behind me—"

Minnie sat back from the table.

"You don't want to hear all this."

Minnie smacked the top of the table. "I wouldn't ask if I didn't want to know. I'm just settling in."

Charlie nodded slowly.

"Now, what about the man at your mother's grave?"

He leaned in on his elbows.

"He said my grandfather knows things he's not talking about—I think this guy was at the house the night before—outside my window."

Minnie stared at him.

"Why do you think someone left this article where you would find it?"

He paused. "I think someone wants me to know what happened."

"And you met the reporter who wrote the article?"

"Right." Charlie nodded. "He said that in 1968 there was Klan activity out in Goochland. He was reporting on it when this Rufus junior disappeared—" He hesitated. "Apparently Rufus junior's father worked for my granddaddy in the country at this garage . . ." He looked at the James River sparkling triangles of light. "My mother grew up there for a time in this apartment on top of the garage. . . . I saw it the other day—there are these iron bars on the windows—"

Minnie's drink suddenly tipped over.

"Oh, I'm so sorry!"

The waiter came over with a towel and sopped up the caramel-colored pool. Charlie regretted the turn of the conversation.

"I'm sorry to bore you with my past."

"No," Minnie said, shaking her head. "I'm glad you told me about your mother."

The waiter finished cleaning the table and the breeze returned.

"Well, let's forget about all that—it could all just be weird coincidences."

She looked at him.

"You don't believe that."

Charlie looked down quickly from her gaze.

"No."

She leaned into the table.

"What do you believe?"

He touched the edge of the shellfish, looking off to the smoky James River flowing silently through the night.

"I believe something happened to my mother down here . . ." He paused. "And I think this reporter was lying to me."

Minnie looked at him.

"Why do you think the reporter was lying?"

Charlie shook his head slowly. "He seemed scared."

"Well, maybe he is."

Charlie looked at her.

"It's been thirty years."

Minnie leaned forward.

"This is the South, darling . . ." She smiled sadly. "Time doesn't mean a thing."

A man was singing country-western songs when they walked into the small bar. They sat around a table crowded among other tables. It was warm and fans blew in open windows. The faces around the singer were pink from the sun. Charlie ordered a beer and a Coke from a teetering waitress.

"I love this song," Minnie whispered closely.

Charlie listened to the twanging voice. He saw two spoons in Minnie's hand lying curve to curve. She beat time on her knee with her hand clapping down in rhythm. Minnie kept her eyes on the singer and the spoons clapped together like the foot snare of a drummer. The song ended and she put the spoons in her purse.

"How did you learn to do that?"

She picked up her Coke, smiling self-consciously.

"Mama taught me. She was from West Virginia; I guess

they used to all get together with their spoons and musical saws."

"You were really good."

"Thank you," she said with no embarrassment. "It used to drive Daddy crazy. He may have come from Thomas Jefferson, but my mother's side was pure hillbilly."

Charlie grinned. "Interesting."

"Most southerners are part linen, part cracker." She leaned closer. "That's what makes us both wild and reserved."

"I wouldn't mind learning how to do that."

Minnie smiled, her eyes slanting in.

"Maybe I can teach you sometime," she murmured, her languid accent floating through the coastal air.

They drove back to the house and Charlie parked opposite the dim white castle behind clinging trees. Old Boy slipped darkly across the sidewalk and vanished into shadow. They sat in the car for a moment. Minnie turned.

"Let's take a walk."

They strolled into the old part of town. Minnie pointed out various homes, talking of people she knew, taking away mystery before adding it again. Charlie watched her stream through the present night.

"How do you like our fair town?"

"I like it," he nodded, touching her hand resting in the crook of his arm.

They passed brick row houses with dark porches. Minnie leaned over, whispering, "Don't you wonder who walked down these streets before us? What men and women may have passed the time as we are?" Her breath tickled around his ear. "You can almost see them on warm nights like these . . . feel how close they are."

"I was just thinking that," he said haltingly, possessed by her burning eyes. They slipped under the harboring shadow of leaves.

"I watch them from my porch sometimes. Just before the night settles. You can feel their graciousness, their refinement."

He suddenly felt he was walking into a forest of trees adorning large country homes with dusk spilling over arbors and resting in stone birdbaths. There was no connection between this part of the city and the highways of flat shopping malls he had seen driving in.

They passed beneath an overhanging tree, the sidewalk wet with the coppery smell of a garden hose. She turned, picking him out of the darkness.

"Now tell me, why did your wife leave you?"

Charlie glanced at her, discerning nothing.

"I wasn't stable enough for her."

A slender hand willowed across the darkness.

"*Pshaw!* Why did she really leave you?"

He paused, toying with truth and fantasy. Charlie looked at her.

"Because I couldn't be there when she needed me," he said faintly, stepping into cold waters. "We had a baby." They passed into the darker shadow of trees. "He died, the immune system wasn't developed—so they said. He was only two months old." Charlie swallowed. "He was really a neat little guy, very happy . . . I—I mean, a very special baby. All babies are special, I know, but his smile . . ." He faltered. "Anyway, we came back from the hospital and there was just nothing to say." Charlie paused. "It was like we were dead too."

He wiped his eyes quickly.

"Anyway, I got drunk and passed out . . . when I woke up

in the morning, Sybil was on the bathroom floor . . . she had vomited up most of the pills."

Charlie waited for the turbulence to subside.

"We separated soon after that."

The light steps stopped and Minnie turned. She took him in her arms, her breath faintly like mint. Charlie could see the glisten in her eyes, and her lips were warm. Then she just held him under the weeping midnight trees.

# CHAPTER EIGHTEEN

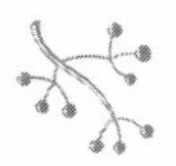

Virginia countryside

*1934–38*

*Austin and his wife run with their daughter along the Virginia shore in modest bathing suits; running on the vacant beaches of the early century. A cottage on a windswept dune hunches against tall weeds of a sea wall; a sagging erosion fence changes to his daughter digging sand with a bucket and shovel. Austin is in double-breasted pinstripes in a black Studebaker and Tamara has a fur wrapped around her shoulders. He smokes on the running board of the car, fashioning himself in the gangster pose of their time, white spats glaring. Tamara walks with hand on hip in model fashion, spinning around with her new fur, prancing with fast, small steps. Austin runs after his daughter on the beach where they are playing with a dog along the surf. He throws a stick and the dog disappears into the foamy water. His mind flickers to a trip to Chicago and the Palmer House. Daughter and wife with matching hats, posing by the steaming train while the porter races back and forth grabbing suitcases in Charlie Chaplin maneuvers. The over-sized cars of the thirties, lined up in rows at the car convention, a hero's welcome for young man with beautiful wife and daughter. There is a summer picnic with fried chicken, cakes, iced tea spread out on the checkered cloth in the country with mother and daughter sitting together in shorts, waving at Father, who is hero to them.*

"*Now!* I guarantee you there is no one that will give you a better price! This Studebaker is the newest model and has more features than any competitor's car has to offer. And what's more—I can beat any price!"

A harvest of snowflakes wafted up like bits of burned paper, dabbing wet on the black hood, imploding around Austin and the man in the overcoat with the automobile gleaming in the twin globes of his glasses. Austin was close enough to see the cold wind contracting skin, bruising his cheeks and nose, swinging the overhead string of bare bulbs.

The man's jaw tightened with some hidden pulse at the temples moving the frame of his glasses, hands deep in the wool overcoat. Austin was at the precipice where every logical argument and coddling emotion had been employed in a carefully orchestrated crescendo. He was at the point of silence. This was the silence Uncle Edwin said can force a hand quicker than a loaded gun.

The man clicked his tongue; a sharp click like a door lock. The newspaper tucked under his arm screamed European war news with black headlines. Austin found his eyes drifting to the paper several times. The man clicked his tongue again, then hunched his shoulders against the cold breath of bad times. Austin felt the harshness of a nine-year depression that had him in the lot at ten o'clock with his tie pulled like Uncle Edwin's, who had died a broken man two years before.

"I think I better wait," he said slowly, a few years older than Austin, with the same lines and dark circles of worry. "Isn't Studebaker having some problems?"

Austin shook his head.

"No sir. Studebaker is doing just fine. You can't read everything that is in the paper nowadays and believe it. We are in a *reorganization* period, and between you and me—" Austin leaned closer to the man, his white shirt visible from the dealership where his two remaining salesmen watched. "Studebaker has staged this whole reorganization to cover for this new line of cars that just arrived. These cars are so far ahead of the other manufacturers' that Studebaker was afraid they would copy the design and bring it out themselves."

Austin leaned back, walking around the sedan coated with fine grit even though Snowball shined the paint with soft rags every morning. It violated Austin's own saying of better days: *"Boys, if the car has dust on it—you aren't doing your job!"*

He opened the car door again.

"Just step inside here, sir, and I think your decision will be made for you when you feel the luxury of this new Studebaker sedan—"

"No, that won't be necessary. I think I better wait . . . thank you, though."

The man walked away with his hard shoes clicking on the cold pavement. Austin knew he should have gone after him. *"Never let a customer walk away—escort him out of the lot and give him your card because I've sold many cars on the way out of the lot."* But he just watched the man hurry into the winter night.

Austin stood by the car, the wind passing through his cotton shirt. He stood by the steel beasts that were trophies such a short time ago. The cars were maddening in their immobility. He used to get a lift seeing new cars lined in his lot. They were the new cars rolling off in his success. He wasn't sure when the slowdown started, but he noticed the same cars outside his office window with the bright red prices he kept lowering.

The red cardboard faded in the sun as he began to let salesmen go, promising he would rehire when things turned around. Austin made the same promise to the mechanics he let go, then to the office girls, then to his creditors. His accountant warned him one blustery night they could not meet their bills. He let him go too.

Austin took over. He told himself it was his own fault. *Of course his dealership was failing! He had not been selling for years.* He charged into the lot that first day, taking the first customer, cajoling, laughing, strutting for the salesmen as the boss rolled up his sleeves. He sold the man a car and plopped the cash down-payment in front of his men.

He let the next few customers go to the eager salesmen. Then the bank called and told him the man had defaulted on his mortgage and they wouldn't finance. He hung up the phone slowly, feeling the sucker punch reeling him back, wondering if he could really stop the slide. He let another salesman go and began to plead for the life of his business with every customer. Suddenly he hadn't sold a car in six months.

Austin touched the fender, looking toward his two

salesmen; the cold wind shaking the lights above the chariots that would carry him no farther.

"Did you sell any today?"

Austin walked into the large house with the unpaid mortgage. He had ceased to think of the house as a home, but as a residence they would abandon to a less expensive place. He put his hat on the rack, smelling the old wood of the hundred-year structure, walking into the dim kitchen.

"Well, did you sell—"

"No."

"Well, why not?"

He looked at Tamara with hot eyes. The dark cloud of his demise had infected her also. They were under a terrible barrage, numbed by the tide of bad times. He explained calmly he was going through a lull in selling and they needed to cut back. Then he saw new dresses and clothes for little Tamara. He ordered her to take back what she had bought.

After he took her checkbook away and closed credit accounts their fights took on an ugly tone. Tamara had tried to attack him, slashing at his face with her nails, eyes blazing queerly. Austin tried to ignore her, guarding his diminishing strength for the battle of business. One time, after a particularly bad fight, he found her in the closet laughing manically.

"Why can't you sell the damn things anymore?"

"Because no one is buying," he answered tiredly.

He saw the man in the lot again, then the salesmen who explained sheepishly they were going to a competitor.

"People think the depression's never going to end and the war's coming."

He cracked open a legal beer—missing the bootlegger's tea-colored bottles of good times. Austin drank slowly, feeling the gentle pull of the alcohol settling over him like a warm quilt. He wondered how long he had been exhausted to the point where he was too tired to think.

"But other dealerships are selling! Did you see what was in the paper today? It said Studebaker is filing for *bankruptcy*!"

He looked at the accusing eyes.

"Reorganization," he snapped, walking out of the kitchen into the dim living room.

"They are going out of business! And where's that going to leave us? I haven't had money to do anything for—"

"You've had plenty of money," he retorted harshly. "Too much. We should have saved some of that damn money and we might not be in the fix we're in."

He turned on the mahogany radio, waiting for it to warm up. Tamara stood over him, dark creases beneath her eyes, breath stale with cigarettes and gin.

"You been having trouble sleeping again?"

Her eyes flashed with the gleam he had come to know.

"*Of course I don't sleep!* You come in at all hours of the night and wake me up. I don't know where you've been half the night and then you ask me why I can't sleep! My mother was right—I should never have come back from California. I could have been a star—"

His eyes flashed. "Saw your mother, did you? She filling your head again?"

Tamara lifted her head defiantly.

"Yes, I went to her store . . . at least *she's* making money!"

Austin finished his beer, war news fading up from the soft yellow dial, punishing his overwrought nerves. He sat in the overstuffed chair like a man in a lifeboat.

"Selling that junk she gets up north," he muttered.

Tamara stood in the middle of the living room.

"Antiques. If you knew anything about culture or

refinement—all you know about is cars . . . and now you can't even *sell* the damn things."

"Watch your mouth," he muttered, feeling the stress flooding his brain with the beer, remembering the time she attacked him and he struck like a man hitting a man. Her eye was closed for a week.

"Well, thank God for my mother. Who would I talk to? *You're* never here—even on weekends!"

"People buy cars on the weekends," he said dully.

"Oh, do they," she drawled out. "Well they don't seem to be buying any from *you*."

Austin sat in silence.

"Do you even know that your daughter won a prize at school today?"

Domestic talk against radio war talk—feeling guilty in the exhausted ether of work stress.

"I'll take her fishing when it gets warm."

"She has school."

"She can miss a day," he said, low-voiced. "Maybe I'll take her in the spring."

Austin looked into the eyes he vaguely understood after sixteen-hour days. He knew his life was at a crossroads; he knew it like the night he talked to Uncle Edwin about the Studebaker dealership. He was powerless to stop destiny's tireless march to some end he could only glimpse. He had ridden some wave, some skimming crest, and inexplicably he had been dashed into the rocky shore. He understood what was happening when the man turned into the icy blast of cold, away from the car. It was almost a relief.

"I'll take her fishing in the spring. It will be warmer then," he decided, hearing the slipper steps fading, the muttering he couldn't begin to know.

• • •

"Daddy . . . is that a storm?"

Austin looked across the wind-rippled water. The bucolic day had been traded for the unstable harbinger sweeping in while he sat with his daughter in the bay. The mushroom hovered like an infected organism with blackened flesh.

"Yes, I reckon it is." He began to click his reel. "Better bring in your line, sweetie."

"Alright, Daddy, I'm bringing in my line!"

Austin looked at the golden-haired girl reeling in the bobber he had painted pink. For a while the world was distant. The sun glimmered off the bay, and father and daughter sat in the creaky sun-gray dinghy with only the buzz of dragonflies and the click of their reels. They laughed when Austin's sandwich fell into the water and a large bass snapped down the bread.

"Reckon fish like baloney sandwiches too."

"Reckon fish like baloney," she sang, eating her sandwich, the bottle of orange soda propped on the slat of the boat.

The small head of yellow sunlight seemed like an angel. But even then, his heart was heavy recognizing the innocence he wished to preserve. Now, water from the swells rolling the boat splashed on his arm. His daughter sang out in six-year-old fun.

*"Wheee, Daddy!"*

The thunderheads churned across the sky, lightning spidering between clouds, turning the bay into a pernicious sea. Austin wrapped the cord rope around the flywheel and pulled. He calmly wrapped the rope again, pulling to a wet splutter that made him think the plugs were wet.

"Start the engine, Daddy!"

"I'm working on it, sweetie."

He pulled again, the boat rising abruptly, tossing him against the middle seat. They were between green phantoms taking turns with the wood dinghy.

"You have your life vest on tight, sweetie?"

She nodded, small among the gray mountains bloating the bay.

"Daddy, I want to go home . . . *I'm scared!*"

His back seared as he hunched over the motor again.

"Just a minute, sweetie, we'll be there in just a minute."

He pulled again, water splashing around his ankles, realizing the black-green phantoms were slowly swamping the boat. Austin looked at the far trees against the slit of horizon light.

*"Daddy!"*

Tamara screamed, water flattening her hair, running from her mouth.

Austin jumped clumsily across the boat, pulling her to him.

"Now, you sit here and be a good girl and hold on tight while I start the motor," he said shakily.

She nodded, wiping water from her cheeks with a small fist. Austin splashed through the encroaching water. Tamara began to cry while he wrapped and tore blisters and calluses open. The boat rolled up suddenly, Tamara's scream in his ears. The boat dropped as if a winch had been cut. Austin was slammed backward, gasping in pain, twisting to see Tamara's contorted face of child terror.

"Are you alright, honey?" he asked huskily, scrambling up with the knives shooting through his back.

Tamara nodded.

"Daddy?"

Something in her voice made him stop. Austin looked at her, water streaming from her chin and down her brow and cheeks. He watched his daughter with rain jumping in the boat water, swells tunneling the craft between two dark mountains. His daughter stared at him with lucent eyes.

"We're going to sink, aren't we, Daddy?"

His vision blurred.

"Well . . ."

Austin stared at the two eyes of his own flesh.

"You can tell me Daddy, it's okay."

"Well now, I don't know," he admitted softly.

Then she held out her hand to him in the darkness.

"Don't worry, Daddy, I understand," she whispered.

Austin held her small hand and could no longer see.

"It's okay, Daddy, don't cry."

Austin then looked to heaven—crying out for any deity to save his daughter. On the last pull, his strength ebbing, the splutter came.

He wept as the wisp of smoke puffed from the dripping exhaust pipe, fearing that the splutter wouldn't last, sobbing when spark found gas, moving the water-laden boat as a slow, lumbering whale.

People were waiting at the shore. The woman who put the blanket around Tamara took her to a car. Austin stood talking to men who marveled he was able to come back. He turned and looked out into the corrugated bay. The wind whipped at his face and rain pelted his cheek. Austin looked up at the black thunderheads; the storm that was now following him.

*Charlie Tidewater*
*465 Marilee Road*
*Southampton, VA*
*August 26, three A.M.*

*Matthew,*

*Sorry to be inundating you with letters, but I met the reporter and he told me this Rufus John Jr. disappeared on the same day King was shot. He said there was a lot of Klan activity in the country at the time. Then I went to dinner with Minnie, that's her name, a judge's daughter, no less. We went to dinner and then a club. Heard some music. When I was driving home—Richmond is pretty far from where Granddaddy lives and there were no cars on the highway—I noticed a car trailing me, keeping a perfect distance between us. I sped up and he sped up and then I floored it. I thought he turned off or something. Then I hear an engine and in the rearview mirror I see a car behind me with the lights off. I must have hit 110 before he finally dropped back. I didn't tell you this, but the first night I was here I thought I saw someone outside my window. He was talking to me. Somebody from a long time ago is out there, Matthew.*

*And he knows who I am.*

*Charlie*

# CHAPTER NINETEEN

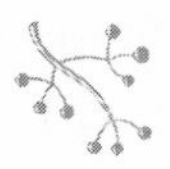

Southampton, Virginia

*August 1998*

Charlie held the phone tightly against his ear and looked down the hallway where Granddaddy was taking a bath. After the fourth ring, a wheezing, like an old accordion, came on the line. Charlie could hear the labor of each breath.

"Junior Pairs?"

"Yas sir," a gritty voice rasped.

"I'm sorry—is this Junior Pairs—sheriff of Goochland County?"

"What can I do fo' you?"

Charlie couldn't believe this man was still alive.

"Mr. Pairs, I am sorry to trouble you, sir—"

The wheezing exploded into a rumble, then a horrible hack.

". . . Who this?"

Charlie ran a hand through his wet hair, running shoes smacking on the linoleum floor of the kitchen. He glanced down the hallway; the bath water stopped with a rickety squeak in the pipes.

"My name is Charlie Tidewater," he said in a lower voice.

There was a pause on the line.

"Tidewatah . . . that is familiar."

The wheezing was more rhythmic. Charlie thought the man might be wearing an oxygen mask of some sort.

"Mr. Pairs, what I wanted to ask you about concerns something that happened thirty years ago."

"What's on yo' mind?"

"It concerns an individual," Charlie continued, pacing back and forth. "He was a black man . . . an African American who disappeared in 1968—the day Martin Luther King was killed—it was a long time ago—"

The phone aired silence.

"What was the Negro's name?"

Charlie looked at the cradle of the phone.

"Rufus John Jr."

The wheezing stopped. Charlie thought he might have hung up.

"I 'member Rufus junior."

Charlie heard the kitchen clock whining its slow evolution. He held the phone tightly to his ear.

"You do?"

"Sho' I do. Colored boy. Trouble from the day he was born."

"Do you know what happened to him?"

There was the slow wheezing.

"Mr. Pairs—"

"Can't say I do—recollect he turned up missin'—they found he gone to Mississippi."

"Mississippi?"

"Yes sir, that's right."

Charlie paced faster. "Was he . . . was he alive?"

"Sho' he was, Mr. Tidewatah, jest like you or me."

"I didn't—"

"You a reportah, Mr. Tidewatah?"

Charlie paused. "No."

"Friend of Rufus?"

"No . . . not really."

There was a long pause and it seemed the breathing had slowed.

"You colored?"

Charlie hesitated, hearing his own short breaths.

"What difference does that make?"

There was another long silence.

"You callin' from Richmond?"

Charlie froze, fighting the urge to hang up.

"Mr. Tidewatah, are you one of them nigger-lovin' Yankees? Are you a goddamn nigger—"

Charlie hung up the phone quickly with the small voice eating air. He ran a trembling hand through his hair. Charlie stared at the phone, hanging quiet, amazed it remained so.

The cold metal scent of rain replaced the aroma of brewed coffee among the clinking chinaware in the kitchen. The judge stood with his hand on the phone, a folded napkin clenched beside his vest. He watched the rain, tasting the first bitter sip of coffee, then returned to breakfast, hearing the voice again.

*"Got to do somethin' Judge . . . don't know who he is but I'm too old to go to jail. Sooner or later somebody's goin' to find out. . . ."*

Minnie was still in her robe and Pearl was feeding

Madelyn. The judge stirred his coffee, then the congealing mush of oatmeal. He didn't touch the morning paper or the strawberries doused with brown sugar.

"What?"

The judge looked at his daughter.

"Beg your pardon."

The thunder rippled across the room, touching air and maybe a tree.

"You are staring at me," Minnie said dully, sleep pushing her back to the pillow she had just left.

He placed cup to saucer.

"How was your date with the young man last night—ah, what was his name?"

"Charlie Tidewater."

"Ah, that's right."

"That rain come out of nowhere," Pearl murmured.

"Did you have a pleasant time?"

Minnie nodded. "I had a very nice time . . . in fact . . ." She turned. "Pearl, can you stay later tonight?"

The judge bumped the table with his shoe, sitting up abruptly.

"You aren't going out with him again?"

"This afternoon." Minnie nodded. "We are going to the country for a picnic." She gazed out the window. "If the rain lets up."

Judge Barrek heard the voice on the phone again. It was a voice of thirty years before.

*"Got a problem, Judge."*

He had squeezed the phone so hard his ring dug into his knuckle.

"I see. . . ." He cleared his throat. "Where in the country?"

Minnie turned her light green eyes upon him.

"Goochland."

Judge Barrek uncrossed his legs and clapped his coffee cup down on the saucer loudly.

His napkin fell from his lap. The light coming in the kitchen window was strangely pale and his heart rose uncomfortably in his chest.

"Now, why would you go out there?" he demanded, watching Madelyn smile at him suddenly.

"He asked me to."

The judge smoothed his mustache several times.

"Well . . . I would think—you just met this man. I think you should wait a proper time before you see him again."

Minnie took a small bite of her bagel.

"He has family here."

The judge pulled back suddenly.

"I have let you know my wishes," he declared, standing, hearing the voice again on the phone and the name he hoped never to hear again.

*"Get hold of Buck and see what we can find out . . ."* The judge's mind raced, careening from one possibility to another. *Buck—why would he use that idiot again? He's still out there? He should be dead.*

He drew himself up.

"I have let you know my wishes and I hope you respect them."

The phone clattered in the hall and Minnie rose. The judge held up his hand. "I'll get it."

He walked briskly into the hallway. The flat midwestern accent with the nasal twang was plain to the judge.

"And who may I say is calling?"

"Charlie Tidewater."

Judge Barrek felt the outsider coming into his home. It was the quality of Yankees he despised most: the utter chaos in which they lived. Judge Barrek clenched his fist.

"Ah, Mr. Tidewater, this is Judge Barrek."

"How are you, sir?"

"Fine, fine . . . I trust you and Minnie enjoyed yourselves last night."

"Yes, sir, very much."

Judge Barrek looked to the kitchen door.

"Mr. Tidewater, I have a little caveat I am going to give you." The judge paused. "We have a tradition down here . . . ah, a way of doing things, let us say—and these, ah, traditions should not be treaded upon."

"Sir?"

The judge lowered his voice. "I know for people in the North the past is of no concern . . ." The judge paused again. "But here, Mr. Tidewater, we take our past deadly serious, and I would say to you—"

The door opened behind him.

"Ah! Here is Minnie now. A pleasure talking to you, Mr. Tidewater, and I do hope you have a safe trip home . . . soon," he finished, handing Minnie the phone, ignoring her glare.

On the front porch the judge paused.

"Three o'clock would be fine." Minnie nodded, her eyes meeting his through the mesh of the screen.

He turned and descended the steps, walking quickly down the sidewalk of rain pools.

*"Got a problem, Judge. . . ."*

# CHAPTER TWENTY

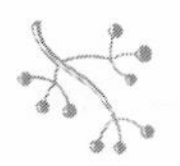

Southampton, Virginia

*August 1998*

Charlie looked up into the attic of the house. He could smell the heated air. The ladder springs echoed into the hollow space as Granddaddy stepped onto the bottom step. He was thinking of his strange conversation with Judge Barrek as he watched Granddaddy put on a sparkly blue helmet.

"Now, wear this," he said, holding out a red helmet to Charlie.

"I don't need it."

"Now, that's what I used to say before I knew better, see." Granddaddy nodded with the chin strap swinging, looking like a daredevil at a turn-of-the-century show. "So, I recommend you put that helmet on."

Charlie looked at the helmet.

"I'll watch my head."

"Don't say I didn't warn you," he muttered, climbing the unfolded steps, springs ricocheting. "Now, let me get the light on up here."

Granddaddy moved out of the opening. A light snapped on. His helmet moved across the bare bulb like an eclipse.

"You can come on up—be careful on them steps."

Charlie reached the top, smelling brown cardboard and hot wood. He stood up.

*"Shit!"*

Granddaddy stood with his arms akimbo, shaking his head slowly, grinning.

"Now, I don't want to be someone who says I told you so . . . but, I did tell you about hitting your head and wearing a helmet, see."

Charlie looked at his hand several times, expecting blood.

"Now, you go and get that helmet and I'll wait here for you."

He descended the rickety stairs and put on the red helmet.

"Now, we need to bring these boxes down with us, see," Granddaddy explained as he reached the top of the stairs.

Charlie followed him, the dry heat feeling like a sauna.

"The boxes are back here, now."

Charlie's eyes adjusted to the dim light. He began to see boxes tucked into the corners of the roof struts. Granddaddy took a pair of glasses from his top pocket and blew dust from a box.

"Now, here's one I want downstairs."

Charlie looked at the box.

"What's in it?"

"Records of things, mostly . . . investments and such."

Charlie hoisted the surprising weight.

"You take that by the stairwell."

Charlie staggered down the center. Sweat tickled his face from under the helmet. He set the box down slowly, standing up carefully in the stifling heat.

"Whooh!"

Charlie wiped his forehead and turned. He saw the glisten of short metal cabinets in the eave shadows.

"Hey, Granddaddy?"

"Henh?"

"What are these?"

"What's that?"

"These toolboxes down here."

Granddaddy came down the planks.

"Now, what are you talking about, boy?"

Charlie pointed to the side of the attic. "Those!"

Granddaddy squinted into the darkness and nodded slowly.

"Now, I been worried about these old toolboxes coming through the roof." He turned to Charlie, the light refracting through the scratched lenses of his glasses like a mad professor. "Those are above my bed, see."

"What's in them?"

"You pull one out and I'll show you."

Charlie walked carefully down the plank, hunching over until he reached the rafters. He pulled on the nearest toolbox.

"What's in these things? Rocks?"

Granddaddy shook his head.

"Don't reckon they're rocks," he murmured.

Charlie grabbed the metal handle with both hands and heaved. The chest shifted slightly. He cradled the chest with his arms and dragged it to Granddaddy.

"Shit!" Charlie sat down on the dusty wood. "*Jesus*, that's heavy."

"Reckon it is—now I'll show you why."

Granddaddy kneeled and lifted the latch. He swung the top back and Charlie saw glinting silver.

"Coins," he whispered.

"Silver dollars," Granddaddy corrected him, picking one of the gleaming medallions off the top and handing it to him.

The coin felt heavy and sounded like a coin tossed across a bar when he dropped it to the floor. He held the dollar up to the bulb.

"Eighteen ninety-nine!"

"Reckon some older ones than that." Granddaddy nodded.

Charlie picked another one out of the chest.

"Nineteen twenty-four."

"Good year," Granddaddy murmured, clinking the coins with his fingers.

"How many are in these?"

He shook his head doubtfully.

"Now, I don't really know—reckon I should."

"Why do you have them up here?"

Granddaddy straightened up and looked down at the toolbox.

"Well, now, I'll tell you. See, I lived through the depression, and when you live through something like that you don't trust the banks. Because in *those days* banks went broke, and everybody lost their money. So, every time I got a real silver dollar I threw it into an empty toolbox." Granddaddy gestured down to the coins. "I knew silver always be worth something, see, money today doesn't have much silver."

Charlie looked at the other blue steel boxes.

"Those too?"

Granddaddy nodded solemnly. "Reckon so."

He whistled.

"You should get these to a bank, Granddaddy."

"No." Granddaddy shook his head. "But, I tell you what I am going to do, and that is give you that coin you are holding there. See, I gave one to your mother when she was a little girl and now I'm giving one to you."

Charlie squeezed the silver dollar in his palm.

"Thanks, Granddaddy."

"Now, don't go spending it," he murmured, closing the lid.

Charlie stared at the coin.

"You're never going to tell me what happened." He looked up. "Are you, Granddaddy?"

He made a hissing noise through his teeth.

"Nothing to tell." Granddaddy looked down at the tool chest. "See, you concerned about the *past* when you *should* be worried about your *future*." Granddaddy pointed down. "It's like these boxes of old coins. These coins meant something to people way back before you were born, see, and now those people are gone and these coins just sit up here in my attic and don't mean a thing." Granddaddy shook his head slowly. "The past doesn't mean anything, see."

Charlie stood motionless in the smothering heat.

"Not unless it catches the present."

Granddaddy bobbed slightly.

"Now, that just shows you how wrong you are, see." He held up his large hand. "The past *can't* catch up with the present."

Charlie looked up at him.

"Why not?"

"Don't you know, boy . . ." His grandfather's blue eyes bored through the attic gloom. "You die before that happens."

# CHAPTER TWENTY-ONE

Richmond, Virginia

*August 1998*

By the time Charlie picked up Minnie the sun had crested the sky and was beginning its descent. The shadow from the fat magnolia by Minnie's porch made him think he had taken too long at the library. He turned from the tree to the griddle-black figure of Pearl.

"She comin', can I get you some lemonade?"

"No, thank you, Pearl."

The screen door clapped shut behind him. Charlie watched the slow circular whip of the sprinkler exploding three times around. The rhythm of the ticking was just slower than the cicadas and the occasional whippoorwill crowding the late-summer afternoon. Charlie looked over the pale August grass, seeing the headlines he had discovered in the library earlier.

## Negro Lynched in Country

*Times Dispatch,* Reporter T. J. Hendricks,
Goochland County, March 4, 1926

A Negro, Willy John, was found burned and lynched in Goochland County. John was a pastor at a local Negro church. He had been missing for two days. Police reported burn marks on his back and legs, reportedly from a blow torch. Authorities have no clue to the perpetrators, but suspect local Klan involvement. This crime comes after a series of Negro church burnings. Willy John was found by his son, Rufus John, hanging in a tree behind their farm.

## Law and Order to Be Kept, Barrek Says

*Times Dispatch,* Reporter John Rolfe, Richmond, April 6, 1968

James T. Barrek, special assistant to Governor Tucker, said law and order will be kept in Richmond. "We don't have a problem down here and if people want to use the assassination of Martin Luther King as an excuse to loot stores and burn buildings then they have another thing coming," he said, making clear the governor's position. "I am acting as a special liaison to the police and we are closing in on pockets of outside agitators who are stirring up this trouble. We will use whatever means necessary to see that the fine, decent people of Richmond are safe in their own city." Barrek said he was also working closely with the sheriffs to keep tabs on agitators who are taking refuge in the Negro churches out in the country around Richmond. "Order will be preserved," Barrek vowed.

Then Charlie found an article he had missed, going through the microfiche several times, passing April 4 and 5, not seeing it until he was just about to leave. He read it several times with redness creeping up his neck.

**Reporter Run Off Road in Country**

*Times Dispatch*, Reporter Todd James,
Goochland County, April 5, 1968

Sherwood Anders suffered a pelvic fracture, a broken leg, and multiple cuts and abrasions after his car was allegedly rear-ended on County Road 500E. Mr. Anders, working on assignment for the *Dispatch,* said he was traveling about sixty miles an hour when he felt a bump from behind. He looked in his rearview mirror and said he thought he saw a white car not five feet behind him before he lost control of his car. Sheriff Junior Pairs in Goochland said he was investigating the incident. "Sometimes people fall asleep and see things, but if Mr. Anders thinks there's a white car out there running people off the road then we'll find him."

Charlie jumped as the screen door slammed shut.

"Ready," Minnie announced with a light kiss.

The gray two-lane outside Richmond shimmered in the false heat of early evening. They passed dilapidated gas stations and empty tobacco barns. Charlie had been driving with her warm hand in his for thirty minutes when Minnie turned in from the window.

"Daddy is acting strange."

Charlie let her hand go. "How's that?"

"He threw a fit about me going to the country with you."

Charlie shifted uncomfortably.

"Why do you think he would care?"

Minnie squinted against the country light.

"I don't really know. . . ."

Charlie glanced at her.

"Maybe you shouldn't have come."

Her hand squeezed his again. "But I wanted to, sugar."

They rested in the steady drone of the tires, Minnie leaning sleepily against his shoulder. Charlie kept his eyes on the darkening road.

"Minnie . . ."

"Mmmm . . ."

Charlie paused.

"What's your father's first name?"

"James," she murmured.

Tall green-and-tan cornstalks riffled past the window. Charlie made out the letters JOH on the leaning mailbox and turned onto a dirt road, a red cloud lingering behind like a dusty halo. The house was far back from the highway and Charlie was amazed this man was listed in the phone book.

The road traveled straight along a gray fence until a leaning house with a washed-pale plank porch appeared at the end of the lane. It was a two-story structure seen a hundred times in old photos of sharecropper shacks. The color had been bleached to pine gray that melted to the trees and farther on to the hills behind. A man in coveralls sat in a rocker. Charlie stopped in the cul-de-sac formed by rain collecting in the swale.

"Wait here . . ." he said to Minnie, staring at the still man in the rocker. "I'm not sure how this is going to go."

Charlie stepped from the car. The roar of insects in the tall corn was a wave of sound not unlike the surf of the ocean. A rusting low-slung car was alongside the house, the door touching the wall. Propped against the porch was a tire worn clear through with the white ply the only dab of color.

"Afternoon," Charlie called out against the insects and lethargy of the afternoon heat. The man's blue coveralls were worn at the knees and his grizzled gray hair covered his head like a fine brush of steel wool. Long hands hung over the arms of the rocker; a glass-blackened kerosene lantern sat by his right boot.

"Ain't the way."

Charlie stopped at the bottom of the steps.

"I'm sorry."

He lifted a hand and pointed across the fields.

"That you is, but highway thataway . . . ain't no battle-fields here."

Charlie smiled.

"I'm not lost."

"Hmm." He looked over his nose. He was a heavy man with a Cherokee bridge between deep eyes filmed with age. The insects crescendoed and the two men waited, the way men in cities wait for a train to pass or a jet to fly clear.

"Who yo' lookin' for?"

"Rufus John."

The rocker creaked and one worn shoe, some type of work boot in better days, slid forward, then his whole body.

"Gov'ment man," he inquired, nodding to the black Mercedes.

Charlie shook his head and put one foot on the lower step. A warm breeze stirred, carrying the scent of honeysuckle and heated fern, and the rich dampness of overgrown fields.

"No . . ." He looked up at the man. "Are you Rufus John?"

The man cleared his throat, fishing a cigarette from his pocket.

"Depend."

"Oh what?"

He scratched a match on the arm of the rocker, spitting a piece of tobacco from his teeth, cuffing the cigarette between two fingers.

"On who you is."

Charlie paused. "I'm Austin Turin's grandson."

The life of heat and time rose and the man touched the loosely rolled cigarette to his mouth with nails long and black. He rocked back, the weathered planks creaking below.

"You still lost," he grunted.

Charlie paused.

"I wanted to ask you some questions about your son, Rufus junior."

The cigarette dropped to the floor and he stubbed it with his boot.

"Know where he at?"

"No . . . but I'd like to know what happened to him. . . ." Charlie paused again. "I'm trying to find out what happened to my mother and this article—"

"Where you from?"

"Chicago."

He gestured to the high corn.

"Go on back to Chicago. . . ." He shook his head. "Ain't nothin' for you here."

Charlie scratched his cheek, sound blotted again by the rattling whisper of summer insects. He wondered if they were against him too.

"I didn't know your son, but it sounds like he was trying to change things, Mr. John."

He lifted his head with eyes like old glass.

"How you know that?"

Charlie took another step toward the porch. "Mr. John, I

feel there's a link between the disappearance of your son and my mother—did he ever say anything to you before he disappeared that—"

"Git on out of here," he snapped, gesturing to the corn again as if he had just thrown something. "Now git on!"

Charlie shook his head slowly.

"Don't you want to find out what happened to your son?"

"I don't give a goddamn about yo' mama," he grumbled, anger sparking his eyes. "My son forgot where he come from." He lifted his hand from the rocker. "Talkin' lot of shit." He leaned forward.

"You lookin' for a whole lotta nothin'."

Charlie looked down at the weathered steps.

"I know they lynched your father . . ." He looked up. "I know you found him."

Rufus rose from the rocker and pointed toward the fields, the chorus drowning his voice in that moment. When it subsided they were staring at each other like two duelers.

"You git, or he comin' fo' you next."

"Who?"

He shook his head. "Never see him 'til it too late," he grumbled, sitting down.

"Who . . . the sheriff?"

"Shit . . ." He rocked slowly. "Sheriff nothin' . . . they come fo' you an' ain't nothin' you can do. . . ." Rufus looked at Charlie, glancing to the darkening trees. "An' he always got a scatter gun . . ." He stared at Charlie. "An' he git you too."

Charlie took a card from his wallet. He wrote Granddaddy's number on the back and laid the card on the porch.

"Call me if you want to talk."

Charlie started back to the car.

"Probably true, ain't it?"

He stopped and turned.

"What's that?"

Rufus sat in the rocker, field light in his eyes, nodding slowly.

"Our chillun pay fo' our sins."

Rufus John watched the spiraling cloud of dust rise above the corn into the slanting light. Then the sound of the car was gone. The rocker creaked; the insects died down. A stick snapped. Rufus turned slowly, willing himself not to panic. He reached inside the door for the double-barreled shotgun, laying it across his lap, cocking back the two triggers silently.

Rufus rocked back, the planks groaning in time. He turned quickly and saw him standing there among the trees, sunglasses reflecting dying sun. Rufus stood and swung the shotgun to his right shoulder and fired. The smoke drifted across the porch. He heard another sound and wheeled and fired again. Rufus fumbled with the shells, smoking cartridges falling to the ground. He snapped the breech closed.

"Hey, Jack."

The voice was behind him.

Rufus cursed silently. *Just a ghost . . . come down that old tobacco road . . .*

Then he laughed nervously. "Oh, that you . . . thought it some old fox . . . yas sir, some old fox I firin' at . . ."

"What'd he want, Jack?"

"Don't want nothin' . . . said he goin' back to Chicago," he nodded, slipping his finger into the trigger ring. "Don't worry 'bout him none."

Rufus turned and saw another tornado coming toward

the house. The red cloud spun behind the car. He looked behind him and the man was gone.

"Where you go," he muttered with the shotgun in his hands.

Wheeling around, Rufus saw the ghost again and fired into the trees. A small pine disappeared. He gripped the second trigger, searching the foliage.

"Where you at, ghost? You comin' fo' me now . . ." He searched the tree shadows, hearing the brush again. "Got you, motherfuckah!" He wheeled and pulled the trigger, shaving a white swath on the side of an oak.

He cracked the breech and picked the shells out, grabbing the box from the corner of the doorframe, dropping the shells. "I knows you comin', I knows you was and I ready fo' you now," he muttered. "Nothin' but crazy, an' never know no difference . . ."

"Should have left well enough alone . . . huh, Jack?"

Rufus froze. One shell was in the breech. He cracked it shut and wheeled to the tree line, seeing the man in a shaft of sun. Rufus raised the shotgun and fired. "Done got you, ghost . . ." He smiled toothlessly. "Ain't so bad after all . . . hauntin' me all these years, shit!" Rufus spat off the porch and laughed. "She nothin' but crazy an' now you ain't goin' to bother me no more . . . yes sir, I goin' to sleep tonight—"

He heard the squeak behind him, the empty shotgun in his hand. He turned slowly to the shack doorway, staring into the glimmering darkness.

"Ghost . . ." he muttered, a fine line of drool falling to the dusty porch floor. The explosion blew him into the red dust. Rufus John whimpered once as the cicadas *shisssshhed* across the heavy air.

The crumpled body spread darkness in the light dirt.

Planks under the chair creaked as the man sat down, watching the squad car flash through the corn rows. He could smell the old damp scent of earth; the hiss in the corn covering all.

# CHAPTER TWENTY-TWO

Virginia countryside

*August 1998*

A line of amber glanced off the oiled wave of his hair, smoke shooting through a slant of light. His hand rested on one boot, crossed at the knee. The shotgun lay on the sofa next to him. He stubbed his cigarette on the floor, listening to the *whump* of two car doors, then the crunch of gravel. The front door squealed below, vibrations coming through dead springs in the couch.

The man heard the second squeal of a door, then steps pianoing toward him. In a liquid movement he swung from the couch and backed into a closet with the shotgun. The room was a slat of light through the doorway. He waited in the recess of dust and mold and the slight scent of mothballs.

The door swung wide.

"This is that apartment I told you about."

"I smell smoke."

The man kept his hand firmly on the trigger.

"I found cigarettes up here once before."

Judge Barrek's daughter came into view. He watched her in her blue skirt and the white blouse of country-club girls.

*The judge's daughter. Judge was sweating, Junior said. Old fucker.*

"I wanted to show you something . . . look at the bars on these windows."

Their voices came from the other side of the room.

"But why have them on the upstairs windows. . . ."

The man came into view and hunched down.

"See, you can see two stains in the wood."

She bent to the floor.

"What do you think it is?"

Minnie looked up suddenly. It was the sound of a board creaking. She stared at the closed door. Charlie followed her line of vision.

"What?"

"That door . . ." Minnie raised her hand unsteadily. "I heard something . . ."

Charlie stood up. "Let's take a look."

"No, *don't*!"

Charlie turned.

"Why?"

She stared at him. "Because there might be something there!"

"That's why we have to look."

Charlie crossed the floorboards and grabbed the doorknob, pulling the door wide. A loud crack echoed in the room and Minnie screamed. Neither of them moved, then he reached down to the floor.

"See—" Charlie picked up the broom. "Just an empty broom closet."

"Charlie . . . let's go . . ."

"Alright, but I want to look in the office downstairs. . . ."

The man heard them thumping down the steps like galloping horses and heard the soft squeal of the closing door. He opened the door and glanced at the broom propped next to the other closet. He settled back on the couch and leaned the gun next to him like a walking stick, blowing smoke into the thin bar of twilight on the ceiling.

Charlie found Minnie standing outside by his car.

"Did you find anything?" she asked, turning around.

"I might have."

Charlie held up a flat envelope.

"What's that?"

"I found it in that old safe." He flipped the envelope open. "Five hundred dollars," he said, holding the greasy, faded greenbacks.

She stared at the money.

"Why would your grandfather leave five hundred dollars in an old safe?"

Charlie shook his head slowly. "I don't know, we were out here twice cleaning the place out . . . why would he leave the safe open, is the other question."

"Are you going to ask him?"

"What's my reason for being out here? That I'm snooping around." Charlie put the money into the envelope and slipped it in his pocket. "I'll give it back to him, but I have to be careful how I do it."

Minnie looked up at him.

"Do you think your granddaddy is in the Klan?"

Charlie again shook his head slowly. "My granddaddy is close to ninety years old . . . I don't think he's in much . . . but he left this here for someone. . . ."

Minnie shivered. "It feels like something bad happened out here."

Charlie looked at her.

"Minnie, I'm sorry about bringing you into all of this."

"Don't be," she said, turning around. "Don't be sorry you brought me here." She turned back to the fallow tobacco rows. "I've been scared a long time . . . the South has always scared me."

"Why don't you leave?"

Minnie looked at him, her eyes sparking.

"And go where?"

Charlie shrugged, feeling he had stumbled. Minnie turned out to the field again, her hair tumbling gold from one shoulder.

"This is where I'm from."

"It doesn't mean you have to stay," Charlie said quietly.

Minnie looked at him.

"That's why I like you, because you aren't from here."

"But I am," he objected mildly.

Minnie took his hand.

"No, you're free."

"You can be free too, Minnie."

She looked at him sadly, light touching one cheek, the world burning down behind her. She kissed him and he felt her breath against his ear.

"That's a nice thought."

The crickets popped away through the tall weeds. The sun was behind the pines and the smell of cool, damp grass calmed them both. Minnie put a wildflower in her hair. They passed between old cars shining dimly among the weeds.

"Granddaddy used to take me through these wrecks when I was a kid," Charlie explained, stopping by a sky-blue Chevrolet with the hood buckled.

A single night cricket sang from the recess of the car's interior. Minnie touched the still-warm fender.

"It's hard to believe someone drove this car and washed it and thought of it as their prized possession."

Charlie looked out at the field.

"All these cars belonged to different lives."

Minnie turned, the yellow flower bright by the dingy wreck. Charlie felt the heat traded casually on the breeze, his eyes drifting back to the dark garage.

"This was my grandfather's life." He turned to the wrecks. "All of this at one time was his business and he lived in that apartment with my mother and grandmother."

"What happened to your grandmother?"

"She died when I was six."

Minnie stood next to him and they watched the land fold into a golden, then pink, field.

"It's funny," she murmured. "I see the South again when I'm with you."

Charlie nodded.

"When I was up north, the South was my difference. I could never quite fit in and I kept this idea of the South as this idyllic place . . . it was my secret weapon, my salvation. Even when things were bad I kept this place with me."

He paused.

"I imagine it would be the same if you came to Chicago."

"What do you mean?"

"I would see Chicago differently with you there. I guess it's true we can only appreciate a place when we leave it."

Minnie smiled and slipped her arm through his.

"I dreamed once of leaving Richmond and living in a big city."

Charlie kept his eyes on the changing landscape, a balmy wind crossing the heated earth.

"That doesn't sound too hard."

"No." She paused, meeting his eyes. "That was a long time ago; this is where I live now."

Charlie turned back to the dark pines rimming the field and noticed a clump of trees jutting from the forest. He couldn't be sure but there was a path of flattened weeds going to the pines. Minnie put her arms around his waist, the perfume of her neck grazing his cheek, nose, then mouth. Her skirt fanned out in the windy field and Charlie kissed her under the Southern sky breaking to stars; a pearl crescent over the man in the open window.

# CHAPTER TWENTY-THREE

Richmond, Virginia

*1941*

"Mr. Turin, scrap man here to take away the sign."

Austin looked up. Snowball was in the doorway of his paper-strewn office, waiting in his coveralls, a white rag fountaining out of his back pocket.

"Alright, tell them to take it on down."

Snowball jammed down his fists, pulling hard on the straps of his coveralls. He shook his head, a steady click from his tongue.

"This sure ain't yo' fault, Mr. Turin."

Austin paused, the box of files between his wing tips.

"I don't know whose it is, then."

"You can't control Studebaker done gone out of business!"

Austin leaned back in his chair, feeling the strain of the

past few weeks since he got the letter. He remembered the drip from a faucet out in the shop, thinking how success has a sound and failure has a sound. The faucet had to be clear across the showroom off one of the bays. It was just him and Snowball left. The phone didn't ring. The mail was bills and letters threatening seizure of assets. People came and looked at cars occasionally. One man said Studebakers would be worth something one day, but even he was not looking to buy. It was a lingering death and many times he wondered whether to bother opening up.

Austin immediately put the house up for sale, but it was when the furniture people came he realized what was happening to him. His daughter was watching men take their sofa, their coffee tables, the high-backed chairs they sat in at the end of long days. Little Tamara sat on the porch swing, watching the men take their home.

"Where are they taking our furniture, Daddy?"

It was a simple question, but Austin couldn't explain that the banks were only too willing to give loans to the youngest owner of a dealership and when his business failed they called the loans due. All he could do was look into the green eyes of eight-year-old innocence and say they were getting new furniture. But he couldn't tell her from where.

"So. You're *broke* now."

His mother-in-law sat behind her desk. There was such vainglory in her voice, he looked up from his hat.

"How are you going to feed your family? I hear you owe money to people all over town."

"I intend to pay them back," he answered quietly.

Austin stood looking down at the deep wood of the mahogany desk, telling himself he must think of his daughter and wife. His own mother had moved to Georgia some time back and was barely able to live herself. There was nowhere else to turn but to this woman who had been a troll waiting under the bridge for years. She was cruel in her galloping tide, crushing three husbands while she furthered any cause of hers. And now she was about to reclaim her daughter.

Miz Drake smoked, eyes glinting in the gloom of Victorian furniture surrounding her in old-world dignity.

"I don't see how you can do that when you don't have money to even *live on*," she snapped.

"I have some money to tide us over."

She stood up.

"You've come to me for furniture after everyone all over town knows you had to return all that *fancy new* furniture you bought on credit! Even if I was to give you furniture, what would you do with it? Where do you intend to live now?"

Austin met the gray eyes sparking in the fainting light of shuttered windows. With her pearl cigarette holder twirling smoke, she looked like a character of the age; a flapper gone bad, gone mean.

"I've got an apartment on the Boulevard."

The pearl baton drew an arabesque line between them, then she gutted it in the round ashtray like someone throwing off gloves. She came up to him, her lips dried to a fading garish red.

"*A rented apartment!* You are going to live in a rented apartment!"

Austin shifted his weight, inspecting his hat carefully, knowing to look at her would be too much.

"Just until I get on my feet."

"I won't have my granddaughter growing up in a rented apartment. She's a *Drake*! And no Drake ever lived in a rented apartment! You can drag yourself down into the gutter, but not with my daughter and granddaughter."

Her eyes flicked over him, the smile drawing out a nefarious line, never better than in her ability to change tactics in midstream. Miz Drake's voice became cool like a peel of blue ice.

"Still wearing the suits of the dandy, aren't you?" She was so close he could smell her old breath—stale, like some cheap perfume. "And you're going to put your wife and child into a *rented* apartment."

She began a slow trek back to her desk, a slight jingle from a diamond bracelet touching her watch.

"I told her about you, but you threw gold dust in her eyes and—"

"Miz Drake—I came to know about the furniture," Austin said, looking up for the first time. "It's not for you to say where we live."

She smiled perniciously and waved away his bluff like the smoke from her cigarette. Miz Drake was sitting back, observing him like a child might observe a trapped fly in a bottle.

"Oh, yes," she drew out slowly. "*It is* for me to say." She pulled open a drawer, drew out a compact, and began to line her lips. She finished and looked up at the man holding his hat.

"You won't get a stick of furniture from me if you go live in that apartment."

Tamara's mother picked up the pearl baton, fitting another cigarette.

"I want you to bring Tamara and my granddaughter to live with me . . . you can stay too, if you like," she offered, putting the antique silver lighter back on her desk, blue smoke rolling toward him. "There are three floors and you can live on the top floor. I think it is the only honorable thing you can do at this point, Austin." She paused, considering the cigarette holder. Her eyes moved to him, chips of gray marble. "A man who can't support his family is one thing, but a man who *deliberately* puts his family into squalor when relatives are offering a helping hand is below all else."

Austin's face darkened. He turned and walked out without a word, hearing the voice behind.

"You bring them over tomorrow, *do you hear*?"

But now, facing the open windows of a child's eyes, he had to make right this terrible wrong as their possessions were carried away.

"We're going to live with your grandmother, sweetie . . . how would you like that? Would you like that? We'll live in her *big* house and you can see Grandmother all day long? Would you like that, sweetie? We'll have lots of furniture there. Now, don't cry, sweetie, we'll get it back, don't cry, we'll get it back . . ."

And facing Snowball in the doorway he felt the same compulsion to smooth over the suffering he felt.

"We'll land on our feet," he said, standing next to his worn-out desk. "We'll just go out there and whip those old bootleggers and anybody else!"

Snowball beamed broadly, the optimism like tonic to a harsh drink.

"*Oh yes sir!* I know we will, Mr. Turin!"

Austin came around the desk, walking with his hands in his suit pants.

"I'm already talking to some people. I'm going to do a little selling. There's a little garage up the country that a fellow wants to get rid of. I think we could do a nice little business up there. When this war ends people will be buying cars again and needing them fixed up!"

He stood in front of Snowball.

"Sure like to work in the country, Mr. Turin."

Austin smiled, feeling the rush of his own momentum, thinking more seriously about the garage he hadn't mentioned to anyone. He jingled some change in his pocket.

"Good. I'll need a first-rate mechanic."

"Yes sir!"

Austin winked at him and walked back to the desk, placing the files from better times in the cardboard boxes. He turned to the window as the men in the truck put a ladder to the steel sign. Austin watched as the sign came down, obscuring his view of the empty street.

# CHAPTER TWENTY-FOUR

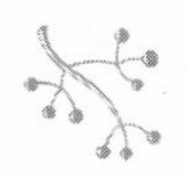

Virginia countryside

*August 1998*

The blue hue of night was on the columns holding the Roman roof above the hill, like some lost capitol. Charlie mentioned his grandfather grew up there, then he was moving the rusty chain across the gravel road, dropping it into the spilled light of tangled undergrowth.

They started down the drive, turning the corner. Charlie jammed on the brakes.

"What the hell—"

"He must need help," Minnie said, opening the door. "*Sir!* Sir, are you alright?"

The old man with long white hair in the wheelchair turned toward the car.

"I'm just waitin' for my son to pick me up, I declare I am," he called, pushing himself to the middle of the dusty road.

Charlie looked around at the trees trellising lightfall.

"I'm sorry, sir—is this your home?" Minnie asked.

The old man leaned his head back.

"Well now, I declare, it is, darlin'! Let me take your hand, you sound like such a pretty thing," he called, holding out a swollen claw.

"Well, you are a pretty thing, I declare you are, darlin'," he repeated, patting her hand.

Minnie looked at Charlie helplessly.

"I am so sorry, you see, his granddaddy used to live here—"

"Many years ago," Charlie added quickly.

"Well now, I declare, is that a fact," the old man said, tilting his head.

"I didn't know anyone was living here," Charlie continued. "My grandfather said it was abandoned and—"

"Obviously it's not." Minnie glanced at him. "Someone is living here."

"Well, now, I declare, are y'all from Richmond?"

Minnie nodded.

"Yes, I'm Minnie Barrek and this is—"

"*Well,* Judge Barrek's daughter!"

Minnie smiled self-consciously.

"Well, it is good to meet you, *sugar*! I known your daddy a long time, I declare I have, and now, how is the good judge?"

"He's fine."

"Well, now, yes he is."

Charlie noticed for the first time the bulky shawl over the old man's lap.

"Now, I declare, it is a small world, darlin'. The judge and I have done business over the years," he continued, patting her hand.

Minnie smiled. "Then you are in the law?"

The old man smiled, showing rotted brown teeth.

"Well, now, I am in lots of *enterprises*, darlin', but the judge is a good man, I declare he is," he repeated, tilting his head toward Minnie.

She glanced up the dark road.

"Do you . . . do you have someone to take care of you?"

"Well now, darlin', don't worry about me, I have my son and my nigger maid." He turned to Charlie suddenly. "Now, I don't believe I've had the pleasure."

"This is Charlie Tidewater; he is visiting from Chicago."

The old man leaned back, his skull-white skin aglow.

"The pleasure is all mine! I declare it is. Now that is a cold climate, Chicago. I imagine you down here to get some of our southern warmth, Mr. Tidewater."

"Yes, that's right."

"I always believe on judging a man for who he is and not where he is from, I declare I do," he nodded to Minnie, patting her hand again. "Now, darlin', you give my regards to the judge, you hear?"

"I'm sorry, sir, I don't know your name . . ."

"Hatfield, Mr. Hatfield."

"Are you going to be alright, Mr. Hatfield?"

"My son is on the way, but y'all go on up to the house and have yourself a visit now." He let Minnie's hand go and turned to Charlie. "I declare, I imagine the house has changed a bit since your granddaddy was here."

"I'm sure," Charlie murmured.

The old man wheeled himself to the side of the car.

"We really don't want to intrude—"

"Well, now, darlin', I declare, y'all go on and make yourselves at home and don't worry about me now, go on now and *enjoy* yourselves."

Charlie turned to Minnie in the car.

"What do you think? Think we ought to leave?"

Minnie stared at the old man sitting by the car.

"Y'all go on, now!" he called out and raised his hand. "It was good talkin' to y'all."

"Well," Minnie shrugged. "He said it was alright."

Charlie put the car in gear, tires crackling over the loose gravel. He took the turn in the road and saw only the pitch darkness behind.

The house soared into the fanfare of stars, both ends of the rambling porch obscured by drooping willow trees.

"I don't see how he lives here," Charlie muttered, watching the driveway vanish into mere ruts, weeds scraping the sides of the Mercedes.

They parked in the horseshoe drive around a decapitated statue and got out of the car.

"Do you think anyone—"

"No." Charlie shook his head. "I don't know who that old man was, but this place is abandoned," he said flatly, surveying the broken windows, a faint tinge of lunar light searing the glass.

The night air flowed across the fields, rustling Minnie's hair and passing lightly through his shirt. Charlie looked out across the land to the wide, unbridled fields under the harvest night. He could see the symmetry of what must have been a large plantation. He turned and walked up the steps behind Minnie.

"See anything?"

"No, he must live in back somewhere."

"Maybe in a tent," he murmured, putting his arms around her.

Minnie turned and Charlie could hear her light breathing. Minnie's eyes toyed with night shadow.

"Charlie Tidewater," she whispered softly in his ear.

"Have you come to rescue me?"

"Both of us," he murmured.

They kissed in the shadow of the column with her back to the window. The same wild breeze creaked the screenless door. Charlie felt Minnie's hair flowing over his bare arm, the plaintive whine of wind in the vanishing darkness. Charlie could feel the world suddenly. The plank wood was under them as they lay in the milky shadows falling over the Virginia countryside. Minnie's eyes and spreading hair were a vision seen only on the warmest nights, something fleeting, then lost.

# CHAPTER TWENTY-FIVE

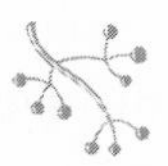

Virginia countryside

*August 1998*

The old man was gone by the time Charlie pulled back onto the empty two-lane. Minnie was asleep and he listened to the music of the tires on a paved road. He heard a rumble and glanced in his rearview mirror. Charlie watched for a moment. He looked forward, then saw something glimmer behind.

"Minnie."

"Hmm."

Charlie looked again in the mirror.

"I think there's someone following us."

Minnie sat up and turned around.

"I don't see anything."

"Keep watching."

She stared into the darkness, then turned around.

"You're just imagining things, darlin'—"

The bump snapped their necks back and sent the car across the highway onto the shoulder. Charlie swerved back onto the highway.

*". . . What?"*

Charlie's neck hit the headrest again, the steering wheel spinning under his hands, seeing white gravel on the shoulder, and then the center lines of the highway were whipping in front of the car. Charlie came out of the slide and stomped down on the accelerator, throwing the car into fourth gear. He saw a chrome grill surface from the darkness.

Charlie gunned the car up to 105.

*"Charlie!"* Minnie scrambled on the seat. "Here he comes again!"

"Put your seat belt on," he yelled, a metallic taste in his mouth.

*"Charlie!"*

The bang punched him back against the seat and threw Minnie against her door. Charlie fought the steering wheel. They careened off the highway and tall weeds whipped down in front of the car. He jerked the wheel back; a wire fence disappeared under the bumper and the highway appeared again.

Charlie fought to keep the trembling in his legs from overtaking him. Minnie turned one way and then another. The white car flew toward them like a spirit. Charlie could scarcely believe they were going 110.

*"Hang on!"*

He swerved into the other lane.

*"Charlie!"*

He jerked back into the lane, bumpers scraping, turning his car as if someone had picked it up. They swerved back and forth across the road; running off the shoulder, skidding on the roadside gravel. A slatted fence sped by, crops flipping like cards. Charlie swerved back onto the road and jumped the Mercedes down a gear, winding the engine to 115. He shifted up and the car surged to 120—the luminous grill flashing the low night toward his mirror. Then the car behind could come no closer. Charlie saw a man with one elbow resting on the door, a cigarette flaring in dark space. He looked as if he were out for a pleasant drive.

The lights of a town flashed ahead. Charlie looked into his mirror and the car had vanished. He stared into the darkness.

"He's gone," Charlie nodded shakily, glancing at Minnie holding on to the handrail like a frozen bus rider.

Car lights flicked on behind; the night split into red swirls.

"Well, it's about time," Charlie muttered, slowing down.

"Don't stop!"

He looked at Minnie. "What, are you kidding?"

"You don't know who it is, Charlie."

"I can't run from the police!"

They came to a stop on the clicking gravel. The old squad car growled up behind. Charlie looked in his mirror, squinting against the glare of the spotlight. Insects wheedled in the high weeds.

"What's this guy waiting for?"

A car door opened. Road gravel crunched underfoot. Charlie turned in toward a flashlight; cold eyes under a tan Stetson flicked over him.

"Did you get that guy?" Charlie asked.

The light flashed to Minnie; Charlie could hear the electric hum of the turning light.

"See your license, sir?"

Charlie squinted into the light.

"Listen, somebody just tried to run us off the road—"

"Your license, sir."

He reached into his back pocket, slipping the license from the plastic. The man walked away. Charlie stared after him with his open wallet in his hand.

"This is bullshit," he muttered, opening the car door. *"Hey!"*

The man pivoted like a soldier.

"Back in the car, boy!"

Charlie froze.

"I said get back in the car," he shouted, taking a step toward him.

"I told you," Minnie said as Charlie shut the door.

He looked in the rearview mirror, watching the officer lean in the car window. "Here he comes again."

The gravel crackled behind, then the door opened.

"Step out of the car."

"What's going on, Officer?"

"Back by the trunk, boy," he commanded, taking him roughly by the arm.

Charlie stopped, turning to the pale eyes.

"Now, wait a minute—"

He felt the wind go out of him as he was slugged to the ground. The fine grit of road dust was in his mouth. The steel butt of the flashlight felt like it penetrated his abdomen. Charlie lay on the ground in front of the old squad car with his eyes closed against the pain. He opened them slowly, seeing a rebel flag painted on the front license plate.

*"Get up, boy!"*

He was lifted from the ground by his shirt and slammed onto the trunk.

"Spread 'em!" Charlie felt his legs kicked apart, trying to get his breath.

"This . . . this is some mistake—"

*"Shut your fuckin' mouth!"*

Hands patted him down as he inhaled the oily exhaust of the car.

"He's clean," the man declared behind him.

Charlie heard another door open.

"Keep yo' head *down*, boy!"

Charlie dropped his head. The heavy steps crackled on the road gravel. A black boot was by his right foot. He felt his blood run cold; a heavy wheezing was behind him.

"Look," he began shakily. "I was almost killed tonight—"

Charlie felt a jolt like a sack of wet sand slamming into his side. His knees buckled and then he was below the exhaust pipe coughing fumes. The world flashed white and he rolled on his side, breath coming in jerky spasms. Another Stetson floated down; a pallid, fleshy face with pig eyes. The man grinned, then laughed, spatting into the gravel by his head.

"Them Tasers sure have a kick, don't they, boy?" The jowled man with pig eyes wheezed. "Man shouldn't be goin' over one hundred miles an hour and resist arrest."

"I was being chased . . ." Charlie groaned.

The heavier man turned, holding his fingers together like a church steeple.

"I just see one black Mercedes-Benz from Chi-cago."

"Bullshit—"

The black boot slammed into his back. Charlie rolled under the car, hands pulling him out by his ankles. The man with pig eyes hunched down.

"Know what happened to me today, boy . . . fella called, wantin' to know about a nigger named Rufus junior." The fleshy face spread into a grin. He spoke slowly, drawing out each word like hot taffy. "And it sounded like a goddamn Yankee boy to me." He paused, tugging on the brim of his hat. A boot came down on the center of Charlie's chest. "If I was you, I'd take my Mercedes and drive on back to Chicago. 'Cause I see you again, boy . . ."—he leaned down toward Charlie, his creased cheeks shiny in the close air—*"they never find you."*

Then two arms were under his, pulling him up. Charlie was amazed he could walk.

"What happened? What did they say?"

"They . . ." Charlie looked at her, feeling an ache in his side, a deep pain in his back. He turned away. "They thought I was racing."

"*What?* What do you mean?"

Charlie saw the red pig eyes in the unsettling darkness.

"I cleared it up . . . they're going after him," he mumbled, jamming the car in gear.

Minnie shook her head in disbelief.

"Didn't they see *his car* too?"

"Oh yeah." Charlie nodded slowly, trying to keep his hands from shaking on the steering wheel.

"They know all about that car."

*Charlie Tidewater*
*465 Marilee Road*
*Southampton, VA*
*August 27, four* A.M.

*Matthew,*

*I'm leaving. They'll kill you down here. Minnie and I went back out to that garage and somebody tried to run us off the road and then a backwoods sheriff threatened me and hit me with a stun gun or something. I can't stop shaking even to write this letter. They can all go to hell—I'm leaving the South and never coming back. I don't care what happened in that garage. I'm going to leave my grandfather a note and when he wakes . . . I'll be gone. . . .*

*Matthew, it's dawn. I should have left by now. The problem is, it will follow me. Something from thirty years ago . . . I've walked into a pocket of time where hatred has lingered. I even think Minnie's father is involved. I'm tired but I'm more tired of running.*

*Charlie*

# CHAPTER TWENTY-SIX

Richmond, Virginia

*1944*

*"How dare you accuse my daughter of being crazy!"*

Light streamed into the wasted redolence of upholstery a hundred years old. Miz Drake sat behind her rosewood desk among the dimensional shapes of lamps, vases, baroque candelabra.

Austin fingered the worn band of his hat, noticing the lion-claw feet of the desk. "I'm not saying she is crazy—I'm saying maybe we ought to talk to somebody about the way she's been acting," he continued in a flat tone. "There are people who can do things for that. You know how she talks to herself and never takes off that robe, and her drinking will kill her if something else doesn't. I found a garbage bag of gin bottles in the basement and I don't know where she's been getting it, but it doesn't help her, it just makes it worse."

Two silver eyes narrowed on the man in the rumpled suit, the elbows and the knees shiny with age. He tucked the threads of his cuffs into his sleeves.

"If there's a problem it's what you've done to her. You're never home."

"I have to sell cars at night, Miz Drake. People don't buy cars during the day, they buy them in the evenings."

"That's a fine excuse for staying out and chasing women around."

Miz Drake called him to her office several times a week, beating him steadily into submission. She had provided a place to live and many times the food on the table. Austin walked the burning streets, wearing holes in the soles of his shoes, passing signs warding off men looking for work. Many times he returned, pleading with the same hard faces. Miz Drake offered to give him money to follow men riding the rails in search of work. Then he found a job selling cars for a man he had once employed.

Austin looked at his hat again, taking the breath of patience.

"What's the matter? The truth hurts, doesn't it. You say Tamara's crazy because she *knows* what you're doing at night! The same way Miz Tyler knows and—"

"Miz Tyler is a bitter woman who lost her husband."

He looked at the woman in the high-collared dress, with her pearl cigarette holder and nineteenth-century broaches, blending in to the antiques. The smoke tickled the shaft of light not blocked by the piled lamps and porcelain figurines.

"There you go. Defaming a decent person who had the bad fortune to marry one of *your* kind."

Austin shifted, keeping up the steady inventory of his hat.

"It would be best if she didn't keep whispering ideas in Tamara's head, because Tamara doesn't know enough about people to know when someone is just spewing poison."

His mother-in-law stomped her foot, rushing at him like the small dogs she kept in her shop. Her eyes, more gray in the gloom, burned at him.

"You just don't want her to know what you've been doing at night!"

Austin nodded slowly, facing the withered face, dried makeup in the lines around her mouth.

"Miz Drake, she knows what I been doing at night. She gets her head filled with ideas, but she knows I been working, because I almost got my debts paid off. And when this war is over people will buy more cars and I'll get a place for us to stay."

She came closer. "If she has a problem, then I'm going to be the one to help her long after *you've* gone and left her. She'll *never* leave this house."

Austin eyed her coolly, thinking she was a porcelain antique with her fat-girl cheeks, small hands and feet; something valued for its sheer years and that's why he couldn't tell her to go to hell.

"Appreciate everything you have done for us, Miz Drake. Reckon I do. And I think once I can quit working so many nights, maybe Tamara won't be so lonely and she'll be right again."

Miz Drake swelled up and stomped her foot again, savaging the oriental rug.

*"There's nothing wrong with my daughter!"*

Austin continued calmly, turning the hat slowly in his hand like an artisan taking inventory of a pot.

"Get out of here! My daughter is not crazy! *You* are the problem. Not her. If *you* leave then she will be fine."

Austin slipped his hat on, tugging the brim.

"Yes ma'am. We're going to leave soon, just as soon as I can manage it," he said, turning and walking for the door.

*"Stop."*

He turned slowly to the yellow teeth, the wickedness of feminine cunning.

"You will never, *ever,* take my daughter from me again."

"Mistah Turin, you think we can sell cars out hyah in the country?"

Snowball stood against the expanse of verdant fields rolling into the curve of land and distance. The narrow gray road wandered down, then up, trickling back into the distant line of bushy trees, disappearing over the next ridge.

"Reckon so." Austin nodded. "People in the country need cars as much as people in the city, and I think we could get a right good repair business going."

Austin turned to the faded garage with three dormer windows pocking the roof. One window reflected the brilliant western light. Another window was a depthless black hole; the third showed perfect white curtains framing square panes. Austin walked across the drive, glass crackling underfoot. Spiderwebs sheened sunlight in the twin globes of the gas pumps. He stared at the two bays overgrown with grass showing through cracks in the cement. He smelled the scent of aged motor oil on the breeze. A hornets' nest buzzed faintly electric.

Snowball shook his grizzled head.

"Just hope people know we here. Ain't no one been comin' down that old highway since we been out here!"

Austin walked out and squinted down the road, rubbing stubble left from a dull razor. He squatted down by the road, scooping up warm gravel, letting it fall slowly by his thin shoes. He didn't afford himself luxuries, nor his wife or child.

*But getting Tamara away from her mother will help her. Although that gleam is always there now, her eyes carrying light like a cracked prism. Talking to herself behind the closed doors; the full conversations going on until I open the door to see if another person is there. And then just shutting the door quietly, unable to stay, because it breaks my heart more than anything else.*

"But if you think, Mistah Turin, that we can make a go of it—then I'm willing to do it!"

Austin looked up from the highway. He regarded his friend of nearly twenty years, long hands by his sides. Austin scraped a short stick through the dusty gravel, then looked down the empty highway. He felt again the sensation that had plagued him since his dealership failed. It was the feeling life was continuing on without him.

"Yep," he nodded, standing slowly, wind picking at his loose coat. "Reckon it's time to try again, Snowball."

He stood in front of the building, looking up to the eaved windows of the small apartment over the garage, jabbing his finger to the sky.

"And that's where we'll live."

*"You bastard! You are going off and leaving me here again!"*

Snowball lifted his head from the hood, the air cleaner in his hand, grease black on his palms and fingers. Rufus John smiled in shadow. Little Tamara and Rufus junior played in the dust by the picture window. The little boy had a metal car.

"My car drivin' up to your doll."

Little Tamara wrinkled her nose, the soft yellow light playing across her features.

"Miss Lady doesn't like your car."

Rufus junior ran his car across the drive. He was a dark-skinned boy, but with softer features than his father. He ran the car up against a tire.

*"Get back here, now!"*

Rufus John looked again at the window, then turned back to Snowball.

"She winding up now," he murmured. "Them white women is sweet as honey, but they is crazy," he continued, holding the greasy carburetor in place.

"You stay away from her," Snowball warned, turning the bolt with his wrench. "They catch you near a white lady and you end up in a tree too."

Rufus John had the same slim smile.

"They ain't goin' believe no crazy lady."

He watched Rufus junior carry a daisy to little Tamara.

"This for you."

The girl looked up from the dust.

"Miss Lady says thank you," Tamara sang, taking the white flower.

"Uh-huh, don't matter she crazy when they stretch you out," Snowball muttered, turning the screws.

Black beads of sweat glistened on Rufus John's smooth head like sprinkled water as he stared up at the window.

Snowball watched Austin's wife spit into the dust below. He shook his head. One time he had to run with Austin to catch her. She was already halfway across the tobacco fields when Austin tackled her. She swung and screamed, slashing with long nails, biting Austin several times. They had to carry her back to the apartment. Snowball had never known anyone who had been normal but then became crazy. It must have been just what Mr. Turin said. Some people went blind for no reason or became crippled, some went crazy. He said there was a place in Richmond for crazy people and he was going to take her there. Snowball thought he had better hurry.

Tamara glowered between the cheap pink curtains framing her face like a veil.

"You leave me out here in the middle of nowhere while you go and see your *whore* . . . what kind of fool do you think I am?"

She spat again, a revulsion welling from her cheeks like vomit. Austin stood in the drive and faced his wife. He stared at the pallid face with red lips hideous and smudged. She had lost the ability to put on lipstick long ago. Her spit fell below and didn't surprise Austin, any more than when she would throw food at him.

"I told you, I had to go into town again tonight," he began evenly, keeping his voice low and calm. "Mr. Fredericks said I could do some selling for him in the evenings until I get this place rolling."

Tamara glared down at the two gold-filled gas globes; Snowball under the hood with Rufus John and the sign down by the cooling two-lane: TURIN MOTORS—CARS BOUGHT AND SOLD—REPAIRS. She watched her daughter play in the dirt with the little black boy.

"This place is *never* going to do anything. How dare you put me out here in the middle of nowhere over a garage! I should *never* have left Mother's!" She leaned out farther, her mouth pursing up. "She was so right about you! *You're nothing but trash!* You have your daughter growing up over a garage, *a garage,* do you know what that means, you trash, you filthy little man, a fucking garage—"

"Now, this is temporary. I just need to get a little bit more business, then we'll get an apartment in town," Austin continued, glancing at Snowball and Rufus John.

It was no longer Tamara speaking. Her ghost skin, the

wildness of her unwashed hair, the way food fell from her mouth, crying pathetically for hours; these were characteristic of the scourge he watched in horror.

"Oh, and then we'll be in a rented apartment! That's something to look forward to! A used-car salesman's wife, that's what I am. . . . Should I wash your clothes for you? Shall I lick the grease from under your fingernails? A hot rented apartment with the brat in the next room while we sweat like pigs in a barn. Why, *niggers* live better than we do! Isn't that right, niggers? Don't you live better than we do? Maybe I should go with you?" She nodded to Rufus John. "A nice big nigger buck like yourself—"

"Tamara!"

"To think I could have been a great star! But now you leave me out here with this brat!"

Austin glanced at his daughter with Rufus junior. They were still playing by the garage wall.

"Don't talk about her that way!"

Tamara laughed, the maniacal laughter making Snowball look up. It was like the devil himself was laughing. She laughed with her mouth open, blood-lipped, the insanity of high, unnatural laughter floating across the highway into the empty fields.

*"Tamara!"*

Austin jabbed his finger at her, the wind kicking dust on his ten-year-old wing tips. He could see the red of her mouth as the laughter finally broke. Her muttering, smoldering mouth was an organism unto itself.

*"You . . ."* she breathed venomously. "You are such a stupid little man . . . of course she understands her mother is insane."

She yelled down to Snowball.

"What are *you* looking at, nigger?"

*"Goddammit, Tamara!"*

Austin shook his finger at her. She regarded him with a contemptuous grin.

"What's the matter? Afraid I'll drive away your nigger mechanics? Your two employees!"

She laughed again, then shook her head slowly.

"What a goddamn fool I was to marry beneath me. A goddamn fool . . ."

The window slid down and there was just the tufting pink curtains. Austin stared in the glow before dark, hearing crickets in the fields. He was in a dark cavern where water, food, and light were the gooey tar of his ill fortune. He felt the eyes, but when he looked, Snowball and Rufus John were under the hood. Austin didn't know human beings could enter such a dark land where trees are skeletons, the earth is rock, water brackish and poisoned. There was little of life now. Only his daughter.

"You better git on to town, Mr. Turin. I finish up hyah and keep an eye on things," Snowball called from under the hood. "You go and sell those cars for Mistah Fredericks," he continued, holding the silver wrench in the gloom cooling his face. "You go on now. I watch over things."

Austin nodded slowly and walked to his car.

"I won't be too late," he called out the window.

Snowball nodded under the hood.

"Yas suh. You just go sell them cars so you can get you a place in the city for Miz Turin an' then she be happy. Ain't nobody I know can sell a car like you. Ain't nobody I know knows automobiles like you, Mr. Turin." He stood up. "You go on and sell them cars, and then you can get Miz Turin to that hospital you talkin' 'bout an' git her some help, 'cause I know she goin' to get better, I know she is, Mr. Turin, you just go on now, you just go on."

"I'll get back as soon as I can," Austin nodded slowly, pulling onto the darkening road that was black when he returned five hours later.

Snowball ran out of the darkness.

"Mistah Turin! Mistah Turin!"

Austin jumped out of the car. A circle of light swirled moths and june bugs by the door.

"What happened?" He felt his stomach grab, seeing death in his friend's face. "Where's Tamara?"

Snowball spoke with lack of breath, fine beads glistening on his high forehead.

"She upstairs . . ." He caught his breath again. "I had to put a board through the door, Mr. Turin . . . *Lord!* I thought she dead!"

*Thought she was dead! Then she wasn't, then the final tribute to my demise had not been paid yet.*

"Now, calm down and tell me what happened."

Snowball wiped his face with a grease rag.

"Rufus John—he jest left . . . I workin' on this car after you left and just after dark . . ."

Austin's taut nerves tingled with what they both heard—the shrieking laughter coming out the window, the fine musical smash of glasses and dishes.

"Go on," Austin commanded.

"Car come down the highway, goin' fast. And Mr. Turin, I don't know why I happen to turn around, 'cause most times I just let that ol' car go on by and never pay no mind to it, but I turn around an' tha' door open and 'fore I can move, Miz Turin runnin' like a hornet after it." He paused for breath. "She runnin' right fo' that car. I start after her and catch her robe and think she might slip out and get hit anyway but it grab her like a puppet and that ol' car swerve so close it slap a corner of her robe, then run off the road. That man must a thought he done seen a ghost or made a ghost!"

Snowball pointed into the rolling darkness. "Went right in that field over there and man come back and see Miz Turin screamin' an' then he start hollerin' while I'm fighting with Miz Turin. She tryin' to get loose, calling me everything, and that man start hollerin', 'She crazy! She crazy! She ought to be locked up, she crazy!' And then Miz Turin cuss a blue streak and he must never heard words like that 'cause he just git in his car and drive away. Miz Turin she never stop fighting with me an' then she jest laughin' an' laughin', beatin' on me an' sayin' things I can't repeat, Mistah Turin."

Snowball wiped his face again, his neck bobbing as he shook his head. "Mistah Turin, she fixin' to kill herself, an' I think she goin' to try again 'cause she say to me, 'Nigger, you can't keep me locked up, I goin' to free myself,' an' she tryin' to break the glass in tha' door. So I lock her upstairs and she been breakin' things and laughin' ever since and I was afraid fo' little Tamara . . ."

Snowball paused, swallowing. The crickets breathed around them in the country dark. He shook his head.

"An' she kept sayin', 'Let me go, nigger. I want to kill myself! You let me go!' I lock the door and then she come out the window, but I watch her an' she go back in then."

The icy, high laughter erupted from the darkened window.

"Where's little Tamara?"

"Found her hidin' in yo' office with Rufus junior. I gave 'em a blanket an' pillow. I think they asleep."

Austin stood in front of Snowball, his tie loosened, the glow of selling a car gone. He looked down.

"Now, I thank you, Snowball, but I won't be selling cars in town for a while. Looks like we'll have to make a go of it out here." He paused, his head low, the steady hum of the car between them. "I think Tamara has been alone long enough."

Snowball nodded, wiping his face again, his eyes catching light from the bulb under the umbrella shade.

"Yes sir. Reckon you right. She a mighty lonely person under all that sickness."

Austin looked at him, then up at the dark windows. He lowered himself down to one knee, picking up a stick from the dust. Snowball rubbed his hands on his coveralls, bending down with his fingers hanging over his knees. Austin stared at the window again, seeing a few stars winking out from drifting ghosts, a scent of rain to come later.

"I wonder if you could get me something, Snowball?"

"What that, Mr. Turin?"

Austin turned to him the way he had when they raced the bootleggers.

"Now, I wonder if you could get me some iron bars about the length of that window there."

The black eyes paused, then rolled up to the darkened curtains.

"Now, I'll need enough iron for the upstairs windows and a dead-bolt lock for the door. You reckon you can get those for me tomorrow?"

Snowball stared at him, then looked down, the tips of his long fingers moving in the forgiving dark.

"Now, you know I will, Mr. Turin, you know I get you whatever parts you need."

Austin nodded slowly, looking across the fields pale under a late moon, seeing in the dead rows the cross of a ragged scarecrow.

# CHAPTER TWENTY-SEVEN

Richmond, Virginia

*August 1998*

Morning was hard and bright, a sharp blue stretching into space. Light etched Robert E. Lee's mouth and cut a triangle under his nose. Charlie waited under the statue while morning traffic hurried by. He felt the sun on his neck and glanced at his watch.

"You sure havin' you a lot of interviews," Granddaddy murmured that morning at breakfast.

"No, I'm fine now," he replied when Charlie noticed his slower movement. "Nothin' wrong with me, just feelin' slow today, is all." He asked him about the pills he took regularly. "They ain't nothin'. . . . Just somethin' for my blood . . . now you go on and get to your interview."

Charlie looked down Monument Avenue and saw a man

walking slowly down the sidewalk toward him. He thought of the conversation with the woman at the hospital.

"Yes . . . we did have a Tamara Tidewater as a patient . . . I had to go back to our microfiche files and—"

"Did she die there?"

Charlie looked at the yellowed invoice from the garage office.

"I beg your pardon."

Charlie closed the door to the phone booth.

"Did she pass away there?"

There was another pause.

"What was the date of death?"

"April 4, 1968."

She came back after five minutes.

"Tamara Tidewater." The woman hesitated. "She passed away on April 4, 1968."

"What was the cause of death?"

"I'm sorry, I can't tell you that."

"I'm her son."

"Then I would say you should know how she died."

Charlie banged on the glass with his fist.

"Can't you just tell me—"

The woman breathed in loudly.

"Just a minute . . ." She paused. "Cancer."

"Could you tell me one more thing. . . . Could you tell me who was the attending physician—who signed the death certificate?"

He heard the woman take a deep breath.

"I really shouldn't, without proper identification—"

*"Please—"*

The woman paused again.

"Dr. E. L. Taylor—"

Charlie opened his eyes on the bench. He heard footsteps

and turned around. Sherwood Anders rounded the statue, a knit tie kicking up against his khaki suit. "I only have a minute," he muttered, sitting down, his mustache peppered with gray in the sunlight.

Charlie watched a black woman push a stroller down the street.

"I want to know about that car . . ."

"What car?"

Charlie turned to him.

"The one that ran you off the road thirty years ago."

Sherwood shook his head slowly.

"I told you what I know."

"Why didn't you tell me about the car?"

"It wasn't relevant."

Charlie nodded slowly.

"It was relevant when the same car tried to run me off the road last night."

Sherwood turned toward him abruptly, then shook his head.

"I'm sorry, I can't help you."

"Why the *fuck* not?"

Sherwood stood up, turning away.

"There are certain things people here just can't accept . . ." He shut his mouth, sweat glistening on his brow.

"I have to go . . . I'm sorry."

Sherwood turned away and began walking. Charlie jumped up.

*"Hey!"*

He kept walking and Charlie ran around in front of him.

"Hey . . . what are you afraid of?"

Sherwood sidestepped and Charlie blocked him again.

"You've got to help me, here . . . you know what's going on but you won't—"

Sherwood stepped toward him violently, shaking his finger.

"*You* . . ." He shook his head. "You . . . you *aren't from here*." His mouth opened, his throat struggling with sound. "You should leave . . . I have to live here . . . these men . . ."

Sherwood shook his head, then turned and walked quickly across the street, disappearing under a tunnel of leaves.

Madelyn was too young to understand what was going on between the grown-ups. She looked to her mother, then her grandfather, then Pearl, who placed her breakfast in front of her. Morning shimmered outside the lace curtains of the dining-room window. Her mother cradled the cup below her mouth, her head slightly bent. The judge stirred the black coffee with the silver spoon he used every morning.

But Minnie found the sound of the silver service particularly annoying. She hadn't spoken to the judge since she arrived home late. Minnie knew he would wait until he had a captive audience to pass sentence. There was little to do until he signaled the first witness. The spoon tinked the coffee cup, then followed to the saucer. The chair creaked back.

"I see you decided to go against my wishes yesterday."

Minnie looked at her father, eyes in the corners like some puppet whose pupils are large. The judge was sitting back, one shiny shoe out to the side, hands crossed over the napkin on his lap. Madelyn's round eyes were watchful.

"Pearl said she would watch Madelyn and I decided to go," Minnie answered evenly.

"I see." The judge nodded slowly. "What does this young man do for a living?"

Minnie was surprised at the clumsiness.

"He is a stockbroker—apparently a successful one."

"He told you that."

"Yes," Minnie answered, raising her coffee.

"Is he married?"

She sipped the coffee and placed it back on the saucer.

"Separated."

"He told you that too?"

"Yes, he did," she replied, tilting her head up.

Minnie was used to this tactic. Impeaching the credibility of the witness.

"Why did they separate?"

"I assume because they weren't compatible."

Pearl went on feeding Madelyn.

"After what happened with Cole, I would think you'd be more careful. We don't want to upset your child's world again."

"Nor mine."

"That's right." Judge Barrek nodded, throwing his napkin to the side. "I hope you had a good time with this man, because you will not see him again."

Minnie turned, raising her eyebrows.

"No?"

The judge nodded.

"There are facts."

She turned suddenly, sensing a trap. The judge quieted her with his hand.

"Charles Tidewater was fired recently for alcoholism."

The judge was speaking quietly now. "It seems his wife had enough of his drinking as well."

"I knew his wife left him," Minnie snapped.

The judge passed, tapping his thick finger against his coffee cup.

"Of course you did . . . but a woman he was married to for seven years decided he was too dangerous to see anymore."

The judge picked up his coffee, averting his eyes. "There is a restraining order against this man, Minnie."

Minnie jumped up from the table.

"You are making all this up!"

The judge set his cup down slowly.

"If you don't believe me, then I would ask him, Daughter."

Madelyn started to cry. The judge stood up and slid his chair into the table.

"I understand his grandmother was quite insane and his mother was in and out of mental institutions. His grandfather was little more than a used-car salesman, Minnie. That is the extent of his *family*."

The judge checked the gold pocket watch in his vest.

"You may not like it . . . but I will not let white trash come into my home." He paused. "I have to protect what is mine."

He hesitated again, then walked into the front hall. Minnie leaned her head down slowly to her hand. Madelyn stared at her mother. A revelation came to her and she put her first word with the fifth word she had learned.

"Mommy . . . *cry*!"

# CHAPTER TWENTY-EIGHT

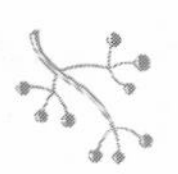

Southampton, Virginia

*August 1998*

Dusk settled on the dogwoods and oaks around the house and glowed beyond the field. Granddaddy and Charlie sat on the deck in the bronze light of an oil lantern. They were silent, somewhat exhausted from the yard work, dreamily full from the pizza Charlie ordered and Granddaddy insisted he pay for. A clear mason jar, taking no light, giving back none, was between them on the iron settee.

". . . so, these old boys finally got tired of paying Snowball and me all their money, see," Granddaddy continued, pointing to the jar that began his story of the bootleggers. "One time I raced them and won and this old boy named Buck said, 'We going to give you something different.' And I thought, What are these old bootleggers going to give me, see, I didn't know . . . I was *hoping* they was going to give me money! But these bootleggers didn't like to keep giving away their money and Buck said I had to follow them into the woods."

Granddaddy sat up in his lawn chair.

"Must have been three or four in the morning, see, and we went down this long dirt road way back in the woods, and Snowball lookin' at me like I was crazy, because in those days the Klan was out in the country." Granddaddy stabbed at the horizon with his index finger. "But—I knew I could always outrun those old bootleggers, or just about anyone else, with that coupe of mine. Next thing you know—we come to a shack in the woods and the bootleggers stop their cars and this bootlegger—he later had a son also named Buck and I think the older Buck was paralyzed in an automobile accident runnin' from the police years later. So—I follow him around to the back of the shack an' we come to this contraption, see, looks like a *great* big kettle with pipes coming out of the top."

Granddaddy leaned back, counting his speech with his finger.

"*Now!* I knew it was a still, because my cousin, Jimmy Lee, who is the great-nephew of General Robert E. Lee, had been making moonshine for years and the Richmond police never bothered him—there was a sheriff who ran the county and he was one of the biggest customers, so they never did have to worry about the law." His voice rose. "*So!* These old bootleggers, Buck that is, takes one of these fruit jars," he continued, pointing to the mason jar on the patio table, "and filled it from the bottom of this kettle and I knew it was white lightning because it is the most awful-smelling stuff in the world! Buck said I could have as many jars as I could fill up and put into my car. Moonshine was just as valuable as money in those days because nobody had any alcohol and people would pay *enormous* amounts of money for it. So, Snowball and I started filling up these mason jars and put them in my trunk and my backseat." He paused, his bottom teeth taking light. "And do you know, I sold every one of those mason jars by the week's end."

Granddaddy was on the edge of his chair, stabbing the darkness triumphantly.

"*And*, I made myself some good money doin' it! And I only kept one jar for myself and that's what you found under the sink and there it sits."

Charlie looked at the seventy-year-old jar of clear alcohol.

"Did you ever drink any of it?"

"Reckon I did," he murmured, nodding to the jar. "But it's right strong and I never did care for the taste. Now, I drank a lot of bootleg whiskey, see, but not moonshine."

Charlie looked at the white lightning again, the clear liquid gelling with evening. He suddenly wanted to taste the crude liquid they drank on dusty roads and on evening-laden porches. He wanted to taste a time when people didn't live so long and wars came up like spring storms and people listened to radios as the marvel of their age. He wanted to taste the young century where an airplane was still a novelty, cars pulled up next to horses, and men who could remember Lee in sixty-five still walked the earth. He wanted to look down from the vantage point of the wild ride to come in the middle of a depression, feel the cheap shoe leather wearing out and the hot black hood of a Model T with the blue oil smoke smelling slightly sweet, raw, primitive. He wanted to taste all those people who sat on saggy springs in heavy Hudsons, Studebakers, Dodges, cars lugging down highways without speed limits or radar traps, lugging down roads where people still waved to a passing car because people weren't overloaded with people yet. He wanted to feel the hit of bootlegged alcohol in a speakeasy or from a flask under a table. *Were these people so original? Why are we such slaves to what they did before us?*

Charlie looked at the jar, wanting to destroy the nagging present with the past.

"You think anything would happen to me if I drank some?"

Granddaddy frowned. "You don't want to drink any of that stuff."

Charlie looked at the liquid again.

"I think I might take a sip—you don't think I'll go blind or anything, do you?"

Granddaddy turned.

"Lord, no!"

"I've just heard of people going blind from white lightning."

"Never heard that before." He turned back to the bottle. "Now, you might feel a little sick from it—but you won't go blind."

Charlie picked up the mason jar, unscrewing the crusty top, vaporous fumes, much like gasoline, escaping.

"You sure this is white lightning, Granddaddy?"

"Reckon I am."

Charlie nodded, bringing the jar to his lips, displacing air with cold noxiousness, thinking once of ghost men with yellow lanterns brewing firewater as he drank of his grandfather's time in one large gulp. He felt his nose drain on his lip, his eyes water, his stomach flaming. He jumped up, slamming the jar down on the table, spitting into the yard.

*"Oh, God!"*

He couldn't stop spitting. He wondered suddenly if he had drunk drain opener, thinking Granddaddy could have easily mixed up a chemical with what might have been white lightning. Charlie felt the boiling torrent roll down into his stomach with the heat of a hot-water bottle pressed to his abdomen. He fell to his knees and considered sticking a finger down his throat to save his life.

"Now! I never seen anyone drink like that!"

Charlie couldn't stop spitting, sucking any droplet of moisture from his tongue, settling for licking his palm to pull the fire off.

"Reckon that stuff is pretty bad after all these years," Granddaddy murmured.

Charlie got off his knees and sat down, the swell in his head coming on like a shot of novocaine. The pain was fading, a fire burning down. The dimming landscape of the yard sparkled clear in three-dimensional beauty. Granddaddy saw the flush of his grandson's cheeks and the hot, soft gleam in his eyes. He turned to the jar swishing light a half inch lower.

"Now, I better have a sip," he nodded to Charlie. "Just to make sure you didn't drink any poison."

Charlie heard him like television or radio where the voice is disembodied. Granddaddy lifted the mason jar, sniffing once with no wrinkle of emotion, drinking with a single bubble belching from the jar. He set it on the table and put his finger in the corner of his eye.

*"Lord!"* He shook his head. *"Whooh!"* He looked at Charlie glassy-eyed.

"Now! *Whew!* I forgot how bad that stuff tastes . . ." He shook his head again, pointing at the jar. "Just goes to show you . . . it's what you get used to. We all used to drink that stuff and got used to the taste, see, because there was nothing else around."

Granddaddy shook his head again.

"But I think we used to mix that with something—I don't

think we *ever* drank it straight—course we might have and thought it was alright—I just can't remember it tasting that bad."

Charlie was released into the warmth of the comforting night, sitting on the back porch of his own childhood. He could see phantoms of past lives floating by in the lucent evening. He looked at Granddaddy, feeling drowsy familial tides rolling over him.

"So Grandmother was in movies?"

Granddaddy nodded.

"Now, I don't know if she was ever actually in any movies. But she went to California and had a screen test; see, I know that much, and that's because I went out there to get her."

"That's when you drove all the way to California?"

Granddaddy nodded, his starched shirt glowing in the half-light, evening in spaces between the trees.

"Yes sir, reckon I did, and it took me four and a half days to get there, but I did it, see."

Charlie felt the pulsing tempo of a thousand nights in the August gloam.

"You must have really loved her."

Granddaddy turned.

"Reckon I did. Drove out there without a penny to my name. Drove out there not yet twenty years old and didn't know anything beyond the city, see, didn't even have a map because most of the roads weren't in yet! I just pointed that coupe to the sun and drove as fast as I could, drove to bring her back." He relaxed slightly, leaning back into the chair. "Reckon I did love her . . . drove 'til I couldn't see and ran off the road so many times I lost count! If you can call them roads," he murmured. "Lot of times they were just dirt and I was the only car, with just the moon to give me light, see." He sat up in the chair. "Car lights weren't like they are today, they were dim, and would get dimmer a lot of times because you lost water in your battery. But I'd turn the lights off if I could see with the moon and at times it was like day out there in that desert with great, big boulders, bigger than buildings, see, appearing out of nowhere." Granddaddy's hand cut across the night. "In those days, there wasn't anyone to help you so I just kept on going, figuring I couldn't stop or I would be stuck." Granddaddy paused, talking to the darkness, his hand wisping down several times. "I just pull into these ghost towns left over from the mining days and park my car up in the main streets and sleep, because wasn't nobody else there, except maybe some old ghosts. . . ."

Charlie looked down at the mason jar again, dulled to the horrible taste. He slipped the jar up, the warmth washing through him again.

"You better watch yourself, boy."

"Don't worry—" He shook his head, shivering wildly. "I'm not . . ." He swallowed again. "I'm not going to drink any more."

Granddaddy cleared his throat.

"Now! What happened with you and your wife?"

Charlie paused.

"I don't know."

Granddaddy leaned on his elbow, his jaw steadied by his forefinger and thumb.

"Now, it must have been something make you split up, see." Granddaddy shifted in the chair. "Did y'all go out much? Did you take her out dancing?"

Charlie grabbed for a mosquito.

"No."

"Maybe that was it, maybe she wanted to go out dancing, see."

*I didn't take her out dancing and why did I become like I*

*did. She just wanted someone to be with her. I wanted to be a good husband but I couldn't take her out dancing. That's all a woman really wants. Just to go dancing every now and then.*

Granddaddy reached for the mason jar, taking a swallow, setting it down with a small tink.

"Now . . ." He cleared his throat. "A woman will not leave unless she is unhappy, see, or she thinks she's unhappy because people tell her she should be!"

Charlie turned slowly.

"Did you make Grandmother happy?"

Granddaddy stared at him.

"Reckon I did. I did *everything* for her." He came back around, nodding slowly. "She was happy; once upon a time, she was happy."

Charlie shut his eyes to the pulsing in his head. The alcohol, which had been so friendly, was now a demon stirring up the mire and muck of bad feelings. He looked at Granddaddy unsteadily, seeing the small man in the chair staring out at an uncaring vista. He leaned forward, glimmering something he couldn't define.

"What about at the end . . . was she happy at the end, Granddaddy?"

Granddaddy paused.

"She was happy," he murmured, staring into nothing. "She just didn't know it. . . . See, I did *everything* for her."

Charlie turned away, figures parading past him in the phantasmal darkness. He sat with the man of his blood by the road they had marched together not knowing, looking out into the playing night warmth of all years unfelt. Charlie was fighting the pounding again, squeezing out all sensation, hearing his grandfather's single word he wouldn't think of until later, breathed in a deep, mournful sorrow.

*"Everything."*

# CHAPTER TWENTY-NINE

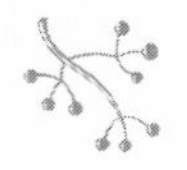

Virginia countryside

*1949*

Austin stared into the aqueous light laying tall shadows of prison bars on the floor, like those in a crazy house. He watched the moon curtains flutter in and could see the glittering wrecks of his life like crystal praying mantises in the high weeds; dead carcasses of fast life pulled in by a wrecker, the parts stripped—only to come alive under a lifeless moon. Austin stared at the open window again with the bars crossing the room in three luminous slashes.

Many times before this he had risen in the night with his wife and daughter sleeping, rising and walking to the window, staring at the contorted, smashed grills and the crazy headlight eyes. The wrecks lay quietly under the broad shadow-play falling across the shingles of his two-story garage. He looked at the wrecks, thinking he was one of them too now. A smashed De Soto, a burned-out Studebaker, a rusting, flipped Hudson. He was one of these lunar wrecks so carefully laid to rest only to shine again when he could see his own destiny out in the sapphire fields of other burned-out machines.

And now he was in the doorway after racing up the steps from the broken lock of the front door. His wife and daughter had left him, completing the picture of the man with the destroyed machines.

He stood in the doorway, seeing the last months in the barred apartment. *"Where are you going?"*

Austin continued tying his shoes, the blood swelling the veins at his temples. He could see the rubbed-off gold flakes from the slippers he bought her so long ago, the slippers smashed flat with holes on the sides. He didn't raise his eyes, keeping his voice steady, giving her nothing to hook on.

"I'm going to work."

He finished and sat up on the edge of the couch, facing a woman with hair unwashed and wild eyes burning queerly, spittle in the corner of her mouth.

"You're leaving me again to go see your whore in town, aren't you!"

He stood up, concentrating on what he was doing.

"You're going to your slut and leaving me locked in this dirty apartment! Why don't you just kill me?"

"Get hold of yourself," he continued in a low voice, looking to the bedroom of his daughter.

Tamara laughed with a short, high shriek.

"Why? She knows what you're doing! She knows you're going off to fuck another woman!"

Austin calmly walked over and grabbed her wrist.

"Get control of yourself, Tamara," he warned.

She glared at him in the stained pink robe.

*"Kill me! Kill me now!* I hate you, you bastard. *Kill me now!"*

He squeezed her wrist harder until she winced—pain a real emotion in the insane. He could see her. She was behind the fuzzed green light. When Austin stood close he could see Tamara in the glaucous web of insanity.

"Calm down. Why don't you take a bath and get yourself cleaned up?"

She smiled perniciously, lips quivering over teeth discolored to black. He didn't understand the physiology of the disease, but it even attacked her teeth.

"Why? So I look good for you when you come back from your whore! Why don't you admit you're going to see her, you coward!"

She spat on him. They stood close together in the center of a sad yellow room, locked in the struggling dance of their weeping Valentine's Day. They stood over the bays that gave everything the slightly sweet scent of a car garage, the dust and disorder of a bachelor apartment evident since Tamara had quit any attempt at cleaning.

"You're crazy—you know that," Austin said in the same low voice. "You're crazy and I'm going to get you some help."

"Crazy, am I! I know the truth! *You're fucking another woman!"*

"You're sick, Tamara, and I'm going to get you help."

"You dirty fucker," she hissed, dropping to her knees in pain, swinging at him feebly.

He felt her soft blows as a velvet hammer on his heart, feeling the rushing warmth of her tragedy. *If she would only be quiet I wouldn't have to do this. If she would only not say these things then at least we could have some sem-*

*blance of a family life. It's not good for a little girl to hear her mother say things like this. It's not good and if she feels pain she will stop.*

He let her go as she tried to bite his hand. Austin scooped up his keys from the kitchen table, crossing the room with his lips pressed into a tight line. He had made another decision, one he had been thinking about for a long time. He paused at the door, seeing his wife huddled on the floor, rubbing her black-and-blue wrist.

"I'm going to talk to your mother and we are going to get you some help."

Then he was getting into his car, her screaming following him from the barred window.

*"Let me out of here, you bastard! Help! Somebody help me! He's keeping me locked up here! You dirty fucker!"*

He started the car, revving it to block out the demented laughter wafting across the empty fields.

"Go on! Go on! Go see your whore!"

He drove directly to her mother's house.

The smoke danced, twirling like a slim white drape, before dissolving. Austin watched the pearl-handled cigarette holder float out of the light, Miz Drake's small lips crinkling around the orange-tipped baton.

Miz Drake inhaled swiftly again.

"So, what do you want me to do?"

Austin stood with hat in hand. He had described the life her daughter had been living. He had been careful not to step on the mines she laid to block him, thinking it was better to describe to the old woman how insane her daughter had become than to defend himself.

"I think we should take her to Tucker's."

Miz Drake's eyes snapped; her entire person was something macabre and beautiful in the hard play of light. She looked at him as if he had struck her.

"Commit her to a mental institution when you are the problem! You'd like that, wouldn't you?"

She was around the desk, knocking papers from the corner, stalking toward him with the determination of a man ready to fight. He could smell decay and tobacco in the warm breath.

"You'd like to say she's crazy! Because then you could have your trollop!"

Austin met the granite eyes.

"She needs help, Miz Drake."

The mouth pulled slightly inward.

"Help getting away from *you*! She tells me how you lock her in that prison when you go to see—"

"It's for her own good. She tries to run into the road," he repeated dully, not telling of the knifes he had removed, the mirrors, glasses, not telling of the night walks around the apartment when he woke to see wild eyes above him.

Miz Drake was picking up her cigarette holder, snapping a flame.

"I'm not going to have any part of putting my daughter in a mental institution."

Austin nodded, putting his hat back on, tugging on the brim.

"Alright. I just wanted to let you know what I intend to do."

He crossed the dark hallway and had his hand on the doorknob when her voice cracked behind him.

*"I'll take my daughter back before I'll let you put her away."*

The voice cracked across the abandoned apartment with the breeze flowing through the window. Austin saw Miz Drake come and tell them to pack their bags and not look back, because she was taking his opportunity away. Austin had agonized over the decision and been out to the hospital talking to doctors, getting their reassurance that they wouldn't just lock her away. He had worked out that he could take her out with him. It was like automobiles. First they would find out what the problem was, then there would be the method for fixing it.

But now Miz Drake had taken back her daughter and his chance to put his family back together.

*"Somebody called tonight."*

Tamara stared, speaking in the saccharine voice more alarming in its sweetness. Austin looked at her in the stained robe, smoking cigarettes she lit one to another. He stopped unlacing his shoes on the couch where he had been sleeping, looking at the closed door where his daughter slept.

"Somebody called tonight and your daughter answered," she continued, her voice sickly sweet with the lipstick smile like a grotesque clown.

The smile quivered on her lips.

"Your precious daughter knows where you go at night."

She laughed in a low voice. He shook his head, continuing to undress.

"I was at work. Go to bed, Tamara."

"At work . . ." She laughed horribly. "You were at work alright!"

The laughter vomited out of her mouth and made him grit his teeth.

"Go to bed, Tamara."

This would be the same as the time she went through his coat pocket, finding touch-up paint and accusing him of having fingernail polish. Or when he came home and found her at the top of the stairs, haranguing him until he slept in his office chair.

"At work . . . that's good," she said smoothly.

Austin turned swiftly. The giddy smoking laughter made him want to backhand her.

"How's it feel to know your own daughter knows you fuck another woman?" She was standing over him with smoke seeping between her teeth. He heard the phone ring again during dinner. Little Tamara answered the phone his wife ignored. He had called many times and Tamara never picked up the line, always his daughter. Austin thought this was another one of her crazy accusations, but then his daughter stared at him in a different way—her eyes uncertain.

Now there was only emptiness. Something slipped across the proud brilliance shining in from the clear sky. Austin watched as the cat he had brought home for little Tamara stopped and sat in a lone square of moonlight, his tail tucked around his paws, meowing in utter loneliness.

Austin woke on the couch with the bar shadows striping his prone body. He washed his face in the sink; the yellow duck with the orange beak still in the soap holder. He kept his mind on what he was doing, dressing in his best suit, pulling out his one unsoiled hat, shining his shoes to a luster.

He hosed down his car, wiping it clean with a soft rag, shining the chrome and glass. Austin set off, driving the speed limit with a constant pressure of his foot. Several times he looked in the mirror, checking his shave, his teeth, the angle of his hat.

He drove into town, parking in front of Miz Drake's home on Monument Avenue. The friendly wide porch was no longer there; the gray-planked veranda was now in need of paint and repair. He walked up the sidewalk, hearing the smart snap of his shoes on the cement. Austin paused as the doorbell rang in the house. He heard his own daughter's fast footsteps come up, then Miz Drake opened the chained door.

Austin smiled, feeling slightly crazy.

"Hello, Miz Drake, I've come to see Tamara," he said, removing his hat.

She looked at the pin-striped suit and the hat years out of style, seeing the begging going on in front of her. Miz Drake's eyes lit in cold, gray triumph.

"All alone now, aren't you? All alone in your pathetic garage with your one nigger in the country."

"Just let me see my family, Miz Drake."

She smiled perniciously.

"They don't want to see *you*." She was back in the shadows behind the door. "You'll be hearing from my attorney tomorrow."

Austin faced the old woman with a half smile frozen on his face like on a mannequin.

"I'd like to see my family."

A strange warmth came into the old face.

"Austin," she said almost kindly. "You don't have a family to see anymore."

The door clicked shut. He was on the outside with the white frilly curtains pulled tight, the steps going back into the echoing hallway.

Austin stood outside the door. He could feel the muscles in his face from the forced smile. He reached for the doorbell when the brass mail slot squeaked open. Austin bent down and saw his daughter's eyes—the clear green of the girl he had fallen in love with.

"Hi, Daddy."

"Hey, sweetie," he said huskily, hunching down, reaching into the slot to hold it open.

"We're going to live with Grandmother again," she whispered, one finger in the slot by his hand.

Austin nodded, staying close to the rectangle of his daughter's face, her warm breath.

"Well, maybe for a time, sweetie, but then we'll all be together again."

She touched his fingers in the mail slot.

"Grandmother says you aren't going to live with us anymore."

Austin shifted his weight, leaning closer, holding on to the small fingers.

"Now, maybe not here, but we'll live somewhere else together, sweetie—"

"*Tamara!* Come away from there!"

She disappeared from the mail slot.

Austin pushed his fingers farther into the slot, pressing his mouth against the cold metal.

"Tamara!"

He could see her walking back into the hallway, holding her grandmother's hand, turning once to her father in the small slot of light. Austin waved, moving one finger, then gradually let the cold brass plate fall into place. He walked slowly down the steps to his car.

Austin drove back to the country in the same measured way he had driven in except he would wipe his hand on his pants leg. By the time he reached the garage his thigh was wet.

# CHAPTER THIRTY

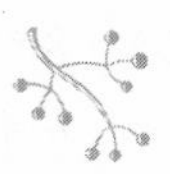

Richmond, Virginia

*August 1998*

Pearl clapped the flame and slipped the lighter under her apron. She kept her eyes on the rabbit, blue smoke elongating like a witch's spell over the cooler air of dusk. The judge was sitting in the parlor with his cigar and her day was over. Pearl rubbed her ankle above the stiff maid shoes, then leaned forward with her hands hanging over her knees.

"Jest you and me," she murmured, staring out into the yard, the cigarette pressed in her lips.

A low rush of cicadas rose out of the shadowy trees and Pearl fingered the nickel-plated .38 in her uniform pocket for the bus ride home to the west side of Richmond. She thought of Minnie in the parlor with the judge.

"She trapped worse than me," she muttered, looking at

the shining eyes of the rabbit, thinking she could see the slight quiver of whisker.

Pearl clamped the cigarette in her mouth again and shook her head tiredly, remembering the first days when she worked for the judge.

"Ain't sleepin' in tha' room no more," she repeated to herself, thinking of the maid's quarters on the third floor.

She touched the hidden pistol and could hear the judge's voice in the heated air like a dog tiredly growling. She rubbed her ankles above the maid shoes again. Her hands drooped over her knees and she sipped the cooling coffee, thinking of the little girl, Madelyn.

"She got to get out someways," she said, rocking slowly, arms folded, the cigarette lodged in her lips.

Pearl stared at the unruffled lawn and saw the maid's room again and the bathroom off the second-floor hallway. The judge's room was across from Minnie's. The judge wore a red-checked robe.

"Judge didn't count on that," she murmured, smoke escaping in small puffs with her hands clenched over her elbows.

The glare of traffic lights fuzzed Charlie's eyes. He noticed the car following him when he turned into downtown Richmond and a white hood flared out of the darkness. Charlie had been thinking of Minnie. He had called three times, and every time, Pearl answered the phone.

"No, no sir, she's not here now, but I tell her you called."

He turned onto a side street and the car closed in. The lull of the white lightning was replaced with short tight thumps under his shirt. Charlie cranked the steering wheel to the left, fast to the right, jamming the brakes. He jumped out as the car skidded short. Charlie whipped the car door open, grabbing the man by his shirt.

"Hey!" The man struggled against Charlie's grip. "You ripped my shirt!"

Sherwood Anders's glasses fell to the street.

"What . . . *you*—"

Charlie let go of his shirt.

"Why were you following me?"

Sherwood Anders glared at him. "You still don't get it," he snapped, trying to piece his shirt together.

"I thought you were the—"

"I'm not!" Sherwood got back in his car and motioned out the window. "Move your car out of the street."

Charlie pulled his car to the side. When he got out Sherwood was limping toward him with a flat envelope. He moved quickly even though his hip and right leg were stiff. He looked at Charlie with flat, dead eyes.

"Rufus John is dead."

"What!" Charlie stared at him. "I just spoke to him—"

"I have a friend in the news bureau . . . they found him shot to death on his front porch—they managed to put the fire out."

Charlie felt as if he had just fallen to the pavement.

"Jesus Christ—"

"Don't open this until I'm gone," Sherwood said, thrusting the yellow envelope into Charlie's hands.

Sherwood limped across the street with one loafer scraping the pavement.

He opened the car door and turned.

"They know who you are."

Charlie stared at him. *"Who?"*

Anders lowered himself into his car and screeched around in the street without looking. Charlie got back in the car and sat with the envelope in his hand. He looked around the deserted street and locked the doors, clawing through the fresh masking tape. A glossy black-and-white photo mirrored light as it slid from the envelope.

Two men leaned against a squad car and faced another man in a suit. The men against the car wore sunglasses, one in a sheriff's uniform, the other a plain white T-shirt. Charlie tilted the picture in the light, and script along the bottom took shape: THE OLD KLAN.

He laid the picture on the seat and looked away twice, then he was sure who the man in the suit was. Charlie drove toward Minnie's house.

*This is what my life will be from now on* is what the parlor clock said to Minnie. She watched her father slowly raise the newspaper into the lamp. The tick resonated across the oriental rug and the polished furniture of Queen Anne. She could smell Pearl's cigarette smoke out the back door of the kitchen. Knocking interrupted the smooth metronome of the clock; the judge's paper fell like a curtain.

Minnie looked up from her book and saw Pearl cross the dark hallway.

"Pearl!"

Minnie heard the door swing back, then Pearl's voice. "Just a minute, I get her." She came into the parlor, her uniform sleeves rolled up, with the red bandanna in her hair.

"Minnie, it's Mistah Charlie—"

"Pearl!"

"That's alright, Daddy," Minnie said, rising from the chair. "I'll get it."

"You'll do no such thing," the judge commanded, rising with the paper.

Minnie and Pearl watched him cross the hallway and Pearl thought of the small rabbit.

• • •

Judge Barrek shut the front door behind him. He paused as if he had forgotten something, then turned around with black eyes under the yellow porch light.

"Minnie will not see you," he said flatly.

Charlie thought the judge might turn and go back in, but he stepped abruptly forward.

"I am going to tell you something else," he continued, backing Charlie into one of the columns. "I don't want to see you near my daughter or my house again," he warned in a low voice. "I don't need Yankee trash down here coming into my home." He took another step, his forefinger and thumb pressed together. "You are lower than a nigger, Mr. Tidewater. I know all about you. If I see you anywhere near my daughter I will have you taken out into the country and strung to a tree with a blowtorch across your back."

Charlie felt his back hit the column.

"Is that what you did to Rufus junior?"

There was a moment of silence, then the judge slapped him with his open hand. The pain flashed across his cheek and Charlie stumbled across the porch. The judge raised his forefinger; a smile played across his lips, his eyes flickering darkly.

"You leave Richmond tonight."

He then calmly crossed the porch. Charlie heard the door lock. The porch light flicked off. He stood in the darkness and could still feel the judge's hand on his face.

*"Psst . . . Mr. Tidewatah!"*

A dark hand willowed against the column. Charlie glanced at the front door and shaded windows.

*"Come hyah!"*

Charlie walked off the porch into the shadows on the side of the house. Cool; leathery fingers grabbed his hand.

"You got to help," Pearl whispered, her teeth glaring in the darkness.

"What—"

"You got to help get Miz Minnie away!"

Charlie shook his head.

"She won't even talk to me."

"Shhh. . . ." Pearl looked around in the darkness like a cat. "She can't—the judge won't let her! He sayin' bad things about you and she don't know who to trust."

Charlie felt the burning on his cheek.

"He just threatened to kill me," he said dully.

She nodded. "He do it too."

Pearl's apron glowed eerily.

"You leave the judge to me. . . . You take Minnie and her daughter away from here 'fore it too late." Pearl looked around again. "I get Minnie to meet you in the park tomorrow at noon. You got to explain yourself then. I can tell you a good man and Minnie trust you, but the judge goin' to try and take that 'cause he don't want to lose her fo' himself." Pearl nodded in the darkness. "But I goin' to get her out. . . . Now go on and be at the park tomorrow."

Charlie hesitated.

"Go on, now! I take care of things."

He nodded, then went down the walk quickly.

Pearl watched him pass through the gate. She fished a half-burned cigarette from her apron, clapping the silver-backed lighter into her pocket. Pearl inhaled deeply and walked back to the kitchen steps. She sat down and looked into the yard, her eyes picking through the darkness. The cigarette flared in the rolling tide of night. Pearl nodded to the still rabbit.

"Jest you an' me."

# CHAPTER THIRTY-ONE

Virginia countryside

*August 1998*

The old man sat on the veranda in the high-backed wicker chair with a dark doorway behind. He kept his hands balanced on the cane, his skin darker in the lunar night.

"You goin' in tonight?"

"Yep," he grunted, putting in the last can of gasoline.

"I declare, they were right on my porch doin' things I can't repeat." He shook his head. "It's a shame for a nice girl like that to get mixed up with trash, I declare it is."

The man grunted again, counting the eight cans in his trunk and lowering it down. He struck light against shadow and inhaled deeply.

"I think the judge is plenty mad and wants that boy strung . . . he goin' to end up like his mama, I declare he is."

The man smoked against the car and watched the fields change hue as a breeze picked at his T-shirt.

"Don't make me no money, Jack."

The old man smiled, skull-white hair in darkness.

"Oh, the judge pays."

He looked at the old man in front of the dilapidated house. He laughed under his breath, then spat into the weedy drive.

"They goin' tear this old house down," the man nodded.

The old man's mouth moved.

"Well, now, I declare, is that a fact?"

He stared at him and shook his head.

"Now, why don't you go in the cellar and get you one of the robes."

He flicked his cigarette into the overgrown drive.

"You keep those musty old things," he muttered, ducking into his car, revving the engine, scattering gravel.

The old man sat with the gravel dust hanging fire in the twilight, the whine of the car fading. The snare of gravel became horses and he wondered if it was the Yankees coming finally. He could hear the troops marching toward him, the flags flying boldly in the setting sun and dust rising far back into the valley from the invading horde of uniforms lined row by blue row. They would see him sitting on his plantation; the last master of land and slave, the South's glorious moment of recognition at hand before it faded forever. He watched the troops come and could hear the fifes and marching drums, the steady precision of timed steps, turning the long drive, coming, finally coming.

"Well now, I declare," he whispered, keeping his hands perfectly still on the cane.

Charlie had a vague memory of opening his eyes in the snowy half-light of his room with the vaporous scent of gasoline in the air. He heard air rushing through a funnel, then his room lit yellow and the magnolia tree on the front lawn was sprouting flames. He ran to the window and saw Granddaddy in his white shirt turn the corner of the house, vanishing like a white caboose. Charlie went out the door and thought the earth was on fire. Flames leaped for the sky, the heat on his skin like scalding paint. He fell back from the cross of fire in the grass.

Granddaddy crossed the lawn with his garden hose and turned the brass nozzle on. He sprayed the fire, one hand in his shorts pocket, as if he were watering tomatoes. Charlie stumbled, the flames hot on his stomach and chest. He followed the six-foot-wide black line left by the retreating fire and suddenly the gas was burned and only the magnolia tree flamed. Granddaddy directed his spray into the branches, sizzling steamy white ghosts.

"Who . . ." Charlie shielded his face. *"Granddaddy?"*

He continued spraying the fire with his hand in his pocket.

"Reckon someone wants to set fire to my lawn."

They both heard the sirens. The fire truck turned onto their street, its syrupy scream wavering near, then far; red-and-blue swirls exploded around them. Granddaddy finished spraying the tree, then directed his spray back onto the smoldering lawn. The black, steaming cross ran twenty feet in both directions.

A large-jowled man crossed the yard, FIRE CHIEF scorched and burned on the front of his helmet.

"Looks like you had a little yard fire."

"Reckon I did." Granddaddy nodded, the hose in his right hand.

The fire chief nodded too, puckering his lips while firemen sprayed the grass with blasts of $CO_2$. He turned to Granddaddy.

"What do you think of this?"

Granddaddy continued his steady spraying.

"Reckon it's just some kids playin' a joke."

The fire chief scratched his creased and bruised cheek, staring at the smoldering cross.

"Now, I can get the police for you."

Granddaddy shook his head, bobbing slightly.

"No, there's no need for that."

The chief took off his helmet and ran his hand through gray matted hair.

"Well, this kind of thing—"

"Uh-huh, that's right." Granddaddy nodded. "Some kids, I reckon."

The chief paused, then put his helmet back on. He shook his head slowly.

"Old enough to know what you want, but I—"

"Reckon so," Granddaddy murmured, hose by his side.

The chief paused, then motioned his men back to the truck. The truck hissed twice, backed into the drive, and dieseled away. There was just the *whoosh* of the water, then Granddaddy turned off the nozzle. Charlie and Granddaddy stood in the uneven patter of water falling from the burned branches; a smoky cross rising like steam from a wet field.

*Charlie Tidewater*
*465 Marilee Road*
*Southampton, VA*
*August 28, morning*

*Matthew,*

*Someone burned a cross on Granddaddy's lawn last night. I woke to flames licking the sky from the lawn. Granddaddy wouldn't talk about it and knows more than he's saying but he's determined to take it to the grave. I haven't written you about this, but he's very ill. He's gotten up every morning at eight A.M. and this morning he was too weak to get out of bed. In the same breath he tells me not to call the doctor. Later he came into the kitchen in a checked bathrobe and stared out the window into the backyard. "Now, the yard still needs raking," he murmured, then looked me dead in the eye. "But you can't finish everything."*

*Minnie won't see me anymore. Her father (the judge) found out about my past (drinking and unemployment—I suppose) and threatened to kill me if I saw her again. He's scared and he's lied to Minnie. She's trapped down here in a way hard to understand, but he has her and he won't let her go. The boundaries down here for southern women are brutal. I'm scared, but I've been alone since that day I woke with my mother gone. I want to find out what they did to her.*

*Charlie*

# CHAPTER THIRTY-TWO

Southampton, Virginia

*August 1998*

The white note fluttered in the morning light against the coal of the car hood. Charlie walked toward the paper the way a person might approach an unknown dog. The folded sheet strained under the windshield wiper. It was coarse, like the construction paper he had drawn on as a child. Charlie lifted the wiper slowly, sliding the paper out.

He opened the single fold and stared at the crude drawings. On the bottom was a square marked GARAGE, then a line went toward squiggly marks with FOREST under it. The line took a sharp left and ended in the center of three circles with an *X*. MIDNIGHT was under the *X*.

Charlie put the paper in his pocket, then turned to the burned lawn. The charcoal cross lay in shadow. The magnolia was a blackened skeleton. Charlie looked again at the cross; he couldn't escape the feeling it was getting larger.

Noon fell upon Richmond and Charlie walked under the trellis of trees. Black women passed him, pushing strollers slowly. Old men sat around a fountain in the center of the park. Charlie sat down on a wrought-iron bench.

He had wanted Minnie last night as he lay in the scent of oily, burned grass. Sleep had come only after he went to the sideboard and drank the scotch. Only then did the gasoline leave his nostrils.

Charlie had hoped in leaving the North he could remake himself as people do in movies. But when Judge Barrek presented his faults like so many bones on a plate he couldn't defend himself. She had finally answered the phone. *"I can't see you anymore, you lied to me. . . . I can't go through that again. . . ."* She hung up then, and what could he have said anyway? There was no defense, really.

Charlie saw Pearl, wearing the gray-and-white uniform of the other maids, guiding a blue stroller. Minnie walked beside her with eyes straight ahead. When he waved only Pearl nodded. She turned to the right and he fell in step with Minnie as if they were spies.

"I only came because Pearl would not leave me alone," she murmured, her hair braided and tied with a bow of gold.

Charlie jammed his hands in his pockets. His long pants were warm and his polo shirt was damp.

"You lied to me and I have had enough of that for a lifetime," said Minnie.

"I didn't tell you everything."

"That's an understatement."

Charlie kept his slow pace.

"I had a life that fell apart, Minnie."

"Apparently," she murmured.

Charlie tried to find a path. He paused, feeling the brash sunlight in his eyes. "Minnie, something has been chasing me my whole life and it destroyed my marriage, my career, and it's slowly destroying me."

She looked at him. A cloud, small and puffy, played through her eyes.

"It's what I'm closing in on here, Minnie," he continued, walking slower. "I have been plagued my whole life by things that were not right. I have to know why I was abandoned . . . why my mother was sick. Why my father was nonexistent . . . When I find out what happened to my mother—what happened to *me*—then I can finally walk away from it."

Minnie's expression changed slowly until the set of her mouth came to a neutral place.

"I was married to a man who would come home drunk and beat me blue," she said briskly. "When I finally left him I swore I would never let that happen again."

Charlie nodded slowly. "I can't deny the past, Minnie, I could explain it all away . . . but it doesn't matter—that was all when I was trying to get away from this thing that has been haunting me—"

"And what do you want me to do . . . *wait*? Daddy would kill me or you if he knew I was seeing you again."

Charlie stopped.

"I want to show you something." He reached into his pocket. "This was on my car this morning."

Minnie's brow darkened with the paper reflecting sun on her face. She looked up.

"You aren't going out there?"

He nodded. "They shot Rufus John to death on his porch, and then, last night, they burned a cross on my grandfather's lawn, Minnie."

Minnie's eyes became small round circles.

"Who is doing all this?"

Charlie paused. "Maybe you should ask your father."

She stared at him, then thrust the paper into his hands.

"Oh, don't be *ridiculous*! Daddy doesn't have anything to do with your mother."

Charlie looked away, squinting into the noon sun. "He threatened to kill me if I didn't leave Richmond, Minnie. There's something he's hiding . . . something he's afraid I'm going to find."

Pearl was circling around the fountain with the carriage. Charlie took Minnie's hand.

"Maybe we both can get free, Minnie."

Pearl was behind them; Charlie saw a man with sunglasses watching them.

"Here's my pager number," he said, pressing an old business card into her hand.

"You're going by yourself?"

Charlie turned around, looking for the man, who had left the bench.

"It's my last chance, Minnie . . . call me."

Charlie turned and walked through the park hurriedly, glancing back toward the man he could no longer see.

Granddaddy didn't smile, but felt his muscles pulling until the pain made him grimace. He stood in the sharp light, pausing from his raking, feeling the early snap that started him thinking about the winter he wouldn't see. Gripping the rake tightly, his knuckles whitening, Granddaddy looked up at the sound of Charlie's car.

*I will see this pain down. I will not cry or beg to this pain. They can burn me up when it is done, but not until I decide it is time will I let the pain engulf me and give myself over. I have endured harder times than this, more pain than this. This will have to wait longer, a little longer before I will acknowledge living is more painful than dying. Not yet, not just yet.*

He watched his grandson and thought of the phone call that had gotten him into the yard. The old doctor's voice was rough.

*"I knew this would happen . . . I knew I should never have done it! I lie awake at night and think of that girl . . . and now I'm about to meet my maker, Austin—I told your grandson I didn't know what he was talking about . . . that I never had a patient by that name . . . but he knows! He must have seen the certificate and it's only a matter of time . . ."*

That was when he had left his bed; even with the pain he was too agitated to lie still. He stood with his rake as his grandson approached.

"Now! You just can't leave things alone, can you, boy?"

Charlie walked up, forgetting the conversation with Minnie, focusing on the pale blue eyes.

"You come down from Chicago. Got no more sense about things here than you did when you was nine, see, and now you go around *botherin'* people about things that don't matter no more."

Charlie stared at him.

"Who got to you, Granddaddy?"

He shook his head.

"Now, it don't matter. See, point is you interferin' with people's lives now and you don't understand what you doin'." Granddaddy pointed at him with a thick finger.

"You just messin' with things you don't understand, see."

"What about the people who interfered with *my life*, Granddaddy?"

Granddaddy swatted his words away.

"You talkin' about things that can't be changed! It don't

make a difference to your life now because you can't change the past, and you keep thinkin' you goin' to change your past by—"

*"I need to know what happened!"*

Charlie felt a swelling emotion, a realization he was the only one who really cared. The old face changed to the sour man of strictness. A line across his forehead creased deeply with the brow's descent.

"I don't know what you talkin' about."

Charlie pulled the greasy envelope of money from his pocket.

"I'm talking about this!"

Granddaddy's eyes darted to the envelope. He shook his head slowly.

"You just a fool—"

He threw the envelope on the ground; it landed at Granddaddy's feet.

"Who are you paying off, Granddaddy?"

"You talkin' crazy, boy."

Charlie took a step forward.

"How about the fucking cross in your lawn, Granddaddy? Is that talkin' crazy?"

Granddaddy turned away.

"You just plum gone crazy, boy."

Charlie stepped in front of him.

"You think you're going to seal the door to the past . . ." Charlie felt the tightness in the top of his throat suffocating him. "But Granddaddy . . ." He fought to steady his voice. "I'm . . . I'm going to find out . . ." He swallowed again, his voice shaking, feeling wave after wave of pent-up emotion, managing only a hoarse whisper. "I'm going to find out what you did . . . *—what you did to Mom.*"

Then he was walking away. Charlie saw the blue-gray

trash can against the house. The metal top was on the cylinder of Granddaddy's rakings, sticks, bits of trash. Charlie paused, winging back with a football kick, exploding the can off the blacktop with the contents splaying out in a rolling scatter. The top rolled like a runaway manhole cover, both can and top coming to a ringing close.

Granddaddy heard the car squeal down the street and watched the small cloud of dust and tire smoke drift. He could see grass clippings blowing back to the lawn, the trash can on its side. Granddaddy reached down and picked up the envelope of money. He stopped and grabbed his side, dropping the rake. Granddaddy limped toward the house holding his abdomen, passing the trash and leaves swirling around in the wind. He stooped to pick up a folded piece of paper from the drive.

Granddaddy went into his bedroom and lay down in the afternoon light. The pain was so acute he looked for blood. He remained still, waiting for the burning knot to subside. He breathed slower, steadier, calming down. *This is not to be it. Not yet, not just yet.* He watched the dust gossamers float slowly to earth, thinking of his grandson, seeing the glassy eyes so much like his daughter's. Granddaddy held the piece of paper to his face, then dropped the crude map as the world quietly darkened.

# CHAPTER THIRTY-THREE

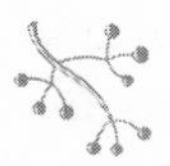

Virginia countryside

*1959*

The highway whispered through the countryside of broad leaf tobacco plants like a vine weaving through a ruffled lawn, a blanket of wet heat hung in slow suspension over the crouched tree line, causing Snowball to squint to see the stick men he knew were television towers in the distance. He shaded his eyes the way men stare down railroad tracks.

A hurtling black dot changed to flashing chrome. The car windshield blazed with reflected sun, slowing in its side passage, but not really slowing at all because it immediately flashed back to a bloated dark hump before dropping from view.

Snowball took a step from the shoulder of the highway. The gravel clicked underfoot as he passed globes half full of gas. He knew Austin kept the old pumps because he didn't have the money to replace them, just as, many times, he didn't have the money to fill the tanks beneath. He walked with the long strides of his purpose, turning over a dead spark plug in one coverall pocket, grasping a screwdriver in the other.

He moved into the slightly cooler shade, passing the OPEN sign in the right corner of the front window; a tin Coca-Cola sign hung between door and garage. He heard the hinge. The metal-on-metal grind bothered him most. The hinge was louder—a steady, rhythmic squeak with the grit of road dust between round surfaces. Snowball glanced to the yellow, rust-pocked Pennzoil sign swinging above the open door.

"Thought they was stoppin', Mr. Turin."

Austin sat in the tan office chair missing the left armrest. He sat with his right arm up and his legs crossed, and could easily have been in front of a checkerboard, contemplating his next move. Snowball settled into the office chair on the other side of the door.

Austin kept his somber expression: the light from the fields burning gas blue in his eyes. He turned and looked at the man who had been his mechanic and friend for over thirty years, pursing his lips slightly, letting Snowball know he was going to speak.

"They opened a filling station just outside of Louisy—reckon people get gas there before comin' out to the country," he said, running a hand over his smooth head, still keeping his legs crossed and the patient, waiting demeanor of a man studying a checkerboard.

Snowball leaned back in the chair against the side of the building, his fingers hanging over the arms, slowly stretching his legs out.

"Ain't had no repairs now fo' three weeks, Mr. Turin. And

seems to me people comin' down this old road less and less. Good thing you workin' in the city, 'cause I don't know how we make it out hyah. Last car you sold was to that Rufus junior and I know you gave him a low price and didn't make no money on it. How come you didn't sell it fo' more, Mr. Turin? I know you could have sold it whole lot more to someone else."

Austin scratched his neck above the bow tie he had started to wear since becoming Mr. Fredericks's personal assistant years before.

"I've known Rufus John and his family for thirty years, and I knew his son needed a car to work, and I figured he didn't have the money to get one. So, I reckon it was good business practice to let him have that one and maybe he'll bring in other people. He and Tamara have been good friends since they were children and he has good character, see."

"You gave him *payments,* Mr. Turin!"

Austin nodded slowly.

"I know Rufus junior is good for the money, like I said, I been knowing his family all these years and he is a boy with great talent . . . whole lot more than his daddy, and what's more, he has a brain, see," he continued, touching his temple.

Snowball palmed his grizzled head, feeling the nappy wool crowning his smooth palate by his ears. He stared at Austin, considering for a long moment, thinking to himself *what people don't know won't hurt them.* Resigning himself with a weary shake of his head.

"Mr. Turin, you know ain't no country nigger goin' to get no bank to give him money for a car. If it weren't fo' you he ain't goin' have no car and that's a fact!"

Austin's hands rested in his lap, his thumbs circling. He

sat and contemplated his next move in the knowledge one moment will be much like the next.

"Now, I'm betting on Rufus junior's future, see, you have to look to the future, always look to the future."

"We have to get some repairs, Mr. Turin. I ain't worked on no cars for weeks," he grumbled.

Austin nodded. "These new cars don't break down as often."

Snowball squinted past the road, seeing the sagging roof of a weathered-gray house. He had the complete change of mood that follows with nostalgia.

"Time sho' is flyin' now, Mr. Turin—I 'member the people who used to live in that old house over there. You 'member them when they moved in? I can't believe we been out hyah all those years, no sir, I can't hardly believe it!"

The Pennzoil sign squeaked in the breeze felt by neither man. Austin looked at the early-century house of weathered boarding, the bowed roof threatening to collapse in on itself.

"That was Mr. Hixon and his family in that house. His daughter used to come over and play with Tamara."

Snowball ran his tongue over his smooth back gums.

"How yo' daughter doin', Mr. Turin?"

"She's good," he murmured, remembering Tamara years before among the blond schoolgirls.

He had been waiting for her to come out of the elementary school for a half hour.

"Hey, sweetie," he called, then hugged the pink-smelling girl clutching her school papers.

"Hi, Daddy!"

"I've come to give you a ride home, sweetie."

She stepped back, small butterflies drawn together.

"Grandma says you were bad to Mommy. And I shouldn't talk to you *any more*."

Austin missed a step, finding it again as he opened the car door.

"I'm sure your grandmother didn't mean—that."

Tamara jumped into the car seat with sun leaping from one blond curl to another as he wheeled around in the street. She shook her head in the taunt of a small girl.

"Grandmother said I should never, ever talk to you again because you were mean to Mommy," she said faintly, a lost nursery rhyme infecting her voice.

Again Austin lost a step, arranging emotions for his daughter while he drove past mothers herding daughters.

"Now, sometimes, Tamara—grown-ups can't work out their problems and so they have to stay apart." He raised his hand. "Your mother . . . your mother has been sick for a long time and I wanted to help her, see," he continued, a timbre of panic entering his voice.

Tamara shook her head, blond curls flying in the car wind with her nose tipped slightly up.

"*Uh-uhnnnn* . . . Grandma says Mommy was fine. But you were mean to her and locked us in the house with bars. She said you made Mommy crazy and I should *never* talk to you again!"

The melodic tone of her voice was replete with child inflection imitating a parent's scolding. Austin turned the car down Monument Avenue, feeling a prickly line of sweat on his upper lip.

"Your grandmother doesn't really understand what's wrong with Mommy," he began, his voice dipping to real emotion. "Mommy is sick. She has been sick for a long time and it is nobody's fault, Tamara. I didn't make her sick. It just happened. . . . Sometimes bad things happen for no reason at all and we don't know why. But your grandmother would like to think it was me, because it's easier to have someone to blame."

Tamara shook her head in simple contradiction, eyes welling with the small fists on her cheeks.

"*Uh-uhnnnn* . . . Mommy says you left us too! She says you were bad and spent your time with another mommy."

"That's not true, Tamara!"

He said it too fast, losing the patriarchal position he had hoped to speak from.

*"Uh-uhnnnnn . . . That's not what the lady on the phone said . . ."*

Austin turned electrically, pulling to the curb in front of Miz Drake's house, hitting the brakes so hard he had to hold her from hitting the dashboard. He stared frantically, feeling the urge to shake her, to chastise her for slapping him so deftly. *That's not what the lady on the phone said!*

"What lady on the phone, Tamara?"

The eyes of his wife, blinking in defiance with the shaking head. *How's it feel to know your daughter knows you fuck another woman?*

"Mommy said not to say anything about the lady to anybody! She said it was a secret and I could *never ever* tell anybody," Tamara repeated, tears in the twin glass windows, brushed away by a small fist with school papers.

*What lady? What lady? What lady?*

"I want to go in, Daddy . . . I want to go in!"

The shaking sob of emotions peeling across her face was too much. Austin put himself aside and got out of the car mechanically. He felt like a man walking on the bottom of a pool. He wished sincerely he could die right there, opening the car door for the little girl of his daughter. He brushed the tears away from the smooth cheeks and bent down to one knee.

"Give Daddy a hug, Tamara."

The small hands were around his neck, the close breath in his ear.

"I love you, sweetie . . ." His voice caught as he understood the forces allied against him. "Take care of your mother."

Then the small steps were running down the sidewalk of the row houses, running up the steps to the porch, dissolving into the gray boarded house he was staring at now.

Austin leaned back in the chair against the wall of the garage.

"*Yas suh!* She look jest like Miz Turin look when she that age," Snowball wheedled, his raspy voice rolling on in Austin's ear. "Jest like her, don't you think, Mr. Turin?"

Austin nodded slowly, watching the soundless wind kick dust across the sparkling two-lane outside the garage, seeing another highway shimmer through his life years before. Years earlier he had become Mr. Fredericks's personal assistant and was driving Mr. Fredericks's black Lincoln Continental on the highway to Florida. Cigar smoke rolled over his shoulder.

"Now, didn't your daughter just win the pageant?"

Austin glanced into the mirror of the leather interior of the Lincoln. He was driving nine hundred miles to the sunny climate of his employer.

"Yes, sir. She sure did, just like her mother did before her."

Mr. Fredericks nodded with the Parkinson's shake Austin had first noticed when he sat in his office three years before. Austin had sat down in the leather-backed chair of the large office with the cars lined on shelves behind the mahogany desk. There was a model sent to Mr. Fredericks for every new car that came out. The cars were fully detailed right down to the engine. The automobile manufacturers wanted to keep the man with dealerships from Virginia to Florida happy.

Mr. Fredericks had called Austin to his office on a sunny

afternoon with a lot full of customers. He sat back, his jowly face hidden by the oversized cigar he lit several times, then shakily put down in a saffron-colored ashtray.

"Now," he began, looking at the middle-aged man across from him. "You been selling cars a long time, Austin, and I'd say you were about the best damn salesman I ever had." He picked up the dirigible again, licking the brown paper, just missing the burnt end with his tongue. "But I have to start to let some of these young fellas out there sow their oats."

Austin sat up straight.

"Yes sir. I been in a slump, but I—"

Mr. Fredericks waved him silent.

"I'm not worried about you, Austin! You been in this business too long not to know what you doin'. But I need a personal assistant now—someone to help Mrs. Fredericks and me now that we gettin' on in our years."

Austin sat back in the chair, fingering the key to a car he was going to show that afternoon.

"Now, I appreciate that, Mr. Fredericks—I surely do, but I love to sell automobiles and—"

Mr. Fredericks waved him silent again.

"How old you, Austin?"

He looked down at the modern indoor-outdoor carpeting.

"Forty-five."

The wildly shaking hand floated back up with the cigar.

"And you still livin' out there in the country above that old repair shop you run with that colored fella?"

Austin kept his eyes down on the keys with the bright tag.

"Yes sir."

Mr. Fredericks's jaw shook with the tremor, the cigar fumbled from his fingers, lying on the desk like a thin piece of dung. He rolled it to the trash can with his fingertips.

"You need some security, Austin. And I got too many

young bucks who want to sell these automobiles. It's a young man's business now! These fast cars are for the young people and I need people that speak their language."

Mr. Fredericks picked up another cigar from the bright colored box.

"You can still sell out of yo' place in the country . . ."

Austin sat facing the old man. He held the key to the new car, squeezed it once, then slowly laid it on the desk.

Austin cleared his mind, concentrating on his driving again. He noticed the gradual change of light that came as they entered Florida. Mr. Fredericks lit the cigar in a glaucous web of blue smoke.

"*Yes suh!* Your daughter is a pretty thing—" Rolling blue smoke wafted over Austin's shoulder as he drove down the familiar highway to Mr. Fredericks's vacation home. "Now, you don't see her much, do you?"

"She's right busy, Mr. Fredericks," he answered, thinking of the road in front of his mother-in-law's house as he dropped off the support check years before.

Austin had pulled the car up to his daughter, amazed at the transformation of girl to woman in the body of a teenager.

"How's your mother?"

Tamara took the envelope of money. At seventeen she was the image of his own love so many years before.

"She's worse," she replied in the fierce heat wavering up from the street.

"Grandma had me sign a paper consenting to those shock treatments again—she gets better, but she doesn't remember a thing."

Austin looked at his daughter in her jeans and loafers. She ran her hand through the same shining blond hair of her mother, her emerald gaze steady.

"Why didn't she sign it?"

Tamara shrugged in teenager nonchalance.

"Guess she doesn't want to be responsible if anything happens."

Austin squinted into the sun, his daughter standing off from the car in the same way of years past when he dropped off the support money. Miz Drake's business had dried up and bad investments had wiped the old lady out. He looked at his daughter holding the envelope of greasy bills.

"Well, I better be getting back—Mr. Fredericks has an appointment—I'll see you next month."

His daughter waved, still chewing the gum she smacked loudly. He drove off from the business between father and daughter.

Austin concentrated on the highway again in Mr. Fredericks's car, breathing the cigar smoke of his employer.

"Now, I hope y'all received that bouquet I sent to your mother's funeral!"

Austin nodded, tapping the steering wheel.

"Yes sir, Mr. Fredericks, and that was mighty nice of you."

"I knew your mother all my life—a more refined woman I did not know—much too good for that pappy of yours! Now, whatever happened to him?"

Austin cocked his head.

"Reckon he's dead—I went out to his place in the country some years back and it was empty. The last the country people heard of him was that he had gone west looking for gold."

Mr. Fredericks shook his head.

"He lived in a shack, didn't he?"

"Yes sir—a log cabin he built with his own hands. I remember going out there as a boy. He would cook great big biscuits for me on a wood stove—he was a tremendous cook and—"

"He deserted a good woman, is what he did!"

Austin nodded. He kept his eyes on the running lines of the highway, driving much like breathing.

"Yes sir—he didn't like the city."

"Didn't like to work!"

"Yes sir, I reckon he didn't," Austin murmured, keeping his eyes on the empty highway with the memory fading to the empty sun-blanched field across from the garage.

Austin heard Snowball's chair squeak back against the building, his arms crossed, his breathing louder, presaging the coming sleep. He looked off into the afternoon light slowing down life to the evening vale. Austin knew the cars were becoming fewer and fewer on his highway and soon there wouldn't be any. He stared across the yellow fields of the country, seeing a small group of people huddled under a tree. Just like a funeral he thought as he closed his eyes.

The dimming twilight surprised Charlie as he lurched out of the tavern, squinting as if it were a clear day in July instead of the ruddy, pink brimming sky of late August.

He struggled drunkenly down the sidewalk, past his own ancestors who walked the streets years before.

*"How is she?"*

*Granddaddy looked at Charlie's father in the fetid wrenching heat of 1967, the hard glass of curbed emotion tight in his voice.*

*"Not good," his father said, head toward the ground. "They found her walking the highway in the country again near that old garage y'all lived in . . ."*

*Grandaddy nodded, his hard eyes small in the Virginia sun.*

*"Now, you let me know if she improves . . . same thing happened to her mother . . ."*

*Charlie's father nodded quickly.*

*"I will." He leaned down. "I'll see you in a couple of days," he said, the heat swallowing him as he walked away.*

Charlie stopped, grabbing on to the hard iron railing, steadying himself against the whiskey urging him to lie down in the cool grass. He could smell wet earth and iron against his nose. The night ran on above him, a great rushing bowl of figures.

He struggled up from the roses in front of Minnie's house. He had made it to the wrought-iron fence, clasping the iron bars, the sidewalk warm under him. He stumbled along the fence until the light parted around the Grecian columns. The porch was in deep shadow, but he saw the dress between the columns.

Charlie opened the gate, swinging with it momentarily. He stood up again, passing through the light near the birdbath.

He paused resolutely, the moment flooding over. He felt the loneliness, the utter grayness of existence. Nobody cared what happened to him.

Minnie stood up from the swing, glittering eyes upon him. Again, the moment engulfed him, knocking him over in what was so obvious. Charlie saw her clearly. *These belles were not to be sullied, but indulged. Their men spent lives supporting their world, becoming their world. Great loves fettered into the hot blowing wind of a thousand dying evenings, leaving brittle reminders and broken people of an age long passed.*

Charlie rested against a column.

"Hello . . . Minnie."

The white dress flowed out from her small waist.

"You didn't call."

Minnie slipped across the porch, peeking into the door.

"*Shhhhh!* Daddy will hear," she whispered, leading him down the steps and through the gate.

"Are you still going out there tonight?"

"—of course."

At times, Charlie careened ahead of Minnie. Her elfin figure glided next to him, the apparition of another time, or was *he* of another time? He stared at her, feeling he was looking at drawn blinds, sunlight bursting between the slats, blindness promised to anyone who dared pull the shutters open.

"How's your daughter?"

"Oh, she's fine."

They passed the yellow lit windows of a home, both feeling the hearth glow of family. Home and sanctity. Mother and daughter, father and son. The tousled hair of sleeping children. They both felt the strong rush of dreams deferred and shattered, dreams as powerful as the desire to breathe.

"If she's beautiful as her mother—"

Minnie turned in, breathing the quiet of their close bond. Trees became sepulchral, branches snaking against the lit sky above.

"Do you think I'm beautiful?" she asked. "Do you think I'm beautiful, Charlie Tidewater?"

He could see her now. She was trapped and he was the unknown traveler. Minnie wanted him now because she would never leave. He had mistaken love for sustenance. She would never get beyond her father. It had all been an act for the Yankee who was good enough to fuck, but never marry. He would take what he could.

He turned in to her, in toward the small mouth and slanting eyes he had desired the moment he saw her. Charlie kissed her under the moon lighting the city on the hills, lying pale gold on the James River rolling off across the leftover country. Charlie kissed the woman as they sank to the grass.

They came apart with Minnie breathing hard. He could feel the dampness on his knees and against the back of his hands, her hair running wild. He could feel the grass matted under them, could smell the darkly rich earth more pungent, more like the musky smell of sex in a closed bedroom. Her mouth burned his ear, his neck, traveling down to his chest, whispering hotly, the ravaged lady, tearing both at her own clothes and his.

Charlie could see everything with amazing clarity. The spidery milk light fell through the trees around them in wild curvations. He was on his knees above her, towering and dark to the woman waiting while he moved through the slowed motion of time. Her dress was up, the perfect white form in the dark grass pulled him down to her in the warm-whispering past, pulling on him until he could smell steam and soap.

"He began to cry."

"It's alright, Charlie . . . it happens." Charlie was on his knees, staring at Minnie as she lay there, the ground spinning, rocking. *His father came in as he lay in the gray tub water, his little-boy's body shivering and thin. His father striding through the bathroom, angry, pointing and shouting at his mother, as she repeated over and over, "It's not clean enough." The bubbles were all gone. The water was cold. "How long has he been in the tub?" he shouted, reaching for Charlie.*

*"But it's not clean enough—he has to stay in longer—"*

*"Tamara. Go take your medicine," his father said. He cradled his son, murmuring. "It's alright, Charlie . . . it's alright."*

The same bewilderment in the damp-wet yard.

"It's alright, Charlie . . ."

Then he was running. He was running through the fantastic streets, passing though the blue-lit night of his own predacious past. Charlie was soaked by the time he reached his car. He was being watched by a thousand glittering eyes, a thousand reflecting eyes waiting for him. He threw the car into gear, spinning around on the slicked street, driving toward the waiting garage.

# CHAPTER THIRTY-FOUR

Virginia countryside

*1998*

Pearl knew the judge was waiting. He was waiting with the paper under the amber lamp light like a patient Buddha. She had seen him mash his cigar and knock the bench into the piano with the keys spilling song like something sloshed on the air. The judge turned toward the door, then crossed back to the chair.

Pearl tapped the cigarette with her forefinger like a carpenter weary with work. She sat with the faintest glow of atmospheric play in the tops of the trees—the earth simmering down after too much heat. Minnie and the judge had been fighting all day and she knew something was at hand. The darkness at least dropped a cloak on their sad play.

She crossed her arms over her lap, wiggling her toe inside

the maid shoes the judge had insisted she wear for the last thirty years. She had to look all over town for them, because the brown oxford shoe with the heel had gone the way of the DeSoto or the Studebaker. But the judge wanted all things to stay the same—even her shoes. Pearl clapped her lighter shut and heard the quick steps on the stairs, then the screen door slammed.

"Where have you been?"

Pearl leaned slightly toward the open door.

"—I went for a walk."

Minnie was standing in the foyer.

"With whom?"

Pearl touched the cigarette to her lips, waiting before she inhaled.

"By myself."

Pearl admired the attempt. There was the pause, the floorboards creaking and she knew the judge was crossing the room.

"You—whore."

Pearl nodded, inhaling the pinwheel just beyond her lips. She expected that. The judge would go for the gut, then shuck the innards. He said it without rancor or a raising of the voice. The judge said it as fact. She was staring at him with those pretty green eyes catching the lamp light. They were in shadow; the judge didn't like overhead lights.

"Don't you touch me, you bastard!"

Pearl froze, her cigarette in midair halfway between her mouth and her knee, with the ember a beacon in darkness. She waited. The sound was sharp and she heard Minnie fall.

"Tell me *whore*—where did he go?"

He was standing over her now with his hand raised up to strike again. Pearl had seen the judge backhand Minnie once before, knocking her across the room. The cigarette stayed where it was. Pearl kept her eyes on the rimming shrubs sparking a firefly every now and then.

"Don't you touch me again, you son of a bitch!"

Pearl blinked, cocking her head back against the screen. She hoped the judge wouldn't kill her. The short harsh sound was followed by the clatter of wood on wood, then a shrill bell. Pearl knew Minnie had crashed into the telephone table in the hall. She dropped the cigarette to the sidewalk below.

*"You tell me where he went!"*

Pearl reached under her apron and brought out the nickel-plated .38. If she killed the judge she would be killing herself. She made the decision the way she had years before.

"Judge only understands one thing," she murmured, hearing his steps coming up the stairs to the third floor. "One thing," she repeated, turning to the screen door with the gun down by her side.

"TELL ME!"

Minnie was crying and Pearl waited with her hand on the screen door, her head down, one finger on the trigger. The short harsh sound was followed by a chair clattering to the floor. Pearl pulled the screen door open, silently stepping inside, the gun reflecting night.

"You little bitch . . . you tell me now!"

". . . he went . . ." Minnie whimpered. ". . . that garage . . ."

Pearl heard the judge's footsteps crossing the room and Minnie moaning from the floor. The phone dinged again and then she heard his voice low and ominous.

Pearl slipped the gun back into her pocket under her apron, stepping outside. She fished out a cigarette, clapping the silver lighter open. Minnie's footsteps were going up the stairs. Pearl inhaled deeply. She would take her up some coffee after the judge calmed down. Pearl leaned against the doorframe. She felt the weight of the gun and thought of the judge walking toward her bed. Her eyes moved out into the unwavering darkness. She fingered the gun again.

"I give her somethin' else."

The moon was behind the clouds like a back-lighted cluster of cotton. Charlie held his tire iron, watching the clouds drift off above the pines. The field offered up glittering chrome and twisted metal. He felt once again for the lost map, deciding he didn't need it as he stared at the clump of trees.

He carried the tire iron like a rifle, both hands ready to swing at whoever would spring from the swishing grass. Charlie smelled the early dew and felt the cool damp on his ankles. He stopped several times with only the crickets chattering back to him.

The line of firs and blue spruce was black. He wiped a trembling hand over his brow and willed himself to look at the trees not thirty feet away. They did not appear particularly evil. Charlie turned around and looked at the garage, thinking of his beeper lying on the car seat. It had gone off several times.

He gripped the iron again between his hands, pushing through the swale of high weeds. There was the grove of trees and Charlie was reminded of the circle with the *X* in the center. He took a deep breath and ducked under the branches into a luminous clearing.

The trees hid the interior like a childhood fort. The grass was short and the turpentine scent of the pines was cool. He halted in midstride. There was a cross in the moonlight. When his eyes adjusted he saw it to be a long spade shovel plunged deep into the earth, a lantern resting next to it.

Charlie leaned the tire iron against a tree and grabbed the

box of matches on top of the lantern. He struck a match, the lantern popped into a white flare, the mantles burning with a small sputter.

The pines emerged light yellow and the grass bleached-white. Charlie hung the lantern on a short, chopped branch and turned it down. He pulled the shovel from the ground, pausing, then thrust the blade into the dirt like a man with a bayonet. Charlie attacked the ground, throwing dirt, hearing his labored breathing. The lantern hissed, the shadows of his own body looming against the trees. He dug wildly for twenty minutes until he fell in the grass from exhaustion. He began to see phantoms around him and thought he saw his mother, then his father.

After another twenty minutes he had a hole the size of a small refrigerator. He leaned on the shovel, gasping for air, sweat-soaked, his shirt hanging wetly and open. Charlie looked into the hole and his breath caught, then began again. He stared into the darkness, seeing spots of light that became his own blurred vision. He set the shovel down and took the lantern from the tree branch. Charlie climbed into the hole and brought the flame-light lower. The cold smell of dirt was in his nostrils as he bent farther down. He leaned forward with the hissing lantern, seeing only the rocky, clodded dirt at first, then the pale white short stick: a finger beckoning him to hell. He leaped out and threw up in the grass.

Charlie retched into the fresh grass twice, sobbing, his head on his arms. He lay there for five minutes, then slowly lifted his head. A tan scuff of leather was just beyond his nose, the other boot squarely on the tire iron. Charlie blinked, wondering if he was dreaming, looking up to a large turquoise-studded belt buckle and muscled forearms. Dark eyes gleamed down at him. The cold steel of a shotgun hollowed a space an inch from his nose.

"Well, boy," Buck nodded, flaring a match to life with his thumb. "You found your mama."

# CHAPTER THIRTY-FIVE

Southampton, Virginia

*August 1998*

Granddaddy ate dinner by himself on the back porch, his fingers dark against the silver tray. He could not shake the premonition gripping him since late afternoon. It was a knowledge. The instinct of an animal leaving for the woods to die.

He watched the earth turn to shadow, seeing the setting sun along the trees, insects streaming through the slanting rays of copper yellow, brilliant saffron, pulling back to the colorless sky between trees he had watched come of age. Granddaddy sat, listening for his grandson's car.

The pain that woke him out of his sleep that afternoon had not subsided. It was bigger than his body and he knew this was the final battle until the body shut down. Granddaddy sat on the back porch and watched the gentle earth turn toward darkness a last time. He listened patiently for his grandson and thought of another time.

*"Mr. Turin—I've got bad news, I'm afraid."*

*He looked at the young man on the couch.*

*"Mr. Turin—Mrs. Turin died last night at Tucker's."*

*The same man he had turned away from, because he didn't want him to see a man crying.*

When it became dark Granddaddy put the folded paper in his pocket. Then he was walking on the tar driveway to his car. The low purr of night and the dome light of the car reminded him of vacations years earlier with his wife and daughter. They would rise in the middle of the night to drive to the beach after packing the night before. He would drive through the deserted streets, as he was doing now, with the feeling of moving between time.

The engine and the tires were loud in the night silence. The steering wheel was slicked and hard in his hands, the accelerator had a pressure to it he hadn't felt before. He could hear the moving parts of the engine running together, visualizing gears and pins, throw weights and fluids, sparks of electricity meted out carefully by the rotating distributor, seeing the perfect red-hot firing of the cylinders.

Usually he had a hard time driving at night, but now the streets were bright as day. He could see the pale light of the retreating moon on the centerline of the highway; trash along the curbs, a mailbox open under a tree, a hose coiled next to a house. He saw things he knew his eyes could not physically receive, yet the world flowed by as if under a spotlight.

Granddaddy drove into downtown Richmond, passing the vacant lot where he had sat with Tamara on her mother's porch. He passed the corner with the fast-food restaurant dark; no trace of the gleaming cars that had lined the lot sixty years before. He drove through the old section of town, passing the dark row-house apartment where he had lived as a boy with his mother. Granddaddy turned out of the old section onto the two-lane highway and headed for the country.

The man drove with the oiled Colt .44 next to his thigh like the muzzle of a dog. He drove with his elbow on the car door and his hand to the right of the twelve o'clock position on the wheel. The car surfed on the hills and floated down into the valleys, leaving behind a blowing piece of paper and a cloud of road dust on the barren two-lane. He passed the burned-out skeletons of tobacco barns and sagging tenant farmhouses with tractors and silos scattered in the fields like so many toys left out to rot.

The wind roared through the car and ruffled his shirt. He kept his eyes on the road, passing an antebellum home on a far hill, pressing further on the accelerator, glancing at the dashboard clock.

The car flew up a hill and the man wasn't sure he didn't leave the ground before the car dropped down into the valley and began to slow. He pulled next to the Mercedes in front of the gas station. He was out in the late-August air, quietly moving toward the open door, the gun by his side. The sour oil smell was acrid in his nostrils. He paused, looking into the bays, seeing nothing but a Coke bottle lambency outside the bay doors.

He turned to the stairwell and pushed the door with one hand while holding the pistol by his head. The man looked up to the doorway, listened, then moved up the steps.

He reached the top, cocked the hammer back twice. He saw the couch and coffee table and the same kerosene lamps. Crazy shadows fell from the open windows onto the floor and cast the room in pale shadow. He checked the bathroom, opening closets as he moved, approaching the back window. Seeing a glow in the trees, he glanced at his watch and crossed the moonlight in a flick of shadow, then was down the stairs, leaving the open front door creaking behind in the windless night.

Pearl wished she hadn't waited so long before she entered the house. She had waited until she heard the clank of the gate, climbed the stairs quickly and knocked on Minnie's bedroom door.

"C'mon baby, open the door . . . *it's Pearl,*" she said just above a whisper, listening for the return of the judge.

She knocked again.

"Minnie, open the door, Judge left . . . *Minnie!*"

Then she had another feeling and knew she was alone. Pearl pushed the unlocked door open.

"Just like when you was a baby," she murmured, walking to the curtain whipping into the frilly pink bedroom of an adolescent.

Pearl looked at the pine clinging to the west side of the house. She watched the wild breeze waving the branches in front of the window and felt the presence of the empty house and her small place in it. She filled her mouth with smoke, crossing one arm under her elbow.

"I knows where you gone," she murmured, the curtains streaming around her in a gauzy white veil.

# CHAPTER THIRTY-SIX

Virginia countryside

*August 1998*

Charlie lay motionless in the grass with the man standing over him. He saw the scuffed rawhide boot standing on the tire iron and swung his left hand, catching the boot at the ankle.

The man kicked out, catching him in the side of the head. Charlie rolled into a dim world.

"Ain't goin' to do that, Jack," the voice continued.

Buck hunched down by Charlie, flicking ash into the hole. He held the black pump-action shotgun in his right hand. He swung it around like a pistol and pointed into the grave.

"Yonder lays yo' mama an' that nigger, Rufus junior, she layin' with."

He squinted, resting one hand on his thigh.

"Reckon that too much for yo' granddaddy."

Charlie opened his eyes to the salmon-colored face more pale in the sputtering lantern. Buck picked the cigarette from his mouth, flicking more ash into the shallow grave.

"Ain't nothin' lower for a white woman than to fuck a nigger," he said, nodding as if there were two people sleeping in front of him. "Reckon yo' granddaddy had enough when he found them layin' together." Buck shook his head slowly. "Come to see what the ruckus 'bout and there's yo' granddaddy standin' with a pistol." Buck nodded to the hole. "An' yo' mama and tha' nigger dead as a couple of barn rats."

Charlie groaned and closed his eyes.

"You're full of shit. . . ."

"Say the same thing, Jack." Buck fished another cigarette from his top pocket, popping a match to life with his thumb. "I helped bury 'em and said to him, 'Austin, you done shot 'em both.' " Buck switched knees, sparking his cigarette into the double grave. "An' he said, 'Yes I did,' and he appreciate I don't say nothin'."

Charlie rolled over and sat up groggily; the creased face hunched down in the lantern light.

"I kept my word, Jack." Buck breathed out tiredly. "I told yo' granddaddy I use a little help an' he leave money safe up yonder." Buck spat into the grave. "Want nobody find what he bury back here."

Charlie glared at him.

"Fuck you—"

Buck nodded, smoke seeping between spaced teeth.

"Well, Jack, don't matter, 'cause judge don't like Yankee trash fuckin' his daughter and you goin' to be layin' next to your mama here. Don't grab the iron again, Jack, or I split yo' skull with my other boot. . . ." He nodded again. "I figured yo' granddaddy pay up after tha' little lawn fire or you'd come out here and I get judge to pay for takin' care of his problem—" He breathed a blue stream into the lantern light. "Figure yo' granddaddy spare you knowin' he was a murderer and yo' mama a whore—"

Charlie lunged and Buck caught him falling back, throwing him into the grave. He fell to his back with the air knocked from his lungs. Charlie could smell the close, damp dirt and felt something sharp in his back. A dark shadow crossed the stars and sharp pines. Buck loomed in the lantern light, pointing down the slick black barrel.

"Well, Jack," he said, pumping the shotgun, swinging it up to his shoulder. "You 'bout to join yo' mama, boy."

Charlie squeezed his eyes shut . . . then was pulled from the darkness, the gun pushed tight on the back of his head. Buck had a vise grip on his neck.

"That you, Jack? Hear you in the trees now, just tellin' yo' boy here how you shot your nigger-lovin' daughter and Rufus junior." A gun double-clicked behind and Buck spun to the pines. The sputtering of the lantern increased.

"Ain't no use denyin' what you done, Jack. I shoot the boy dead and you dyin' anyway—I do the job and y'all be in the same plot here."

Charlie felt the grip tighten around his neck, the round barrel pushing his head.

"Count of three. Then I finish the job here. . . ." Buck moved slowly around the grave like a shadowboxer. "One . . ."

"Now, Buck, I been knowin' you all these years . . ."

The gun left Charlie's head and swung toward the trees, exploding, chopping a pine branch to the ground. Buck shucked the shell and moved again, pressing the warm barrel behind Charlie's ear.

"Known your daddy too, see . . ."

"Two, Jack."

The gun flashed again over his shoulder and a branch fell as if someone had sliced it with a machete. Buck took another step, shucking a shell by Charlie's feet, the hot pipe pushing against the back of his head. Charlie's ears rang from the concussion.

"I been right good to you, Buck, but only one thing a person like you respond to, see."

*"Three, Jack—"*

The pines exploded; the lantern flamed into a pyre of fire and Buck flew away as if grabbed from behind. Then Charlie was running from the trees in the clear moonlight of the field. He ran through the tall weeds, falling twice, not feeling himself falling. Charlie could hear his own labored breathing. He ran to the garage and fell against the wall, gasping for air, looking back across the shining wrecks. He leaned against the side of the garage, shaking wet, his mind on fire. Charlie struggled to his feet, feeling his way along the plank wood to the front of the garage. Charlie wiped a trembling hand across his forehead, looking up as a car came slowly down the highway.

Buck crouched down in the Hudson, the cushion tickling his cheek and his blood pooling on the seat and floor. He held the shotgun to his chest and could hear people walking in the weeds. He would have only one chance with his strength draining onto the seat. He swore shots had come from two different directions in the pines.

"Ambush," Buck whispered, thinking of betrayal by the judge, his mind racing.

*. . . treat me no better than a nigger, done their dirty work and treat us like we dirt . . . no better than a nigger, Jack . . . no*

*better than nigger layin' in a ditch. . . . Been serving the judge an' got nothin' to show. Always been the judge and people like him . . . they treat us like dirt and nothin' lower . . .*

Buck pushed himself backward along the seat, holding his side where blood flowed between his fingers. He stared into the shadowy landscape, then pushed himself up in the car. Buck swore softly, his eyes fixed on the woman walking toward him. The judge's daughter was coming through the weeds.

He stood up from the car, just another shadow as he leaned his arm across the top of the Hudson to steady the shotgun. He sighted up, pinning his aim to her head.

"One's for you, Judge," Buck muttered, squeezing the trigger just as his forehead was slammed to the roof.

There was a silence, then weeds rustled behind the car. A man walked forward with an oiled .44 by his side, smoke wafting from the barrel, hanging in a small cloud in the damp air. He approached cautiously with the grass swishing, stopping behind Buck lying spread-eagled on the roof; a black pool gleamed on the car roof.

He paused, looking for any sign of life.

"Got you, you crippling son of a bitch," Sherwood Anders muttered.

# CHAPTER THIRTY-SEVEN

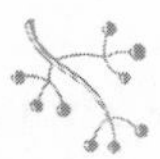

Virginia countryside

*August 1998*

Sherwood Anders crossed the field, clutching the smoking gun in his hand. He had on a checkered shirt with jeans and hiking boots. He looked at Charlie, then Minnie, turning back to the Hudson with Buck sprawled across it like some exhausted runner.

"Don't worry about that son of a bitch anymore."

Sherwood holstered the long pistol.

"Your granddaddy's still down in the trees," he said, turning.

"*You* were in the pines?"

Sherwood swept his longish brown hair to the side.

"After Minnie called me and told me you were coming out here, I called your granddaddy . . . he's quite a shot. I went for that lantern, but your granddaddy picked him right off."

Charlie looked at Minnie and thought of the iron pipe he had picked up when he saw the judge's car coming down the road, the glimmer of moon stopping him before she opened the door.

"Before that son of a bitch crippled me . . ." Sherwood's voice was tight. "I was a different man. . . ." He paused and looked at Charlie. "The same night your mother was killed, Buck ran me off the road."

He turned and Charlie thought Sherwood might shoot Buck again. Charlie noticed how the gun sagged on his one good leg, the strange position of his hips.

"That article you found was written by a colleague of mine when I was in the hospital." He paused. "Judge Barrek and Sheriff Pairs have been in the business of terror a long time. . . ." Sherwood looked at Charlie and Minnie. "It all comes down to one damn thing . . . a southern man can't stand the idea that a white woman would ever be attracted to a black man. That's what got Willy John lynched and that's what killed your mama and Rufus junior." He looked at Charlie. "Rufus junior and your mama . . . were together. Your mama came from good family, a First Family of Virginia, and there were certain things you didn't do if you were in that elite group," he continued, turning again to the car. "I had become friends with a deputy out here and he told me she had started coming out to the church when Rufus junior was speaking." He paused and looked at Charlie. "They talked to your daddy . . . I don't think he knew what to do about it. Your mama had her problems. . . ." Sherwood took another breath. "Then she and Rufus junior started meeting in that old garage. I think it went on for some time." He nodded slowly. "They knew when she was there, sometimes she didn't even bother to park the car around the back." Sherwood turned to Charlie. "The judge visited your father and I think he gave them the go-ahead to teach them a lesson, probably just to scare them . . . but I knew from the deputy they were going to do something—he called me that night . . . April 4, 1968." He turned to the form on the car. "Buck went to the garage." Sherwood glanced at the car again. "Buck's daddy was an old moonshiner and Klansman from way back . . . I think he was probably involved in lynching Willy John."

Sherwood looked down at his gun. "So I grabbed this old gun and drove for the garage—see, I was a different man then, I didn't have the fear yet . . ." He wiped his eyes quickly. "When I got there, Rufus junior and your mama were already dead. Then Buck knocked me cold. He must have thought shooting me would be too much to hide."

Sherwood turned once again to the gleamless Hudson.

"So he waited until I started driving for Richmond and ran me off the road." He looked at Charlie and Minnie with the gun holstered to his thigh. "I was afraid to leave my house for a year after that."

He breathed heavily and patted the gun in the long holster. Sherwood Anders looked up, his crooked glasses gleaming moonlight.

"Now, do you know . . ." He paused, his eyes glistening. "For the first time in thirty years, I don't feel like a cripple."

Sherwood struck light to darkness a second time, hanging the lantern close to where the first one had been. They stood in a small circle of a funeral gathering around the shallow grave. Granddaddy held the gun Charlie had seen the night Buck broke into the house.

"Your daddy and I both felt if we could keep it quiet then

you could have some sort of a normal life." Granddaddy spoke to Charlie, talking down to the beckoning finger. "See, somebody called me and told me to go on out to the garage," he explained. "I got here and found them already dead . . . and that's when Buck comes up and says I killed them and reckon I figured I could say I did and he'd be quiet, see." Granddaddy nodded slowly, like a man before a fire. "I told Rufus John and his wife . . . they wanted to keep it quiet too, because in those days people liable to do anything and they didn't want any more trouble."

Granddaddy paused.

"Now, Buck was always in some kind of trouble and I thought I could get him to help me bury them and get him to stay quiet . . ." Granddaddy didn't break his reverential stand. "But then he started wanting money. So I started leaving it for him in that safe, but the boy wanted more and more. So, when I knew I was dyin' . . ."

Charlie looked at him sharply.

"I thought he just go away, but he didn't," Granddaddy murmured. He looked at Charlie. "Then you came down. Reckon he figured I pay up then, to keep it from you," he said, turning. "That's the money you found, see." Granddaddy pursed his lips with the heavy old pistol between his hands. "Now, I probably shouldn't have gotten that old doctor to make up the false death certificate, see, reckon I should have called the police, because I think I have caused more trouble trying to cover it up."

Charlie stared down into the dirt of his mother's grave. He listened to the crickets and the few morning birds. He reached for his granddaddy's hand, feeling old calluses, tired from life.

• • •

They left the police station and sat in the lawn chairs on the back deck. The gray was in the tops of the trees with a brimming pink. Granddaddy gripped the plastic of the lawn chair, his knuckles whitening several times.

"How long have you had it?"

Granddaddy squinted.

"Reckon over a year now. . . ." He shook his head. "See, I just thought it was old age, but it got to the point where I couldn't even pick up a rake." Granddaddy nodded to the trees. "So, I went in and they told me I had something wrong with my water . . . my blood, leukemia." Granddaddy sat up straight. "And do you know that was the first time I went to a doctor in thirty years?" He nodded again. "That's right . . . and they find I have leukemia, see. So, you shouldn't go to doctors because you just find out you have something wrong with you . . . you better off not knowin', see."

Charlie nodded, smiling in spite of himself. They sat for a few minutes, listening to the whippoorwills in the trees.

"What happened to my mother, Granddaddy?"

He nodded slowly.

"Now, your mother, she was fine up 'til just after you were born. Then she started to act the same way your grandmother did, see." He turned with the chicory light on his face. "She became a mighty unhappy young woman . . ." Granddaddy held out his wide hand with his fingers spread. "I think her and your daddy were havin' some troubles back then." He paused. "She started to disappear for a time—just up and leave and not tell anybody, see. Your daddy and I would go looking for her and one time we found her out in the country . . . close to that garage. . . ." Granddaddy shook his head. "Then she started to see Rufus junior . . . they knew each other as children when I lived out at the garage—

playmates, see. Now, Rufus junior was a man who bettered himself. His daddy was a no-'count, drank all the time, petty thief, but the boy managed to get himself to college and when he came back he was a changed man, see. Wore a shirt and tie, a right good-looking man, smart, spoke about civil rights and what King was talking about at the time." Granddaddy cut the air with his right hand. "Pulled himself up by his bootstraps, see." He shook his head slowly. "Now, I don't know when they met again, but after thinkin' on this for most of thirty years now, I reckon they were seein' each other for some time . . . in other words, they were a couple."

He lowered his hand slowly and looked at his grandson.

"It was your daddy who called that night. He was mighty upset. Said Judge Barrek and Sheriff Pairs had come by and said she was out in the country with Rufus junior."

Granddaddy shook his head.

"Your daddy was afraid something was going to happen, see, so I drove on out there and that's when I found them."

Charlie felt a great compassion for his mother suddenly, putting his head down on his hand, trying to grasp the world his mother had faced. He kept his head down for a full five minutes.

When he looked up he saw the house next door as if for the first time. The morning was different, the air, the light, the flowers. Charlie saw a woman staring at them from a window.

"Your neighbors are going to think there's a couple of nuts sitting back here," he said, watching her pull the blinds shut.

Granddaddy smiled slowly.

"Now, maybe there are."

They sat quietly as the unpainted dovecote in the backyard emerged in the tree shadows. The sky was brightening.

"Now. I been having these dreams for the last week." He looked at Charlie. "And they have been the strangest thing." Granddaddy put up his hand. "I been seeing my whole life, well, not my whole life, but *most* of it, anyway."

Charlie stared at him.

"But now . . ." Granddaddy said, turning, holding his wide hand toward the sky. "I have about dreamed my whole life, see, and I'm almost scared to go asleep again and see what I'll dream next."

Granddaddy turned back to the yard, looking at his hand, spreading out the wrinkled knuckles, the corroding fingernails.

"But I can't stay up for the rest of my life," he murmured.

Charlie watched him, fighting his own prescience to stop what was evolving in front of him.

"I'm sure you'll be fine, Granddaddy. We should probably go to the doctor tomorrow."

Granddaddy stared at his hand.

"I wonder," he murmured, pausing. "Now, do you suppose . . . do you think that maybe this is all there is?"

The wind slapped Charlie squarely in the face and if he had a hat he would have turned and run to get it. Instead he spoke into the void, hollering against night, ending weakly all the same.

"No," he said, shaking his head. "That's not all there is."

Granddaddy nodded, bringing his hand down slowly in the new light.

# CHAPTER THIRTY-EIGHT

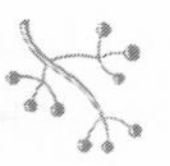

Southampton, Virginia

*August 1998*

Austin squinted down the sparkling country highway running past his closed place. He looked for Snowball in the doorway and wondered why he hadn't opened for business. Austin gripped the Studebaker steering wheel tightly, staring at the golden-haired woman, with the little girl, standing by the dusty side of the road. He stopped in the swaddling Virginia heat and got out of the car.

"Now, what are y'all doing out here?"

Tamara smiled, beautiful in the late-twenties dress she had worn just after they were married, beaming with the radiance of a movie star. His daughter was in the white dress they had bought for her sixth birthday.

"We were waiting for you, darling!"

*"We were waiting for you, Daddy!"*

His daughter ran to him, putting her close warm hands around his neck as he picked her up, holding her above the verdant country streaming off into the white glare of southern sun. Austin held her, smelling the clean skin of his daughter—the faint talcum of their family years.

"We've been waiting for you *so long,* Daddy," she breathed into his ear, small hands gripping tighter.

"I've been waiting for you, sweetie," he whispered, kissing the warm neck, looking over his daughter's shoulder at Tamara with her smooth skin and russet hair of evenings with the scuppernong, wisteria, and the drooping willow trees protecting them.

The heat wallowed in long waves on the time plane around his daughter and wife.

"I've been waiting for you, sweetie," he repeated over and over, holding the daughter of himself.

*"I love you, Daddy,"* echoing in the small close mouth as he held what he couldn't before, light overhead bringing the mica highway to life.

Austin put his daughter down, hugging his wife in the washing warmth.

"You look so beautiful, honey," he said to the love of his life, his arms around her, running his hand through the pure gold of his capacity to dream beyond himself.

"I'm so glad you came back," she whispered. "I knew you would. We've been waiting so long!"

They walked toward the car slowly, holding hands, Austin in the middle.

"Where are we going, Daddy?"

He looked at little Tamara as they approached the car together.

"We are going on a long, long trip, precious."

Then Austin was driving, holding the steering wheel, the quick centerlines slipping under them in fast denominations as the wind-roar poured in. Austin drove, feeling the engine in the car, the full-power hum moving them down the road faster and faster into the country of his first days, passing all they had seen and running back into the warmth of the cradle. Austin turned to speak to his beautiful love with his daughter leaning over the seat, her warm breath by his neck, the starred highway a rushing gray milky way.

"Now, do you know," he said to the loves of his life. "I could drive forever—"

The sheets were cool and slippery, luxuriantly soft on Charlie's feet and back. He watched the light blare in through his bedroom window, stopping short of his bed, containing itself to the mahogany dresser and gleaming on the dime from his pants. Charlie listened to the christening birds rustling through the trees outside his window. He stretched the full length of the bed, balling his fists like a child. He felt the warm glow again, remembering last night's conversation with his grandfather.

"Now! Don't you worry about your life, boy," he had said, talking as a friend, as two men mulling over the day. "You are from good people!" Charlie smiled at the old-world logic. "Now, maybe you already thought of this, but in my opinion, and from what I've seen of you, I think you would make a mighty fine teacher!"

Charlie stretched again, thinking about his mother, reordering the resentment of a child not loved, seeing the sweat on the white toilet, the small square tiles counting out into three-dimensional illusion, a dust web up behind the sink. His mother was leaning over the dirty water, staring at him, not saying anything at all. She handed him the plastic bubble-bath container that was empty before but full now, covering the dirty water and himself with frothy white suds of color spinning bubbles.

Then Granddaddy was coming in, taking him out of the water and he was no longer wet but dressed.

In the rosy light of family life, Granddaddy pushed him through the air in his swing. He flew up, Granddaddy floating behind him. He hurled through the air, with Granddaddy propelling him, making him feel the child delight.

Charlie laughed, feeling the tickle down in his stomach like a thousand Ferris-wheel rides, turning up and then coming down, Granddaddy kicking behind him like he was swimming as they rode up to the corner of the room.

*"Wheeeee!"*

Charlie couldn't stop laughing; he was turning and twisting and flying all around.

*"Wheeeeeeee!"* He sang out, hearing Granddaddy's cackle just behind him.

*"Wheeeeee! Wheeeeeee! Wheeeeeeeeee!"*

Charlie flew up and up, then just as suddenly he floated back down to the floor and Granddaddy was gone.

Charlie finally opened his eyes in the sepia pitch of late afternoon. He sat up in his clothes, disoriented with the strange hour. He sat in the orange light that made him think it must be five or six. The house was very quiet. Charlie thought Granddaddy was still asleep.

He walked through the house, passing through still rooms, stopping outside Granddaddy's room. There was a pause in the air like nature's inhale. He knocked softly several times, listening for the vibration, the rhythm of sleep.

Charlie opened the door quietly, hearing the fast tick of the bedside alarm clock first, smelling the age of cloth, furniture, man. The room was frozen silent. The windows were closed against the unseasonable cool.

Charlie walked to the four-poster canopy bed next to the antique bedside table with the hand-worn clothes brush in the middle. His eyes moved to the small mound in the covers, to his grandfather on his side with his mouth open and eyes pinched closed.

"Granddaddy," Charlie whispered, clasping the small hard shoulder that didn't move.

He sat down slowly on the bed next to the gnarled hands of his grandfather with the open mouth of life exhausted.

"Oh, Granddaddy," Charlie breathed, taking the cold hand that was like so many cloth-covered sticks.

"Granddaddy . . ." he breathed again on the edge of the bed, holding the man's hand he had held just so long ago and now the tear of his sorrow on the bed of life.

"My granddaddy died," he whispered, crying alone in the twilight, crying for both of them.

# CHAPTER THIRTY-NINE

Virginia countryside

*September 1998*

Charlie walked behind the sheenless robes. He followed the group to a cross of displaced earth next to the grave of his mother. The people formed a circle behind the robed men with suit pants peeking out below. A man held a small black box with both hands while the clergymen read from books. His dark suit held the sun and his glasses were red.

Charlie stood, listening to the words, thinking of earlier that afternoon. He had wandered around the house in the midst of the forced conviviality before the funeral. He pulled down the springing steps to the attic, ascending into the hot breath of baked wood, wandering under the low glare of the clear bulb. He opened boxes of Christmas ornaments, coats, lampshades, loose scrapbooks. Charlie sat down in the heat, turning the pages of the last eighty years—seeing Granddaddy holding a drink, toasting his wife, Granddaddy cutting down a tree—shading his eyes against the interminable sun—an old radio script from his Studebaker dealership (typed with mistakes), a canceled check from a girls' school for his daughter, Granddaddy on his wedding day, Granddaddy in front of his dealership, Granddaddy holding Charlie up with pride of a grandfather.

Then he found the envelope with Granddaddy's address on the corner. Charlie pulled the letter out and his mother's elegant handwriting began talking to him.

*April 1, 1968*

*Dear Charles,*

*I write this letter with the premonition that events are drawing to a close. What has been happening to me, to us, is rooted in the past and events I cannot reconcile. I am sorry if I have hurt you. But there is something you must know. I cannot carry it any longer. Do you remember the young man who worked for us for a time? His name was Rufus junior and I had known him as a child. Remember, he worked in the yard for a while and you loaned him books to read. At that time you and I were going through a troubling period. We had been trying to have a baby and could not. You were blaming me and I didn't know what to do. I was desperately unhappy, I didn't feel attractive anymore. You were away on business trips for weeks at a time. I was lonely and it was a long hot summer in 1958. Rufus junior had come over to work in the yard and there was just the heat and the dark shade inside the house. I was already drinking by noon. I was just so alone, Charles, and feeling unwanted. He came in and I gave him a glass of water and there was always a certain friendship between us. We had gone through things together and we started talking. I didn't feel so alone then. It should have ended there, but, Charles, we became friends . . . and ultimately we became lovers. When I became pregnant, I considered an abortion, but in those days there was nowhere to turn. And I already desperately loved that baby. I didn't see Rufus junior again, until recently. I feel I must resolve some things and he is, after all, Charlie's father too. I cannot carry this secret any longer. But I feel, also, that this is something people will not accept and so I say now with deep foreboding, if something happens, and we do not meet again, know that I loved you and Charlie with all the heart I had to give—always and forever.*

*All my love,*
*Tamara*

Charlie sat in the attic with tears of perspiration falling on the old paper. He thought of his father and the distance he had always felt. He looked at his hand and it was still white. Charlie touched his face, feeling the structure, the bones, the shape of his head.

Charlie waited for some significance, some percussion of this knowledge to hit him, but all he felt was a strange completeness. He had never really regarded his father as his own. Charlie then wondered what his father had done with this knowledge . . . he wondered if this was the reason he turned Judge Barrek loose on his mother and Rufus junior.

"Rufus junior was my father," he said. He paused. "A civil rights leader . . ."

Charlie looked at the postmark on the letter. His father

must have sent it to Granddaddy just after his mother's funeral. Charlie realized then that his granddaddy had known about his real father all along.

"That's why he was paying Buck," he murmured slowly.

He held the letter, started to put it back in the box, then slipped it into his pocket.

Later in the day, Charlie had the letter with him in the tight pew of the Episcopal Church with the blades above the rafters fanning a gentle breeze over the people in the four rows. He looked out the narrow rectangle of day framing houses and fields under a brilliant blue sky.

" 'Yea—though I walk through the valley of the shadow of death—I will fear no evil . . .' "

Then, miraculously, Granddaddy broke through and everyone remembered the man.

"He *loved* automobiles! He could tell you *anything* you wanted to know about automobiles! Youngest man in the state to have a Studebaker dealership! *Loved* to teach people about automobiles! *Loved to drive!* He could drive and drive and I remember he used to tell me how he would drive Mr. Fredericks straight down to Florida and *never* stop. . . . *Loved automobiles.*"

But Granddaddy was lost in the Bible verses while the man held the black box in front of the dirt cross. Charlie stared at the man with his blooded glasses and duty stance. The minister finished his pronouncements, stepping back while the man walked to the shallow grave.

"I'd like to pour the ashes."

The man looked to the robed clergymen. They hesitated, then nodded. Charlie took his granddaddy from the man and held the weighted cardboard box between his hands.

*A man is not so heavy as this. This life reduced to this box of density. And so this is what it comes to, and so this is what it comes to . . .*

Charlie heard the black robes rustle in the heated air that would thunder come evening. He held the box carefully, shakily pulling the tape off the lid, looking at the earth beneath the lawn, then tilting the gray-and-black ash across the bottom of the earth cross, pouring the life back.

Charlie closed the lid and stepped back from the gray-speckled cross. He held the empty box with the fine coating of gray dust inside, and stood in the silent roar of heat.

*Charlie Tidewater*
*465 Marilee Road*
*Southampton, VA*
*September 3, 1998*

*Matthew,*

*A bitter wind blows from the north into my window. It's all over. Lot of details I'll fill you in on over a beer, but my mother was murdered in 1968 for being with a black man—my father. He was working for my parents at the time and they had an affair. He was murdered next to my mother for that. Rufus John Jr. was his name. A civil rights leader, one of the proponents of change during the period of Martin Luther King. I don't know what their relationship was, but it is enough my mother was with him.*

*My grandfather has died and has been buried alongside his wife and daughter. It's comforting to know the magnolia leaves will fall on their graves together. Strange there should be constancy in a world so uncertain. Maybe even symmetry—it may be human nature to want the thrill of reckless abandon, but I see now it's the constancy of a mother's admonishment, or galoshes worn in rain, or the woolly smell coats get in a closet, that is really the barometer of the lived life. My granddaddy had his share of problems, but in a way he was always there.*

*I'm leaving, but I'll come back. Virginia is that way. One comes back eventually, and then, forever. I guess the leaves in the Midwest will be red and gold before long and there will be a touch of woodsmoke in the air.*

*Ah, well, Matthew, time to go home.*

*Charlie*

# CHAPTER FORTY

Southampton, Virginia

*September 1998*

Charlie stood in the slanting sun. He breathed in the kerosene air and stared at the phantasmagoria of tools and parts, engines and cleaners in the bright colored boxes of faded years—a tube of glue from 1930 next to a brilliant plastic key chain. Charlie picked up the toolbox into which he had thrown some of Granddaddy's tools, remembering the voice at the door on the day of the funeral.

"Yes sir, I'm sorry for being late but I come to pay respects fo' Mr. Turin."

A tall, gray-grizzled man in a black droopy suit stood in the door.

"My name is Robert Jones—but my other name is Snowball, and maybe you hear Mr. Turin speak of me."

The black man walked stooped-over into the array of food and drink, greeted by relatives who knew him better than Charlie knew him. He ate the food toothlessly, drinking his Coca-Cola with long wrinkled hands. When he went outside to bring in more soda, Charlie found him standing in the garage. He was staring at the tools and parts lined up on the walls.

"Yas suh, Mr. Turin an' I, we built many a car with them tools," he nodded, his sadness starker in the light-bulb glare. "Could do jest about anything with an automobile—knew how it worked, take it apart an' put it back together again—an' he built his own race car. Yas sir, he did. From bottom up he did, an' nobody could catch up with us, neither—beat them old bootleggers with it every time!"

He looked at Charlie, smiling broadly.

"But he talk 'bout you plenty—he always talking 'bout his grandson an' what he doin'," he said. "Talk 'bout his daughter too. Even when she not seeing him all those years—he talk 'bout her being a model for department stores, an' winnin' the beauty pageant an' how smart she was!" He nodded with a gentle smile. "He sure loved yo' mama!"

Charlie nodded slowly.

"Snowball, did you know Rufus junior?"

He licked his lips, pulling at the loose collar, moving his shoulders under the worn baggy suit.

"Yes sir, but I knew his father, Rufus John, better an' he was a troubled person."

"But his son weren't like him—and he play with your mama all the time when they was children." He nodded slowly, "No, sir, never seen two kids closer than Rufus junior and your mama."

"But Mr. Turin, he real good to me," Snowball said. "Yes sir, Mr. Turin was . . . he was a right kind man . . ."

he said, his voice fading as Charlie picked up the heavy toolbox.

Charlie walked to the door and paused, smelling years of lost time, the dust-filled slant of light touching the floor. Then he turned and walked out into the September sun.

Charlie turned off the expressway and drove into Richmond. The antebellum houses faded by on the green-and-yellow-splashed street as he drove slowly down Monument Avenue in the afternoon.

Charlie turned onto another street and parked under a shady willow. He walked down the sidewalk, remembering Minnie's presence at the funeral as if she were a dream. He had wanted to call her, but something kept him from doing so. Charlie approached the black iron gate to her house, surprised to see Pearl coming toward him.

". . . Is she here?"

She stood up straight, eyeing him suspiciously.

"You leavin'?"

Charlie nodded. Pearl's brow descended as she shifted her handbag to her side.

"She on the porch."

Charlie watched her stomp down the sidewalk, then he turned and walked up to the house. He expected the judge to appear, but Minnie said her father had been away from the house since the police had come to the door. Charlie had seen a series of articles appearing under the banner OLD KLAN AND MURDER IN THE COUNTRY. The judge's picture had been in the paper.

The swing flitted between the columns. Minnie had on jeans and a white oxford shirt. She seemed suddenly normal to him. Charlie walked in from the sunshine and onto the wooden porch.

"A gentleman caller."

"Hello, Minnie."

Charlie looked out at the yard colored with roses and azaleas. She moved slowly on the swing, one small foot forward.

"I've come to say good-bye."

Her delicate eyebrows arched.

"I know." She looked straight out. "Everyone leaves sooner or later." Her eyes came around to him. "Don't they?"

He nodded, forgetting all explanation or promises.

The swing creaked slightly. Charlie looked down, feeling the long moment of Minnie's life.

"I hope you find happiness," she said softly.

He looked at her and started to speak, then nodded.

"I hope you do too."

Charlie glanced at her. Sunshine was on her cheeks, her beautiful eyes dancing with light. He stood up off the banister, looked out from the long porch and then back at Minnie. The light was slowly leaving her face.

"Please, no pity," she whispered, wiping her eyes quickly.

Charlie paused a moment longer.

"Take care, Minnie," he said huskily, then he was walking down the sidewalk, stepping over Old Boy stretched out for the day's end.

He clicked the gate shut quietly, looking back at the sleepy southern home. The porch was graciously empty.

Charlie walked with his head down.

"So you jest goin' to leave her!"

He stopped, nearly running into Pearl. Her coal-black face and angry eyes were in front of him.

"Beg your pardon—"

"Don't *beg my pardon*! You jest leavin' her and Madelyn with that old judge and after all she done to help you!"

Charlie opened his mouth.

"Ain't no reason for her not have a life! Ain't her fault the judge is her daddy and don't know he ain't supposed to be doin' the things he been doin' to her . . . but you know better and you jest leavin' her to die!"

Charlie held his hands out.

"What do you want me to do?"

She nodded coolly, lighting up a cigarette.

"Uh-huh," she murmured, shooting a stream of smoke. "You from here and you got out. Ain't nothin' for her or her daughter here no more, jest old folks with their niggers an' ain't no reason for judge to have two prisoners when one do."

Pearl trapped the cigarette in the corner of her mouth.

"You run off to Chicago, but you leavin' somebody behind." Pearl glared at him. "An' if you love her—an' you leavin', you worse than the judge."

She pushed by and Charlie watched her go down the sidewalk. He couldn't help but notice her bright new tennis shoes. He turned and began walking. His feet slowed until he stopped by the iron fence. Charlie looked down the long path disappearing into the twilight gloom. He saw a little boy far down the sidewalk. Charlie felt a visceral pain, taking a step toward him. The boy vanished into shadow and Charlie stood still, not able to move. He concentrated, fighting the old feelings, the old crushing uncertainty. With all the sorrow in his heart . . .

Charlie took a step.

Pearl settled down on the back stoop; the short clap of the lighter mixing with the hurried rush of early evening. She leaned forward and heard the front door close, the heavy steps.

*"Pearl!"*

"I's out here," she yelled, not getting up.

The screen door whined open.

"Have you seen Minnie?"

Pearl turned back around and raised the cigarette to her mouth.

"Can't say I has, Judge."

She felt the stare on her neck and breathed out slowly, dropping her cigarette between her legs the way she dropped the judge's name.

"There is something I must speak to her about . . . it's very important and—"

"Like I says, can't say I seen her lately . . ." she murmured, looking to the center of the shadowy back lawn.

Again she could feel the black eyes and heard the squeak of the door opening further.

"Have we decided we don't like the shoes I require anymore?"

Pearl looked down at the flashy white tennis shoes.

"Feel good, Judge . . . lot better than those old maid shoes."

The heavy silence was there.

"When you address me—"

"Ain't addressing you no more. This here's my notice," she declared, turning her body this time and looking him in the face.

They stared at each other and Pearl thought she saw something flicker behind the black eyes. The judge's face reddened, then he retreated behind the screen door.

"Very well, if you see Minnie before you leave . . . tell her . . . tell her I will be in the parlor . . ."

Pearl kept her eyes on his. Then he was gone and she turned back to the yard. She slowly brought her cigarette up.

"She gone, Judge," she murmured, keeping her eyes on the yard, grinning for the first time in years.

"An' rabbit done gone too."

• • •

Charlie drove north, the sun peeking between the line of trees. The road danced in front of him, ignited by the bending rays.

"Now, we have never been on a vacation before, have we, Madelyn?"

The little girl looked at Minnie, shaking her head with the soft wind blowing back her curls.

"You are in for a treat, precious, Chicago is a *big* wonderful city with tall buildings and carnivals and a lake we can take a boat on," Minnie continued, turning around and squeezing Charlie's hand.

"That's right, Madelyn," he said, driving with one hand on the wheel. "We'll see it all, it's colder, but the people are nice. And there's lots and lots of snow!"

The little girl opened her mouth, reaching forward from her car seat.

*". . . shnow!"*

"That's right, shnow!"

He looked down the two-lane leading out of Richmond.

". . . straws!" The little girl screamed, pointing with her finger.

"Stars, she's pointing to the road," Minnie explained.

Charlie stared at the highway and slowly nodded.

"Now, do you know why the road does that, Madelyn?" Charlie pointed over the steering wheel. "See, there's *mica* in the gravel in Virginia and it makes the road sparkle."

Charlie nodded slowly, lifting his wide hand from the wheel.

"Now, when I was little, Madelyn, I used to think that *all* the highways sparkled like this." He looked at the little girl again and then at Minnie.

"But, when I got older, see . . ." Charlie smiled. "I realized only our *own* highways sparkle this way."

Charlie put his hand on the steering wheel, looking to the highway flaming out as the earth gems died in quiet reverberation.

"Only our own, Madelyn," he murmured, driving down the long road of departing light.

# ABOUT THE AUTHOR

Born in Virginia, WILLIAM ELLIOTT HAZELGROVE was raised in Richmond, Baltimore, and Chicago. He attended Western Illinois University where he received his Master of Arts in history. He settled in Chicago and began writing full time. His first novel, *Ripples,* was published in 1992 and awarded "Editors Choice" by the American Library Association. His critically acclaimed second novel, *Tobacco Sticks,* was published in 1995. He lives with his wife and son in Chicago.

LEE COUNTY LIBRARY SYSTEM
3 3262 00213 9595